LINCOLN'S DREAMS

LINCOLN'S DREAMS

CONNIE WILLIS

BANTAM BOOKS
TORONTO · NEW YORK · LONDON · SYDNEY · AUCKLAND

LINCOLN'S DREAMS

A Bantam Book / May 1987

*Grateful acknowledgment is made for permission to include
the following:*

*Quote from "John Brown's Body" by Stephen Vincent Benet
from* Selected Works of Stephen Benet. *Holt, Rinehart &
Winston, Inc. Reprinted by permission of Brandt and Brandt
Literary Agents, Inc.*

Excerpt from Mr. Lincoln's Army *by Bruce Catton. Copyright
1951 by Bruce Catton. Reprinted by permission of Doubleday
Publishing Company.*

Library of Congress Cataloging-in-Publication Data

Willis, Connie.
  Lincoln's dreams.

  1. United States—History—Civil War, 1861–1865—
Fiction. I. Title.
PS3573.I45652L5 1987   813'.54   86–47886
ISBN 0-553-05197-0

Published simultaneously in the United States and Canada

PRINTED IN THE UNITED STATES OF AMERICA

DH 0 9 8 7 6 5 4 3 2 1

To
Courtney and Cordelia

Special thanks to my research assistants, the Smiths—Brooke and Karolyn, Brien and Julie—for wandering among the tombstones of Fredericksburg and Arlington, asking questions and taking notes, searching for clues.

It may be that life is not man's most precious possession, after all. Certainly men can be induced to give it away very freely at times, and the terms hardly seem to make sense unless there is something about the whole business that we don't understand. Lives are spent for very insignificant things which benefit the dead not at all—a few rods of ground in a cornfield, for instance, or temporary ownership of a little hill or a piece of windy pasture; and now and then they are simply wasted outright, with nobody gaining anything at all.

Bruce Catton
Mr. Lincoln's Army

CHAPTER ONE

They bred such horses in Virginia then,
Horses that were remembered after death
And buried not so far from Christian ground
That if their sleeping riders should arise
They could not witch them from the earth again
And ride a printless course along the grass
With the old manage and light ease of hand.

                    Stephen Vincent Benet

Traveller died of lockjaw two years after Robert E. Lee died. I looked that up one day in February, the day I went out to see where Abraham Lincoln's son Willie had been buried. I had been looking for the grave for over a year, and when I finally found it in a biography of Mary Todd Lincoln, I ran out of the library still carrying the book. It set off an alarm, and one of the librarians came out on the steps and shouted after me, "Jeff, are you all right? Jeff!"

It was snowing hard that day, a wet spring snow. It took me nearly an hour to drive out to the old cemetery in Georgetown. I don't know what I thought I'd find, some clue maybe to where Annie was and what had happened to her, some message that would tell me what had happened to all of them,

Tom Tita and Ben and the rest of the soldiers who had died in the Civil War and were buried together under granite squares no larger than a scrap of paper.

But there wasn't anything there, not even Willie Lincoln's body, and I went back to Broun's house and got out Freeman's four-volume biography of Lee and tried to find out what had happened to Traveller.

As with everything else that had happened, there were both too many clues and not enough. But eventually I found out what I needed to know, the way I had found out where Willie had been, the way I had found out what was causing Annie's dreams. After all, that was what I was good at, wasn't it, looking up obscure facts? Traveller had lived two years. He had picked up a nail and gotten lockjaw. They had had to shoot him.

I met Annie two years ago, the night of Broun's press reception. The reception was supposed to be an advance publication party for Broun's twelfth novel, *The Duty Bound,* with bound galleys passed out to the press, but there weren't any galleys. There wasn't even a finished book.

The press reception had been scheduled for the last week in March, but at the end of February Broun was still fiddling with the copyedited manuscript, making changes and then changing the changes, and a week before the reception I was back in West Virginia, trying to find out exactly when Lee had bought Traveller.

It was a detail that didn't matter one way or the other to the book, since Lee had definitely been riding Traveller at Antietam in September of 1862, but it was the kind of thing Broun had been fussing over the entire book, and it worried me.

He was having all kinds of trouble with *The Duty Bound.* He usually turned out his Civil War novels like clockwork: proposal to outline to manuscript to corrected galleys, which was why his publisher, McLaws and Herndon, had gone ahead and scheduled this reception before they had the copyedited manuscript back.

I might have done the same thing. In the four years I'd been doing research for Broun, he'd never missed a deadline. But with *The Duty Bound,* he hadn't made a deadline yet, and when I called him from West Virginia he was still making major changes.

"I'm thinking of adding a chapter at the beginning of the book, Jeff," he said. "To explain why Ben Freeman enlists."

"I thought you'd already sent the copyedited manuscript back," I said.

"I did, son. Three weeks ago. But then I got to worrying about Ben. He signs up just like that, for no reason. Would you do that?"

"No, but a lot of recruits did. Listen, I'm calling because I've run into some trouble with Traveller. In a letter to one of his daughters, Lee says he bought Traveller in the fall of 1861, but the records here show he didn't buy him until 1862, during the Carolina campaign."

"They must have had some reason for enlisting," Broun said. "What if Ben's courting a girl who's in love with somebody else?"

McLaws and Herndon would kill him if he started adding new characters at this late date. "I think the beginning's fine," I said. "Ben doesn't have to have a good reason to sign up. Nobody else in the Civil War did. Most of the recruits couldn't have told you what the war was even being fought about, let alone why they were in it. I'd go ahead and leave it as is, and that goes for Traveller, too. I'm going up to Lewisburg tomorrow to check the courthouse records, but I'm almost sure Lee didn't buy the horse in 1861."

"Will you be home in time for the reception?" Broun asked.

"I thought they'd postpone it since the book's late."

"The invitations were already out. Try to get home for it, son. I need you here to explain why the book's taking so long."

I wanted to ask him to explain it to me, but I didn't. Instead, I chased all over Greenbrier County for three days, trying to find a scribbled note or a preliminary agreement that would settle the matter one way or the other, and then drove home through an awful snowstorm, but I made it in time for the reception.

"You look like you've been through a campaign, son," Broun said when I got there late in the afternoon.

"I have," I said, pulling off my parka. The snow had

followed me all the way from White Sulphur Springs and then turned into icy rain fifty miles from D.C. I was glad Broun had a fire going in his upstairs study. "I found out what you wanted to know about Traveller."

"Good, good," he said, taking books off a straight-backed chair and setting it in front of the fire. He draped my wet parka over the back of it. "I'm glad you're home, Jeff. I think I've finally got a handle on the book. Did you know Lincoln dreamed about his own assassination?"

"Yes," I said, wondering what on earth this had to do with a novel about Antietam. "He dreamed he saw his dead body in the White House, didn't he?"

"He dreamed he woke up and heard the sound of crying," Broun said, dumping his Siamese cat out of his big leather armchair and pulling it around to face the fire. He didn't seem to be in any hurry, even though the reception was supposed to start at seven. He was wearing the ratty-looking gray cardigan he usually wrote in and a pair of baggy pants, and he apparently hadn't shaved since I'd left. Maybe they'd canceled the reception after all.

Broun motioned me to sit down. "When he went downstairs he couldn't see anyone," he went on, "but there was a corpse lying in a coffin in the East Room. The corpse's face was covered by a black cloth, and Lincoln asked the guard standing at the door who was dead, and the guard answered, 'The President. He was killed by an assassin.' "

He was looking at me eagerly, waiting for me to say something, but I didn't have a clue of what that something was supposed to be. "He had the dream, what, a month before he died?" I said lamely.

"Two weeks. April the second. I'd read it before, but while you were gone, McLaws and Herndon's publicist called and asked me what book I was going to do after *The Duty Bound*. She needed it for the press release they're going to pass out at the reception tonight, and I told her I didn't know, but then I got to thinking about the Lincoln book."

The Lincoln book. That was what all this was about. I supposed I should be glad. If he got involved in a new book, maybe he'd quit messing with *The Duty Bound*. The only problem was that the Lincoln book wasn't a new book. Broun called it his midlife crisis book, even though he hadn't started it till he turned sixty. "I was afraid I'd die before I wrote anything important, and I still might. I never could get a handle on the damned thing," he'd told me laughingly when I first came to work for him, but I suspected he was more than half serious. He'd tried working on it again a year later, but it still wasn't much more than an outline.

"Tomorrow I want you to go out to Arlington, Jeff." He scratched at the grayish stubble on his cheek. "I need to know if Willie Lincoln was buried there."

"He's buried in Springfield. In the Lincoln tomb."

"Not now. During the Civil War. His body wasn't sent back to Springfield until 1865, when Lincoln was assassinated. Willie died in 1862. I want to know where he was buried for those three years."

I had no idea what Willie Lincoln had to do with Lincoln's assassination dream, but I was too tired to ask. "You aren't still having the reception, are you?" I said, hoping against hope that he would say no. "The roads are terrible."

"No, it's still on." Broun looked at his watch. "I've got to go get dressed. Those damned reporters always come early." I must have looked like I felt, because he said, "The battle won't be joined till eight o'clock, and I'll take care of the preliminary skirmishes. Why don't you go take a nap?"

"I think I'll take you up on that," I said, and heaved myself up out of the chair.

"Oh, would you do one favor for me first?" Broun said. "Would you call Richard Madison and make sure he's coming tonight? His girlfriend said they'd be here, but I'd like you to call and make sure."

Lincoln's dreams and Willie Lincoln's body and now my old college roommate. I gave up even trying to look like I knew what he was talking about.

"He called while you were gone," Broun said, scratching at the stubble. "Said he had to get in touch with you right away. I told him I didn't have a number for you but you'd be calling in and could I give you some kind of message, but he just said to tell you to call him, and then when you called I didn't have a chance to pass the message on, so I called him to tell him you'd be back today."

There had to be a connection here somewhere. "You invited him to the reception?" I asked.

"I invited the girlfriend to the reception. Richard wasn't there. The girl said he was at the Sleep Institute, and I asked her what he did there, and she said, 'He tells people what their dreams mean,' and after I hung up I got to thinking about Lincoln's dreams and wondering what a psychiatrist would say they meant, so I called her back and invited them to the reception so I could ask him. But since I never talked to Richard and since he wanted you to call him, I think it would be a good idea for you to call and make sure they're coming. And then you'd better go lie down, son. You look like you're about to fall over."

He went out. I stood in front of the fire for a minute, wondering why Richard had called me. We'd been good friends when we were roommates at Duke, but we'd hardly seen each other in the six years since we graduated. He'd gone to New York to do his internship and then come back to D.C. for his residency at the Sleep Institute, which meant he was too busy to see anybody. He'd called me exactly once in the last year, and then it was to make me a job offer. One of his patients, a Pentagon big-wig, was doing a study on the long-term effects of the Vietnam war and needed a researcher.

"Not interested," I'd said. "I haven't figured out the long-term effects of the Civil War yet."

"This would be a job where you could do something important instead of wasting your time looking up obscure facts nobody cares anything about for some hack writer," he'd said.

I had just spent that whole day trying to find out why General Longstreet was wearing a carpet slipper at Antietam. He'd had a blistered heel, a fact that Richard would most certainly put in the category of "facts nobody cares anything about." Longstreet had probably cared, though, since he was trying to run a war, and so did Broun, which was why I worked for him, but I hadn't been about to try to explain that to Richard.

"If this Pentagon job is so great, how come the guy's a patient of yours?" I'd said instead.

"He has a sleep disorder."

"Well, I sleep great nights," I'd said. "Tell him thanks but no thanks." I wondered if he was calling now with another job offer. Broun had said Richard wouldn't tell him what he wanted to talk to me about, which meant it probably was, and I was in no shape to listen to it.

I took a hot shower instead and then tried for a nap, but I found myself still thinking about Richard and decided to call him and get it over with. I went back into Broun's study to use the phone. I thought maybe the girlfriend Broun had talked to would answer, but she didn't. Richard did, and he didn't have any job offers.

"Where in the hell have you been? I tried to call you," he said.

"I was in West Virginia," I said. "Seeing a man about a horse. What did you want to talk to me about?"

"Nothing. It's too late, anyway. Broun said he'd have you call me," he said almost accusingly. Why was I constantly finding myself in conversations I couldn't make heads or tails of?

"I'm sorry I didn't call. I just got home. But listen, whatever it was, we can talk about it tonight at the reception."

There was dead silence on the other end.

"You are coming, aren't you?" I said. "Broun's really anxious to talk to you about Lincoln's dreams."

"I can't come," he said. "It's out of the question. I have a patient I—"

"We're closer to the Sleep Institute than your apartment is. You can give the Institute Broun's number, and they can call you here if there's an emergency. I'd really like to see you, and I want to meet this new girlfriend of yours."

Another dead silence. He said finally, "I don't think Annie should—"

"Come with you? Of course she should. I'll take good care of her while you talk to Broun. I'll tell her all about your wild undergraduate days at Duke."

"No. Tell your boss I'm sorry, but I don't have anything to tell him about Lincoln's dreams that he'd want to hear."

Somewhere along in there I started to ache all over. "Then tell him that. Look," I said, "you don't have to come for the whole thing. The reception starts at eight. You can talk to Broun and still have this Annie person home in bed by nine watching her rapid eye movements or whatever it is you psychiatrists do. Please. If you don't come, Broun'll send me to Indiana in this blizzard to look up nightmares Lincoln had as a kid. Come on, for me, your old roommate."

"I can't stay after nine."

"No problem," I said. I gave him Broun's address and hung up before he could say no, and then just sat there in front of the fire. Broun's cat jumped on my lap and I petted it, thinking I should get up and go lie down.

Broun woke me up. "How long was I asleep?" I said, rubbing my hands over my face to try and wake up. However long it had been, the aches were worse than ever.

"It's six-thirty," Broun said. He had changed into a dinner jacket with a pleated shirt and string tie. He still hadn't shaved. Maybe he was trying to grow a beard. If he was, it was a terrible idea. The grayish black stubble seemed to take all the color out of his face. He looked sharp and disreputable, like an unscrupulous horsetrader. "I wouldn't have wakened you, but I wanted you to take a look at this." He thrust a sheaf of typewritten pages into my hand.

"What's this?" I said. "Willie Lincoln?"

He poked at the fire, which had died down to almost nothing while I was asleep. "It's that first scene, the one I was worried about. I just couldn't see Ben signing up for no reason at all, so I rewrote it."

"Do McLaws and Herndon know about this?" Broun's cat jumped off my lap and started batting at the poker.

"I'm calling it in to them tomorrow, but I wanted you to look at it first. Ben had to have some motivation for enlisting."

"Why? What about later in the book when he falls in love with Nelly? He doesn't have any motivation for that. She gives him one spoonful of laudanum, and bang, he's ready to do anything for her."

The cat wrapped a paw firmly around the poker, but Broun didn't notice. He stared into the fire. "It was the war.

People did things like that during the war, fell in love, sacrificed themselves—"

"Enlisted," I said. "Most of the recruits in the Civil War didn't have any motivation for enlisting. There was a war, and they signed up on one side of it or the other." I tried to hand the scene back to him. "I don't think you need a new scene."

He put the poker back in the stand. The cat lay down in front of it, tail switching. "Anyway, I'd like you to read it," Broun said. "Did you call your roommate?"

"Yes."

"Is he coming?"

"I don't know. I think so."

"Good. Good. Now we'll run this dream thing to ground. Be sure and tell me when he gets here." He started out the door. "I'm going to go check on the caterers."

"Hadn't you better shave?"

"Shave?" he said, sounding horrified. "Can't you see I'm growing muttonchop whiskers?" He struck a pose with his hands in his lapels. "Like Lincoln's."

"You don't look like Lincoln," I said, grinning. "You look like Grant after a binge."

"I could say the same thing about you, son," he said, and went downstairs to talk to the caterers.

I tried to read the new scene, wishing I had the time to run a few dreams of my own to ground. I felt tireder than I had before the nap. I couldn't even get my eyes to focus on Broun's typing. The reporters would be here any minute, and then I would stand propped up against a wall for endless hours telling people why Broun's book wasn't ready, and then tomorrow I would go out to Arlington and poke around in the snow, looking for Willie Lincoln's grave.

If I could find out where he was buried, I might not have to spend tomorrow out wiping snow off old tombstones. I put down the rewritten scene and looked for Sandburg's *War Years*.

Broun has never believed in libraries—he keeps books all over the house, and whenever he finishes with one, he sticks it into the handiest bookcase. I offered once to organize the books, and he said, "I know where they all are." He might know, but I didn't, so I had organized them for myself—Grant and the western campaign in the big upstairs dining room, Lee in the solarium, Lincoln in the study. It didn't do much good. Broun still left books wherever he finished with them, but it was better than nothing. I had at least an even chance of finding what I needed. Usually. Not this time, though.

Sandburg's *War Years* wasn't where I'd put it, and neither was Oates. It took me almost an hour to find them, Oates in the upstairs bathroom, Sandburg down in the solarium underneath one of Broun's African violets. Before I even got upstairs with them, a young woman from *People* showed up and tried to pump me about Broun's new book.

"What's it about?" she asked.

"Antietam," I said. "It's in the press release."

"Not that one. The new one he's starting."

"Your guess is as good as mine," I said, and turned her over to Broun and went back into the study with the books I'd found and looked up Willie Lincoln. He had died in 1862, when he was eleven years old. They had had a reception downstairs in the White House while he lay dying upstairs. And probably people had kept ringing the doorbell, I thought, when the doorbell rang.

It was more reporters, and then it was somebody from the caterer's and then more reporters, and I began to think Richard wasn't coming after all, but the next time the doorbell rang it was Richard. With Annie.

"We can't stay very long," Richard said before he even got in the door. He looked tired and strung out, which wasn't much of an endorsement for the Sleep Institute. I wondered if the way he looked had anything to do with his having called me when I was in West Virginia.

"I'm glad you both could come," I said, turning to look at Annie. "I'm Jeff Johnston. I used to room with this guy back before he became a hotshot psychiatrist."

"I'm glad to meet you, Jeff," she said gravely.

She was not at all what I'd expected. Richard had dated mostly hot little nurses when he was in med school, and Washington's Women on the Way Up since he started working at the Institute. He had never so much as glanced at anyone like Annie. She was little, with short blonde hair and bluish gray eyes. She was wearing a heavy gray coat and low-heeled shoes and looked about eighteen.

"The party's upstairs," I said. "It's kind of a zoo, but . . ."

"We don't have much time," Richard said, but he didn't look at his watch. He looked at Annie, as if she were the one in a hurry. She didn't look worried at all.

"How about if I bring Broun down here?" I said, not at all sure I could get him away from the reporters. "You can wait in the solarium." I motioned them in.

It was, like every other room in the house, really a room for Broun to misplace books in, even though it had been intended for tropical plants. It had greenhouse glass windows and a heater that kept it twenty degrees hotter than the rest of the house. Broun had stuck a token row of African violets on a table in front of the windows and added an antique horsehair loveseat and a couple of chairs, but the rest of the room was filled with books. "Let me take your coats," I said.

"No," Richard said with an anxious glance at Annie. "No. We won't be here that long."

I tore up the stairs and got Broun. The caterers had just set out the buffet supper, so he wouldn't even be missed. I told Broun that Richard was here but couldn't stay and herded him toward the stairs, but the reporter from *People* latched on to him, and it was a good five minutes before he could get away from her.

They were still there, but just barely. Richard was at the door of the solarium, saying, "It's almost nine. I think . . ."

"Glad to meet you, Dr. Madison. So you're Jeff's old roommate," Broun said, putting himself between Richard and the front door. "And you must be Annie. I talked to you on the phone."

"Yes," she said. "I've been wanting to meet you, Mr. Brou—"

"I understand you wanted to talk to me about Abraham Lincoln," Richard said, cutting across her words before she even got Broun's name out.

"I do," Broun said. "I appreciate your coming. I've been doing some research on Lincoln. He had some mighty strange dreams," he smiled at Annie, "and since you told me Dr. Madison here tells people what their dreams mean, I thought

11

maybe he could tell me about Lincoln's dreams." He turned back to Richard. "Have you had supper? There's a wonderful buffet upstairs if the reporters haven't eaten it all. Lobster and ham and some wonderful shrimp doodads that . . ."

"I don't have very much time," Richard said, looking at Annie. "I told Jeff on the phone I didn't think I could help you. You can't analyze somebody's dreams just by hearing a secondhand account of them. You have to know all about the person."

"Which Broun does," I said.

"I mostly need some information on what the modern view of dreams is," Broun said, taking hold of Richard's arm. "I promise I'll only take a few minutes of your time. We can all go up to my study. We'll grab something to eat on the way and—"

"I don't think . . ." Richard said, with another anxious glance at Annie.

"You're absolutely right," Broun said, his hand clamped firmly on Richard's arm. "Why should your young lady have to be bored by a lot of dry history when she can go to a party instead? Jeff, you'll keep her company, won't you? Get her some of those shrimp doodads and some champagne?"

Richard looked at Annie as if he expected her to object, but she didn't say anything, and I thought he looked relieved.

"Jeff'll take good care of her," Broun said heartily, like a man trying to make a deal. "Won't you, Jeff?"

"I'll take care of her," I said, looking at her. "I promise."

"The dream I'm having trouble with is one Lincoln had two weeks before his assassination," Broun said, leading Richard firmly up the stairs to his study. "He dreamed he woke up in the White House and heard somebody crying. When he went downstairs . . ." They disappeared into the roar of noise and people at the top of the stairs. I turned and looked at Annie. She was standing looking up after them.

"Would you like to go up to the party?" I said. "Broun'll be upset if you don't have some of the shrimp doodads."

She smiled and shook her head. "I don't think Richard will be that long."

"Yeah, he didn't seem all that enthusiastic about the prospect of analyzing Lincoln's dreams." I led the way back into the solarium. "He kept talking about having to leave. Is one of his patients giving him a rough time?"

She went over to the windows and looked out. "Yes," she said. "Richard told me you're a historian."

"Did he also tell you he thinks I'm crazy for spending my life looking up obscure facts that don't matter to anybody?"

"No," she said, still watching the rain turn into sleet. "That's a term he reserves for me these days." She turned and looked at me. "I'm a patient of his. I have a sleep disorder."

"Oh," I said. "Can I take your coat?" I said, to be saying something. "Broun keeps this room like an oven."

She gave it to me, and I went and hung it in the hall closet, trying to make sense of what she'd just told me. Richard hadn't contradicted me when I'd called her his girlfriend, and Broun had told me she answered the phone at Richard's apartment, but if she was his patient, what was he doing living with her?

When I came back into the solarium, she was looking at Broun's African violets. I went over to the windows and looked out, trying to think of something to talk about. I could hardly ask her if she was sleeping with Richard or if her sleep disorder had anything to do with him.

"I've got to go out to Arlington National Cemetery in this mess tomorrow," I said. "I've got to try and find where Willie Lincoln was buried, for Broun. Willie was Abraham Lincoln's little boy. He died during the war."

"Do you do all of Broun's Civil War research for him?" Annie said, picking up one of the African violets.

"Most of the legwork. You know, when Broun first hired me, he wouldn't let me do hardly any of his research. It took me almost a year to talk him into letting me run his errands for him, and now I wish I hadn't done such a good job. It looks like it's turning into snow out there."

She put the flowerpot back down on the table and looked up at me. "Tell me about the Civil War," she said.

"What do you want to know?" I asked. I wished suddenly that I had had that nap so I could give my full wits to this conversation, tell her stories about the war that would get that 'somehow sad expression out of her blue-gray eyes. "I'm an expert on Antietam. Bloodiest single day of the Civil War. Possibly the most important day, too, though Broun will argue with that. General Lee needed a victory so England would recognize the Confederacy, and so he invaded Maryland, only it didn't work. He had to retreat back to Virginia and . . ."

I stopped. I was putting myself to sleep, and God only knew what I was doing to Annie, who had probably never heard of Antietam. "How about Robert E. Lee? And his horse. I know just about everything there is to know about his damned horse."

She brushed her short hair back from her face and smiled. "Tell me about the soldiers," she said.

"The soldiers, huh? Well, they were farm boys mostly, uneducated. And they were young. The average age of the Civil War soldier was twenty-three."

"I'm twenty-three," she said.

"I don't think you'd have had too much to worry about. They didn't draft women in the Civil War," I said, "though they might have had to if the war had gone on much longer. The Confederacy was down to old men and thirteen-year-old boys. If you're interested in soldiers, there are a whole slew of them buried out at Arlington," I said. "How would you like to go out there with me tomorrow?"

She picked up another of the potted violets and traced her finger along the leaves. "To Arlington?" she said.

Richard and I had roomed together at Duke for four years. I had never even looked at one of his girls, and tonight I had told him I would take care of her for him. "Arlington's a great place to visit," I said, as if I hadn't spent the last three days and nights living on No-Doz and coffee and wanting nothing more than to get back to Broun's and sleep straight through till spring, as if she weren't living with my old roommate. "There are a lot of famous people buried there, and the house is open to the public."

"The house?" she said, bending over another one of the violets.

"Robert E. Lee's house," I said. "It was his plantation until the war. Then the Union occupied it. They buried Union soldiers in the front lawn to make sure he never got it back, and he never did. They turned it into a national cemetery in 1864. I've done a lot of research on Robert E. Lee lately."

She was looking at me. And she had put her hand in the flowerpot. "Did he have a cat?" she said.

I turned and looked behind me at the door, thinking Broun's Siamese had come down here to get away from the party, but it wasn't there. "What?" I said, looking at her hand.

"Did Robert E. Lee have a cat? When he lived at Arlington?"

I was too tired, that was all. If I could just have gotten a nap instead of looking up Willie Lincoln and talking to reporters, I would have been able to take all this in—me asking her out when she was living with Richard, her asking me if Lee had a cat while she scrabbled in the dirt of the flowerpot as if she were trying to dig a grave.

"What kind of cat?" I said.

She had pulled the violet up by its roots and was holding it tightly in her hand. "I don't know. A yellow cat. With darker stripes. It was there, in the dream."

I said, "What dream?" and watched her drop the empty flowerpot. It crashed at her feet.

"I've been having this dream," she said. "In it I'm at the house I grew up in, standing on the front porch, looking for the cat. It's snowed, a wet, spring snow, and I have the idea that he has gotten buried in the snow, but then I see him out in the apple orchard, picking his way through the snow with little, high, funny steps."

I did not know what was coming, but at the words *apple orchard* I sat down on the arm of the loveseat, looking anxiously over my shoulder to see if Richard and Broun were coming. There was nobody on the stairs.

"I called to him, but he didn't pay any attention, so I went after him." She was holding the violet like a nosegay in front of her, tearing the leaves off in absent, desperate movements. "I made it out to the tree all right, and I tried to pick the cat up, but he wouldn't let me, and I tried to catch him and I stepped on something. . . ." She had torn all the leaves off now and was starting on the flowers. "It was a Union soldier. I could see his arm in the blue sleeve sticking out of the dirt. He was still

15

holding his rifle, and there was a piece of paper pinned to his sleeve. Somebody had buried him in the orchard, but not deep enough, and when the snow had started to melt it had uncovered his arm. I bent down and unpinned the paper, but when I looked at it, the paper was blank. I had the idea it might be some kind of message, and that frightened me. I stepped back, and something gave under my foot."

There was nothing left of the violet but the roots, covered in dirt, and she crushed them in her fist. "It was the cap of another soldier. I hadn't stepped on his head, but where the snow had melted I could see him lying face down with his gun under him. He had yellow hair. The cat went over and licked his face like he used to lick mine to wake me up.

"Whoever had buried them had just shoveled sod over them where they'd fallen, and the snow had hidden them, but now it was melting. I still couldn't see them except for a foot or a hand, and I didn't want to step on them but everywhere I stepped I went through to the bodies underneath. And the cat just walked all over them." She had dropped what was left of the violet and was looking past me at the door. "They were buried all over the orchard and the lawn, right up to the front steps."

I could hear somebody clattering down the stairs, and I moved, for the first time that night, as if I were wide awake. I reached past Annie and scooped up a handful of dirt and torn leaves off the floor. When Richard came in with his coat over his arm, we were both bending down, heads together, picking up the shards, and my hands were as dirty as hers.

I straightened up with a handful of dirt and clay triangles. "Did you two figure out what was causing Lincoln's dreams?" I asked.

"No. I told you I couldn't tell him what he wanted to know," Richard said. He looked past me at Annie. "We've got to go. Get your coat."

"I'll get it," I said, and went out to the hall closet.

Broun came plummeting down the stairs. "Is he still here?"

I motioned toward the solarium. He hurried in, and I followed with Annie's coat. "I'm so sorry, Dr. Madison," Broun said. "That damned *People* reporter caught me on the way down. I wanted to say . . ."

"You asked me my opinion, and I gave it to you," Richard said stiffly.

"That's right," Broun said. "I appreciate your giving it to me. And maybe you're right, and Lincoln was heading for a psychotic break, but you have to remember, there had been a number of attempts on his life already, and it seems to me that it would be normal for him to . . ."

Richard shrugged on his overcoat. "You want me to tell you the dreams are normal? Well, I can't. A dream like that is obviously a symptom of a serious neurosis."

I looked at Annie. She hadn't moved. She was standing beside me, her hands full of leaves and pieces of flowerpot, with an expression on her face that told me she had heard all this before.

"Lincoln was in need of immediate professional help," Richard said, "and I'm not going to stand by and say nothing. It's my duty as a doctor to . . ."

"I think Lincoln is pretty much beyond help even for a doctor," Broun said.

"We have to go," Richard said angrily, buttoning his overcoat.

"Well, even though we disagree, I'm glad you came," Broun said, putting his arm around Richard's shoulder. "I'm just sorry you can't stay and have some supper. Those shrimp doodads are wonderful." He led Richard out into the hall.

I held the gray coat and wondered if I were really asleep and dreaming all this. Annie came and took the coat off my arm, and I helped her into it. "What was the cat's name?" I said. "In your dream?"

"I don't know," she said. "It's not my cat." She looked down to button her coat, and then looked back up at me. "It's not my dream," she said. "I know you won't believe me because Richard doesn't. He thinks I'm heading for a psychotic break, and you probably think I'm crazy, too, but it's not my dream. I'm dreaming it, but it's somebody else's."

"Your . . . he's getting the car," Broun said, taking in the whole scene.

"I'm sorry about your African violets," Annie said. "I was looking at one of them and . . ."

"No harm done, no harm done." He led her to the front door and out, talking the whole time. "I'm so glad you could come to our reception."

When he came back, I was on my hands and knees in front of the bookcase, looking for volume two of Freeman. "I had a very peculiar conversation with your roommate just now," he said. He sat down on the arm of the loveseat and looked at the pile of dirt and flowerpot fragments that had been his violet. He scratched his scruffy beard, looking more than ever like a horsetrader. "He told me that Lincoln's dream was a symbol for some deep-seated trauma, probably in his childhood."

I found *The Gray Fox* and looked up "Cats," and then "Lee, love of pets," in the index. "Well, what did you expect from a psychiatrist?" I said, wishing he would go back to the party so I could find out whether Lee had had a cat.

"I told him I thought the deep-seated trauma was probably the Civil War, and that it seemed perfectly normal for him to dream about assassinations and coffins in the White House. Did you know Willie's coffin was put in the East Room?"

"Did Robert E. Lee have a cat?" I said.

Broun looked at me. "Lincoln had cats. Kittens. He loved kittens."

"Lee, damn it, not Lincoln. When he lived at Arlington, did he have a cat?"

"I don't know," he said, and it was the same placating tone he'd used with Richard. "Maybe Freeman says something about a cat."

"Maybe it does, but I don't have a goddamn clue as to where Freeman is. You keep volume one in the attic, volume three under your bed, and volume four you tear up for mulch and use in your African violets. If you had a library like other people instead of this goddamned disorganized mess . . ."

"Your roommate said," Broun went on, "that all the half-buried bodies in the dream showed that Lincoln was obsessed with death."

I looked up from the book. He was watching me with his

bright little horsetrader's eyes. "Do you have any idea what he was talking about?" he asked.

"No," I said. I picked up the scattered books and started to put them back on the shelf. "I'm going to bed. I've got to go out to Arlington in the morning."

He stood up then and patted me on the shoulder. "Don't bother with it," he said. "It can wait. You've just gotten home from a long trip, and I know you're tired. Go on to bed, son. I'll take care of that mob upstairs." His hand was still on my shoulder. "Did you get a chance to read that scene I gave you?"

"No," I said.

"I had Ben have a fight with his brother over a girl. I wonder how many soldiers did that, enlisted because of some girl?"

I looked down at the book I was holding. It was the missing volume two. "I don't know," I said, and moved away from him.

CHAPTER TWO

Robert E. Lee first saw Traveller during the Big Sewell Mountain campaign in western Virginia. He was riding Richmond then, a big bay stallion that had been given to him by a group of admirers in Richmond. The horse Richmond didn't have the stamina or the disposition for war. He tired easily and squealed and bucked whenever there were other horses around. When Lee was ordered to the south, he didn't take Richmond. He took a horse called the "Brown Roan," who later went blind and had to be retired. After Manassas, General Jeb Stuart gave Lee a gentle mare named Lucy Long to spell Traveller. In 1864 Lucy gave out, and Lee sent her behind the lines to recuperate. She was stolen by stragglers and sold to a Virginia surgeon.

I didn't wake up till ten the next day, and when I did it was with the idea that the phone had been ringing. It must have been. The message light was on. I turned on the answering machine and listened to the messages while I got dressed. There were two of them. The first was Broun. It had the grainy sound of his car phone. "Jeff, I'm on my way to New York," he said. "I called my editor this morning. He says it's too late to add a scene, that they're already printing the galleys, so I'm taking the scene up to him myself and making sure it gets in. I'll be back tonight. Oh, and forget about going out to Arlington. I got to thinking this morning, Arlington wasn't made into an official cemetery until 1864, and Willie died in 1862. We'll figure out where he was buried later. Stay home and get some rest, son. It's supposed to snow. Oh, and I straightened up the books."

I looked out the window. It had apparently just sleeted enough to put an icy glaze on the streets last night and then stopped, but now it was starting again. There were only a few large flakes, and they were melting before they even hit the sidewalk, but it had started that way in West Virginia, too, and then turned into a blizzard.

The message was over for a while before the machine and I realized it. Broun had refused to buy a regular thirty-seconds-and-beep kind of machine. "Nobody worth talking to can state his business in thirty seconds," was what he said, but what he really wanted was to be able to read long passages of the galleys over the phone or have me dictate the research I was doing in Springfield onto a tape that he could listen to and I could transcribe when I got home. He had had a whole elaborate setup built into the wall behind his desk, with a voice-activated tape that could hold up to three hours of messages and all kinds of fancy remote codes and buttons for fast-forwarding through messages and erasing them.

I pulled on a sweater and waited for the second message. It was Richard. "I'm at the Institute," he said. "I want to talk to you." He sounded as angry over the phone as he had when he left last night.

I erased both messages and called Annie at Richard's apartment instead. "It's Jeff," I said when she answered.

"I just tried to call you," she said, "but your line was busy. Do you still have to go out to Arlington to do your research? I want to go with you."

"I was going out this morning," I said. "Are you sure you want to go? It's supposed to get pretty bad." The snow was coming down faster now and starting to stick to the sidewalk. I could imagine her standing at the phone in Richard's living room, looking out at it.

"It isn't snowing very much over here," she said. "I'd like to go."

"I'll pick you up," I said. "I'll be there in about an hour."

"Don't come all the way across town. There's a Metro station right outside of Arlington. I'll meet you there, all right?"

"Okay," I said. "I'll be there in half an hour."

I got a Styrofoam cup and put what was left of Broun's breakfast coffee in it to take with me. I had been up half the night, trying to find the answer to Annie's question about whether Lee had had a cat. It hadn't been in volume two of Freeman either, or in Connelly's *The Marble Man.* I'd found a letter from Lee to his daughter Mildred that mentioned Baxter and Tom the Nipper, but they were Mildred's cats, and anyway, there was little chance that they had made it through the many moves of the war. Robert E. Lee, Jr., had annotated the letter with the remark that his father was fond of cats "in his way and in their place," which seemed to indicate that Lee hadn't had any special cat after all. Nothing I could find in the mess of Broun's books said anything about the family owning a cat when they lived at Arlington. I had finally had to call one of the volunteers who guided tours at Arlington House. I woke her out of a sound sleep, but even half-awake she knew the answer. "It's in the letters to Markie Williams," she said, and told me where to find it.

The snow turned into something that was half-rain, half-snow, and slicker than either as soon as I pulled onto the Rock Creek Parkway. It took me almost twenty minutes to get past the Lincoln Memorial and across the bridge.

Annie was waiting on the sidewalk next to the stairs of the Metro station, hunched against the sleet in her gray coat. She was wearing gray gloves, but she didn't have anything on her head, and her light hair was wet with snow.

"I've already been in this storm once on my way back from West Virginia," I said as she got in. I turned the car heater up to high. "What say we forget the whole thing and go have lunch somewhere?"

"No," she said. "I want to go."

"Okay," I said. "We may not be able to see much of anything, though." Arlington was always open, even on days like this. It was, after all, a cemetery and not a tourist attraction, but I had my doubts about the house.

The sleet was coming down progressively harder. I couldn't even see as far as the Seabees Memorial, let alone back across the bridge. "This is ridiculous," I said. "Why don't we . . ."

"I asked Richard if he'd take me out to Arlington last night. On the way home. And again this morning. He wouldn't. He says I'm trying to project repressed feelings onto an exterior cause, that I'm refusing to face a trauma that's so terrible I won't even admit it's mine."

"Is that what you think?" I asked.

"I don't know," she said.

"How many times have you had the dream about the dead soldiers in the apple orchard?"

"I don't know exactly. I've had it every night for over a year."

"Over a year? You've been at the Sleep Institute that long?"

"No," she said. "I came to Washington about two months ago. My doctor sent me to Dr. Stone because I was what they call pleisomniac. I kept waking up all the time."

"Dr. Stone?"

"He's the head of the Institute, but he was in California, so I saw Richard. I stayed at the Institute for a week while they ran all kinds of tests, and then I was supposed to be an outpatient, but the dream started getting worse."

"Worse? How?"

"When I first started having it, I couldn't remember very much of the dream. The dead soldier was in it and the snow and the apple tree, but it wasn't very clear. I don't mean fuzzy exactly, but distant, sort of. And then, after I'd been at the Institute for two weeks, it suddenly got clearer, and when I woke up from it I was so scared I didn't know what to do." Her gloved hands were clenched tightly in her lap.

"Did you go back to the Institute?"

"No." She looked down at her hands. "I called Richard up and told him I was afraid to stay alone, and he said to get a cab and come right over, that I could stay with him."

I'll bet he did, I thought. "You said the dream was clearer? You mean, like focusing a camera?"

"No, not exactly. The dream itself didn't change. It was just more frightening. And clearer somehow. I started noticing things like the message on the soldier's arm. It had been there all along, but I just hadn't seen it before. And I noticed the apple tree was in bloom. I don't think it was in the first dream."

The windshield wipers were starting to ice up. I opened my window and reached around to smack the wiper against the windshield. A narrow band of ice broke off and slid down the window. "What about the cat? Was it in the dream from the beginning?"

"Yes. Do you think I'm crazy like Richard says?"

"No." I pulled very carefully away from the curb and onto the wide road.

I couldn't see the curving stone gates until we were almost up to them, and I couldn't see Arlington House at all. You can usually see it all the way from the Mall across the Potomac, looking like a golden Greek temple instead of a plantation, with its broad porch and buff-colored pillars.

"Robert E. Lee had a cat, didn't he?" she said.

"Yes," I said, and turned in at the iron gate that led to the visitors' center, flashed the pass Broun had that let him drive into the cemetery instead of parking in the visitors' lot, at a guard in a raincoat and a plastic-covered hat, and drove on up the hill to the back of Arlington House. We still couldn't see more than a bare outline of the house through the sleet, even after I'd parked the car at the back of the house next to the outbuilding that had been turned into the gift shop, but Annie wasn't looking at the house. As soon as I'd parked the car, she got out and walked around to the garden as if she knew exactly where she was going.

I followed her, squinting through the snow at the house to see if it was open to visitors. I couldn't tell. There weren't any other cars in the parking lot, and there weren't any footprints leading up to the house, but the snow was coming down fast enough that it could have hidden them. The only way to tell would be to go up to the front door, but Annie was already standing in front of the first of the tombstones at the edge of the garden, her head bent to look at the name on the wet tombstone as if she wasn't even aware of the snow.

I went over and stood next to her. The snow still wasn't sticking to the grass except in little isolated clumps that melted and refroze, making webs of ice between the blades of grass, but the wind had blown enough snow against the tombstones to make them almost unreadable. I could barely make out the name on the first one.

" 'John Goulding, Lieutenant, Sixteenth New York Cavalry,' " Annie read.

"These aren't the soldiers who were originally buried here," I said. "Those were all enlisted men. Officers were buried on the hill in front of the mansion."

The second gravestone was covered with snow. I bent and wiped it off with my hand, wishing I'd worn gloves. "See? 'Gustave Von Branson, Lieutenant, Company K, Third U.S. Vermont Volunteers.' Lieutenant Von Branson wasn't buried here till 1865, after Arlington had become a national cemetery." I straightened up, rubbing my wet hand on my jeans, and turned around. "Then Commander Meigs had the enlisted men moved to—"

Annie was gone. "Annie?" I said stupidly and looked down the row of tombstones, thinking maybe she had gone past me, but she wasn't there. She must have gone into the house, I thought. It must be open today after all.

I walked rapidly back along the gravel path and up the slick steps onto the porch. The wind was blowing snow up onto the brick-tiled porch and against the buff-colored pillars so they looked almost white.

I tried the door and then pounded on it. "Are you open?" I shouted, trying to see in through the windows. There weren't any footprints on the porch except mine, but I kept on pounding for another full minute, as if I thought Annie might have gotten locked in, before my rational self told me she'd probably gotten cold and gone back to the car, and I went back around the house to see.

She wasn't in the car, and the gift shop was locked up tight, and I gave up all pretense that I wasn't worried and went tearing back to the front of the house to look down the hill at the lawn where the bodies had been buried.

The wind had picked up in the time it took me to get to the car and back, and I couldn't see more than a few yards down the hill. "Annie!" I shouted.

I wasn't sure I'd be able to hear her if she answered, but I shouted again, ready to take off down the hill, and then I caught a glimpse of gray moving between trees on the far side of Arlington House and took off running after her. She must be on the Custis Walk, the wide cement sidewalk that came up from the road below. It made a wide curve around the hill so the view of the house wouldn't be spoiled, and I wondered as I ran if that was why they had moved the bodies, too, because they had spoiled the view.

The walk was hardly snowy at all, protected as it was by the big trees that were planted all along its length, and I took the cracked, uneven steps two at a time, trying to catch up with her, and found myself suddenly at the curved wall and marble terrace of the Kennedy Memorial. The eternal flame burned on the grave in the center of a circle of rough, smoke-charred stone, melting the snow around it as it fell.

I looked back up the hill. The snow was blowing almost horizontally across the hill and I couldn't see Arlington House, but I could see Annie. She stood halfway up the hill behind a low wall, looking down at the snow-covered lawn where nothing was buried anymore. I must have gone right past her, missing the turnout in my headlong pitch down the stairs. She didn't see me, standing there looking helplessly up at her, or the eternal flame that seemed to flinch away from the wet flakes of snow falling on it, but I could see her clearly in spite of the snow and the distance between us. I could see the expression on her face.

She had looked frightened last night, telling me her dream, but it was nothing compared to the terror in her face now. I could see them, the yellow-haired soldiers with their arms flung out across the snowy grass, their rifles still under them, and the ink on the scraps of paper pinned to their sleeves beginning to blur as the snow hit the paper and melted. I could see all of it, even the cat, reflected in Annie's face, and I knew I had had no business bringing her out here.

"Annie!" I yelled, and sprinted up the steep slope, my shoes slipping on the icy grass. "Hold on!" I shouted as if I thought she might fall. "I'm coming!"

I scrambled over the pebbled cement wall. "I lost you," I said, trying to get my breath. "Are you all right?"

"Yes," she said, still looking down the hill. "Tell me about Robert E. Lee."

The shoulders of her coat were covered with snow. Her hair was wet past curling. She must have been standing there the whole time I was looking for her.

"I had no business bringing you out here," I said. "You're going to catch your death of cold. Let's go back to the car."

"Did he ever come back here?"

"I know a great place just across the bridge. Big fireplace. Great coffee. We can talk about Lee there." I took hold of her arm. "I'll tell you whatever you want to know."

She gave no indication that she even felt my hand on her arm. "Did he come back here after the war?"

"No," I said. "He saw it once. From a train window."

She nodded as if I had confirmed something she already knew.

"Let's at least go up on the porch of Arlington House. We'll be out of the wind there."

"He was a good person, wasn't he? They always say that, that he was a good person, don't they?"

I wanted to get her in out of the snow and out of her wet coat and sopping shoes and in front of a fire so she wouldn't catch pneumonia, but I was never going to get her to budge until I had answered her questions. I let go of her arm. "He was a good person, I guess, if you can call anybody who directed the slaughter of two hundred and fifty thousand men good," I said. "He was brave, dignified, forgiving, kind to children and animals. Everybody loved him, even Lincoln."

"His soldiers loved him," Annie said. She had taken off her gloves and was twisting them in her hands.

"Yes," I said. "One time at Cold Harbor, a column of his soldiers saw him resting under a tree and passed the word that

27

'Marse Robert' was asleep. The whole column went past him practically on tiptoe so they wouldn't wake him up. His soldiers loved him. His horse loved him."

"Two hundred and fifty thousand men," she said. "If he was a good man, how could he bear that, all those young boys? He wouldn't ever be able to get over it, would he?"

"I don't know."

"Maybe that's why he can't sleep. Because of all those boys." She turned to look at me. "This is the house in my dream. In the dream it looks like my house, but it's not my house. It's this house. And it's not my dream." She turned and looked back down the hill at the Kennedy Memorial. The eternal flame, burning inside the circle of blackened stone, looked like a soldier's campfire. "Tell me about the cat."

"Did you ever have a cat? When you were a child?" I asked.

"No," she said. "You think I'm crazy, don't you?" she said. She had dropped both gloves. Her hands, flat on the low rough wall, were red and wet.

"No."

"Richard says something happened to me when I was little, something I don't remember, that's causing me to have the dreams, and that the apple tree and the bodies and the cat are all symbols for what happened. He says the blank paper pinned to the soldier's sleeve is a symbol for the message my subconscious is trying to send me only I'm too afraid to read it."

"Robert E. Lee's daughter had a cat named Tom Tita," I said. "A yellow tabby. He was left behind accidentally when the Lees left Arlington. When a cousin, Markie Williams, went to Arlington to get some of their things and send them to the Lees, she found the cat. It had been locked in the attic, living on mice."

"What happened to it?"

I stooped to pick up her gloves. "I don't know." I handed them back to her. "She didn't say anything about taking it with her. I suppose she left it there with the Union soldiers who were occupying Arlington. I don't know what happened to it."

"I feel cold," she said, and walked ahead of me back to the sidewalk and up to the house.

The porch wasn't much protection. The snow was starting to pile up on the wooden steps and had blown across the hexagonal brick tiles in curving drifts. "Why don't we go sit in the car and talk?" I said. "It's freezing out here."

She sat down on a black painted bench. "Did you find that in a book?" she said. "About the cat?"

"In a letter," I said.

"I could have read it, too, a long time ago, and forgotten I'd ever read it. I could have read somewhere that Arlington was Lee's house and forgotten that, too."

"Like Bridey Murphy," I said. "She was hypnotized. She didn't have dreams."

"Richard says dreams aren't really the way we remember them. That they're emotions projected as images or symbols, but the second people wake up they try to hide the meaning of the dream from themselves by adding things and forgetting things so it means something else. Maybe that's what I'm doing. I'm making them dead Union soldiers and they're really something else."

"What?" I said.

"I don't know."

"What kind of gun did the soldier have? The one you stepped on. You said he was still holding on to his rifle. What kind of rifle was it?"

"I think it was a toy gun," she said. "It looked like a rifle, but it had a roll of paper caps in it, like a toy pistol." She looked up at me. "Does that mean I shot somebody with a cap pistol in our apple orchard, and then made myself forget it?"

The snow was coming down like a curtain around us. I could barely see past the edge of the porch. "One of the guns used in the Civil War was the Springfield rifle. It fired a minié ball by using a paper roll of percussion caps, like the roll of caps in a toy pistol."

"I had another dream last night," she said.

"We can't sit out here. You can tell me about it in the car," I said, and stood up, offering her my hand. She took hold of it with her icy one, and I helped her up, wanting to grab both her hands and hold them against my chest, rubbing some warmth back into them, but she let go as soon as she was on her feet, and put her sodden gloves back on. We walked back to the car.

I started it and turned up the heater and the fan as far as they would go. I didn't turn the windshield wipers on, and the collecting snow shut out the sight of the house and the garden and the graves.

"I was standing under the apple tree, only it was on a hill and down at the bottom of it was a stream, and where my house was supposed to be was the Presbyterian church that I went to when I was a little girl," she said. She took off her gloves, started to twist them in her hands, and then stopped and stuck them in her pocket.

"It was afternoon, and Richard was there. He was wearing his slippers, and he was looking down the hill, but I couldn't see what he was looking at, and I was angry that he was doing that instead of helping me look." She stopped and stared at the blinded windshield.

"Helping you look for what?" I said.

"The message. There were supposed to be a hundred and ninety-one of them, but one of them was missing, and I said to Richard, 'We've got to find it,' but he wouldn't put down the telescope, he just pointed down the hill and said, 'Ask Hill. He knows where it is,' and at first I thought he meant the hill we were standing on, but then I saw a man on a gray horse and I went down and said angrily, 'Where is it?' but he didn't pay any attention to me either. He was trying to get down off his horse, but the horse had fallen forward, onto its knees sort of. Its knees were bent under . . ."

She tried to show me, but her elbows wouldn't bend the right way, and I already knew how the horse had looked. I shut my eyes.

"He had one foot in the stirrup and he was trying to get his other leg over the saddlehorn, but he couldn't, and after a while I went back up the hill to Richard and said, 'We've got to find it.' He didn't answer me either because he was looking through his telescope past the church to the south. I was going to take the telescope away from him, but just then I saw what he was looking at. It was a whole line of Union soldiers, coming up from the south. I said, 'Whose troops are those?' and Richard handed the telescope to me, but my hands were bandaged and I couldn't hold it, so I made him look again, and he said, 'They're Federals,' and I said, 'No. It's Hill,' and just then the man who'd been on the horse that was on its knees came riding up on another horse, only now he was wearing a red wool shirt, and I was so glad to see him because it meant that even though we couldn't find it, he had still gotten the message."

I didn't say anything. I ran my hands around the rim of the steering wheel and thought about how I should take her home before the snow got any worse and we were both trapped up here.

"Maybe Richard's right," she said, "and whatever's in that lost message is whatever it is I can't remember."

"What about the bandages on your hands? What about the Confederate soldiers in blue uniforms? And the number one hundred and ninety-one? What are they supposed to mean?"

"I don't know," she said lightly, and put her gloves back on. "Richard will have to tell me. He's the psychiatrist."

"Broun's new book is about Antietam," I said. "I've spent the last six months researching everything in print about that battle."

"And you know why my hands are bandaged?"

"Lee broke his right hand and sprained his left just before the march into Maryland. He was still wearing the splints and bandages at Antietam. Lee had sent an urgent message to A. P. Hill at Harper's Ferry, telling him to bring his men up as fast as he could, so when he saw some soldiers coming up from the south he hoped it was Hill's troops, but the soldiers were wearing blue uniforms.

"He asked one of his aides, 'Whose troops are those?' The aide told him they were Union soldiers and offered to let Lee use the telescope, but Lee held up his bandaged hands and said, 'Can't use it. What troops are those?' The aide looked again, and this time he could see the Confederate battle flags.

"It was A. P. Hill's men, just up from Harper's Ferry after a forced march of seventeen miles. Hill was riding ahead of them. He was wearing a red shirt." I gripped the steering wheel. "They were wearing Union uniforms they had taken from the Federal stores they captured at Harper's Ferry."

Annie turned and looked out the side window at the graves she couldn't see. "I want to go home," she said.

CHAPTER THREE

Lee didn't buy Traveller "in the mountains of Virginia in the autumn of 1861," as he wrote his cousin Markie Williams after the war, but he thought of the horse as his from that meeting on, calling him "my colt" when he saw him again in North Carolina and going out to the stables to visit him. The hostler complained that he was "always pokin' 'round my horses as if he meant to steal one of 'em."

Broun had called again, from New York, and left a message on the machine. The weather was even worse to the north. He hadn't been to McLaws and Herndon yet, but he'd seen his agent, and she'd hit the roof about the scene. She'd told Broun that the galleys had already gone to press and there was no way they'd be willing to stop the presses for a scene Broun's editor hadn't even okayed, but Broun was going to try anyway. He'd be home tonight if the weather let up. Otherwise, he'd come back tomorrow morning.

"I want you to call your friend Richard and see if he knows anything about prodromic dreams." He spelled the word, and then, as if he knew what he was asking was impossible, he said, "Or better yet, call Kate at the library and see if you can get a bibliography on them. And see if you can find out where Willie Lincoln's buried. Lincoln dreamed about Willie after he died. I'm determined to run this dream thing to ground."

I looked at the books lying jumbled on the shelves under the African violets. Broun must have been at them again after he straightened them up. There was a biography of Lincoln lying open on top. I rescued a Freeman from the mess and then put it down again.

I wondered what Annie was doing. I hoped she had gotten out of her wet clothes and taken a hot bath, had something to eat, gone to bed, but I had an image of her standing, like myself, looking out at the snow, still in her gray coat, dripping all over the carpet like I was, and beginning to shiver.

I picked up the biography of Lincoln and went up to the study to put it away. The phone rang.

"I want you to stay away from Annie," Richard said.

"Are you asking me as her doctor or her boyfriend?"

"I'm not asking you at all. I'm telling you. Stay away from her. You had no business taking her out to Arlington."

"She asked me to drive her out," I said. "She told me she asked you to take her, and you refused. So I figure you had your chance."

"Annie's emotionally unstable. By taking her out there, you could have sent her into a complete psychotic break."

"Like that nutso Lincoln?" I said. "You told Broun old Abe was heading for a psychotic break because he'd dreamed, of all things, about his own assassination. Are you trying to tell me that anybody who dreams about the Civil War is crazy?"

"She's not dreaming about the Civil War."

"Then where in the hell did the Union soldiers come from?"

"You did this, didn't you? While I was upstairs talking to Broun, you were filling her head with a lot of nonsense about soldiers being buried in the front lawn out at Arlington, encouraging this neurotic fantasy of hers. You told her Robert E. Lee had a cat, didn't you?"

"He did have a cat."

"And as soon as you told Annie that, she told you the cat in her dream was exactly like Robert E. Lee's cat, didn't she?"

I didn't answer him. I was thinking of Annie clutching the

African violet and saying, "Did Robert E. Lee have a cat? A yellow cat? With darker stripes?"

· "During dream recall the dreamer's extremely suggestive," Richard said. "Anything that's told to the dreamer then can influence his memory of the dream. It's called secondary elaboration."

"Like telling her she'd shot somebody with a cap pistol?" I said. "The Springfield rifle had a percussion cap, did you know that? It looked just like a kid's cap pistol. The Springfield rifle was used in the Civil War."

"Did you tell her that?" he said, sounding almost frightened. "You had no business telling her that. You're interfering with her therapy. As her psychiatrist, I have a duty to . . ."

"To what? Hit on your patients?"

"I wasn't trying to hit on her, damn it. It just happened. I was trying to help her. She was afraid to be alone at night. It just happened. Damn it, you've seen her."

I'd seen her, standing in the solarium in her gray coat saying, "You won't believe me either." I would have driven her out to Arlington right then, in spite of the snow, if she had asked me to. I would have scaled the locked gates and broken into the attic with an ax to look for Lee's lost cat. I would have done anything to help her. Help her. Not take advantage of her fear and her helplessness.

"So you told her she was crazy and then climbed on top of her?" I said. "Is that how you helped her?"

"Keep away from her. You're interfering with her therapy."

"Is that what you call taking your patients home and fucking them when they're too scared and tired to say no? What other therapies are you using, Doctor? Have you thought about drugging her so she'll cooperate?"

He waited so long to say anything that even Broun's patient answering machine would have switched off. I waited.

"You know what's really ironic," he said bitterly, "I tried to call you last week, but you weren't there," and hung up.

I looked out at the snow some more and then called the clinic to find out if Richard had phoned me from there. His secretary said, "I'm sorry. He's not in right now. Can I take a message?"

"Will he be in at all today?"

"Well . . ." she said as if she were looking at an appointment book. "He has a general staff meeting at four, but that may be canceled because of the weather."

I didn't wait for her to ask for my name. "Thanks. I'm a friend of his from out of town, and I've got to catch a plane in about five minutes. I just thought I'd give him a call while I was in Washington."

The phone rang as soon as I pressed down the button. I had the crazy idea that Richard had been listening in on the call and was going to threaten me again, but it was Broun.

"I didn't make it up here with the last two pages of that damned scene," he said. "It's probably on my desk. Can you look for it?"

I rummaged through the pile on his desk. He had stuck it in Randall's *Lincoln the President*. "It's right here," I said. "Do you want me to Federal Express it?"

"There's no time for that. They've got the book all set up to print. If these changes don't go in right now, they don't go in at all. You'll have to read it over the phone. McLaws and Herndon are set up to record your call at this number." He gave me the number.

"Are you going to try to come home tonight?"

"No. It's a real blizzard up here," he said, and then seemed to catch something in my voice. "Are you all right?"

No, I thought. I've just had a conversation I would never have believed I'd have with my old roommate over a girl I've just met, and I want you to come home and tell me she's not crazy. I want you to come home and tell me I'm not crazy. "I'm fine," I said. "I was just wondering."

He still sounded worried. "You got my message this morning, didn't you? You didn't go out to Arlington in this mess?"

"No," I said. "The weather's terrible here, too."

"Good," he said. "I want you to take care of yourself. I thought you looked kind of peaked last night." He paused, and I could hear voices in the background. "Listen, they're getting impatient on this end for that scene. Get some rest, son, and don't worry about anything till I get back."

"I'll call it in right away," I said.

I hung up and then wished I hadn't. What would Broun say if I called him back and told him I'd gone out to Arlington after all, and with somebody who'd dreamed about the battle of Antietam and Lee's lost cat?

He would say, "There's a logical explanation for this," and I had already told myself that—that and a lot of other things. I had gone through every argument there was last night, one after the other, the way I had gone through Broun's books looking for Tom Tita.

They were only dreams. She was ill. She was crazy. It was all an elaborate scam so she could get close to Broun. There was a logical explanation for the dreams. She had read about the cat somewhere. She'd been to Arlington as a child. It was all a joke. She'd been put up to it by Richard. It was some kind of dopey Bridey Murphy phenomenon. It was just a coincidence. Lots of people dreamed about yellow tabby cats. They were only dreams.

There was no point in calling Broun back. He wouldn't be able to add any new arguments to that list. Worse, he might not even try to convince me there was a logical explanation. Fascinated as he was by Lincoln's dreams right now, he might say, "Has she ever dreamed she saw herself in a coffin in the East Room? Do you think you could try to get her to dream Lincoln's dreams?"

I called the number Broun had given me for calling in the scene, and they put me on hold. I read the scene over while I was waiting.

"You can begin recording now," a woman said, and I heard a click and then a dial tone. I called again, but the line was busy, so I set the machine to redial the number every two minutes, plugged in the auxiliary mike, and read the revised scene onto the answering machine:

The picket fire slowed up toward dark, and Malachi went back into the woods a little way and built a cookfire.

"What you Rebs havin' for supper over there?" a voice called from across the river.

"Yankees," Toby said, and then ducked as if he thought they'd shoot at the sound. There was laughter from across the river, and another voice called, "Any of you Rebs come from Hillsboro?"

"Yeah, and we are on our way to Washington," Toby shouted back. He put his gun down and leaned on it. "Myself, I hail from Big Sewell Mountain. What you want to know 'bout Hillsboro?"

The voice across the river shouted, "I am looking for my brother. His name's Ben Freeman. You know him?"

Toby stepped forward in plain sight to say something funny. Ben stood up and fired across the river. There was a rapid volley of rifle fire, and Toby dived for the ground, his arms around his gun. Ben walked into the woods and sat down by Malachi's fire. Malachi didn't say anything, and after a minute Ben said, "I don't think we should go talking to the enemy thata way."

Malachi stirred the fire and hung a can over it to boil the coffee in. "How'd you and your brother come to be on opposite sides of this thing?"

"We just did," Ben said, staring at the can.

Toby came up to the fire and squatted down in front of it. "You and your brother fight over some girl?"

"We didn't fight." Ben reached for his rifle and laid it across his lap. "He just one day signed up, and I knew I had to, too, and there we was, enemies."

"Me, I was drafted," Toby said. "I bet there was a girl in it somewheres, you signing up thataway."

"You keep on like that, you might get yourself shot," Malachi said mildly, "setting yourself up for a target that way."

I rewound the tape and waited. The call-completed button came on. I picked up the phone and gave the editor the remote code so she could receive the recorded message without redialing and waited again while she set up a recorder on her end.

"We're all set here," she said.

"Call me again if it doesn't work," I said, and hung up.

It was two-thirty. The snow looked like it had let up a little. Richard should be able to make it to his staff meeting. If he wasn't sitting by the phone making sure I didn't talk to Annie.

I picked up Randall's *Lincoln the President*. Maybe he knew where Willie was buried. If he knew, he wasn't telling, but he did say what Willie had died from. It was something called bilious fever, and God only knew what that was. Typhoid probably, though that was already a disease with a name in 1862, and a lot was made of his having caught a cold from riding his pony in bad weather, so it might have been a simple case of pneumonia.

Finding out what people died of a hundred years ago is almost impossible. Letters written by the grief-stricken relatives say that the daughter or son died of "milk fever" or "brain fever" or frequently just "a fever," and even that is something. Sometimes the patient simply died, "having progressed weaker and more sickly through the winter till we held out little hope."

Doctors' accounts are no better. They diagnose agues and heavy colds and "diffusion of the heart." Robert E. Lee, who had almost certainly suffered from angina throughout the war and died of a heart attack, was variously diagnosed as suffering from rheumatic excitement, venous congestion, and sciatica. The modern diagnosis had been pieced together only because somebody thought to write down the symptoms. Otherwise, nobody would have the slightest idea what he died of.

At any rate, Willie Lincoln "took cold" and died of pneumonia or typhoid or possibly malaria—whatever it was was probably contagious, because his brother Tad was sick, too—or something else altogether, lay in state in the Green Room, and then was moved to the East Room for the funeral.

The funeral was well documented, though I had to put down Randall and rummage through the mess in Broun's study to find the details. The government buildings were closed on the day of the funeral, which irritated Attorney General Bates, who commented that Willie had been "too much idolized by his parents." Lincoln, his son Robert, and members of the Cabinet attended, and Mrs. Lincoln didn't. The Reverend Dr. Gurley performed the service, Willie was bundled into a hearse, and then, like Tom Tita the cat, dropped out of sight.

Randall stopped cold after the funeral; everyone else I read quoted Sandburg, and Sandburg said blithely that Willie's body had been sent back west for burial. It had, but not until 1865. I was sure of that. Lloyd Lewis had chronicled every detail of Lincoln's funeral and the long train trip to Springfield, including Willie's coffin, which lay in front of his father's in the funeral car, so it wasn't "sent back west" for over three years, and Sandburg, of all people, should have known that.

Sandburg had known Lewis back in the Chicago newspaper days. He had called him Friend Lewis when he wrote the introduction to Lewis's *Myths After Lincoln*. I wondered if Sandburg had forgotten what Lewis wrote about Willie, or if something else had happened between them, something that made Lewis no longer a Friend, something that meant they didn't read each other's books anymore. And was there a girl in it somewhere?

But even Lewis, who was a treasure trove of Lincolniana, didn't say where Willie's body had been for three long years. Was I supposed to assume that it lay in the East Room all that time, giving Lincoln bad dreams? Or had they buried it in the front lawn of the White House?

It was a quarter of four. I put the books back where maybe they would be next time I wanted them and called Annie.

She sounded sleepy, and that reassured me. She hadn't been standing by the window in her wet coat looking out at the snow, listening to Richard tell her she was crazy. She had been asleep.

"How are you?" I asked.

"Fine," she said, but slowly, with a question in her voice.

"Good. I was worried about you. I was afraid you might have caught a chill out at Arlington." Caught a chill. I sounded like a Civil War doctor.

"No," she said, and this time she sounded a little more sure of herself. "Richard fixed me some hot tea and made me lie down. I guess I fell asleep."

"Annie, does Richard have you taking anything? Any medication?"

"Richard?" she said, and that faint note of questioning was there in her voice again.

"Is Richard there?" I asked.

"No," she said, and it was the only thing she'd sounded sure about so far. "He's at the Institute."

"Annie," I said, and felt like I was shouting to her from the bottom of a hill, "are you taking any medicine, any pills?"

"No," she said through a yawn.

"When you first came to the Sleep Institute, did Richard prescribe anything for you? Any medicine?"

"Elavil," she said, and I grabbed my notes on Willie and scribbled it in the margin. "But then he took me off of it."

"Why?"

"I don't know. He just took me off of it."

"When did he do that?—take you off the Elavil?"

It took her a long time to answer. "It was after the dreams got clearer."

"How long after?"

"I don't know."

"And he didn't put you on anything else?"

"No," she said.

"Listen, Annie, if you have any more dreams or if you need anything, if you want me to take you somewhere, anything, I want you to call me. All right?"

"All right."

"Annie, last night you said you thought you were dreaming somebody else's dream. Are you sure it was a dream?"

There was another long wait before she answered, and I was afraid the question had upset her, but she simply said, "What?" as if she hadn't heard the question.

"How do you know it's a dream, Annie? Could it be something that really happened?"

"No, they're dreams," she said, and her words were blurred a little, as if she still weren't awake.

"How do you know?"

"Because they feel like dreams. I can't describe it. They . . ." She all of a sudden sounded more awake. "What message was I looking for? Was it the message I sent to Hill at Harper's Ferry?"

"No," I said. "On the twelfth of September Lee issued campaign orders for the drive into Maryland. One of them was lost. Nobody knows exactly what happened, but a Union soldier found the order and gave it to McClellan."

"There couldn't have been a hundred and ninety-one copies of it, though," she said, as if she were trying to convince herself. "Lee didn't have that many generals. There probably weren't that many generals in the whole Civil War."

I said, "You've had a rough day. I don't want you to catch pneumonia. Go back to bed, and we'll talk about this tomorrow."

"If there weren't a hundred and ninety-one copies, why did I dream that number?"

"It was Special Order 191. It was addressed to D. H. Hill, the man you saw on the gray horse in your dream. He claimed the message was never delivered."

She hung up. I stood there holding the receiver until the phone began beeping. Then I went and stood by the window and looked out at the snow till it got dark.

It had started snowing again, thick heavy flakes that would cover the graves at Arlington like a blanket. I hoped Annie was asleep and dreaming of something pleasant, a dream without dead Union soldiers in it, a dream without messages.

She hadn't asked me about D. H. Hill, and I hadn't told her. Hill had ridden a gray horse at Antietam. He had been surveying the troops on an exposed knoll when Lee and Long-street rode up. They dismounted to scan the field, but Hill stayed in the saddle in spite of the artillery fire. "If you insist on riding up there, and drawing the fire, give us a little interval," Longstreet had said angrily.

Hill didn't even have a chance to answer. The cannonball took the horse's front legs off, and it plunged forward onto its stumps. Hill had had one foot in the stirrup, and when he tried to get off the horse he had been unable to get his other leg over the croup of the saddle, just the way Annie had described it. Just the way she had seen it. In her dream.

CHAPTER FOUR

Traveller was a Confederate gray gelding with a black mane and tail. He was probably not a thoroughbred, though historians have gone to incredible lengths to provide him with aristocratic breeding lines, one of them even claiming he was descended from Diomed, the famous English Derby winner. He did have a thoroughbred's intelligence and courage and incredible endurance. "He never needs whip or spur," his owner wrote to Lee, "and will go anywhere."

I got up early and went to the library to see what I could find out about Elavil. The drug compendium said it was a fairly mild tricyclic antidepressant with a sedative effect, and that it was frequently used in connection with insomnia. It had an assortment of minor side effects and a couple of major ones. It was contraindicated for patients with heart conditions and those who had shown a previous hypersensitivity. It didn't say anything about dreaming of dead Union soldiers. In fact, if Richard had had Annie on Elavil she shouldn't have been dreaming at all. The tricyclic antidepressants increased the amount of time spent in delta sleep and decreased REM sleep, which was the stage most dreams occurred in.

I asked the librarian what she had on dreams. "Not much," Kate said. "Some pseudoscience things and Freud's *Interpretation*.

No, wait, I think that's checked out." She hit some buttons on her computer and waited for the book's status to come up. "Yeah, that's checked out till April ninth. Do you want to reserve it?"

"I was really looking for current research."

She tapped some more buttons. "We've got a few things in the one hundreds, but nothing very up-to-date. If you know exactly what you want, I can get it through interlibrary loan. If not, I suppose the Library of Congress. Have you tried the Sleep Institute? They've got a really good reference library."

"I'll take my chances in the one hundreds," I said.

Kate was right. There wasn't much, and what there was was do-it-yourself dream interpretation: "To dream about a house means you are sexually repressed," that kind of thing. Cats were a symbol of animal instincts, guns of sex, dead bodies of—surprise!—death. Horses with their front legs shot off weren't mentioned.

I asked Kate to see if she could put together a bibliography on prodromic dreams for Broun, and went home.

The phone was ringing when I opened the door. I had set the answering machine to "message" before I left. It shouldn't have rung more than twice before the taped message kicked in, but I counted three rings while I wrestled to get the key in the door and one more on my way up the stairs. I burst into the study.

Broun was hanging up the phone. "Who was that?" I demanded breathlessly.

"It wasn't anyone," he said mildly. "Whoever it was hung up before I answered. Jeff, I want you—"

"It rang four times, and you were standing right there. Why didn't you just leave the damn thing on 'message' if you weren't going to answer it?"

"Dr. Stone and I were going over some material on dreams," he said, still mildly, and gestured toward his club chair. "Dr. Stone, I don't think you've met my researcher, Jeff Johnston. Jeff, Dr. Stone is head of the Sleep Institute."

The man who had been sitting in the club chair all this time stood up and extended his hand. "How do you do?" he said. My first thought was that Richard had sent him over to tell me to keep away from Annie, but he was smiling a polite, mildly ingratiating smile, the kind you use when you meet a total stranger, and Broun was smiling, too. My name obviously hadn't been brought up before I got there.

"I think I may know a friend of yours," he went on. "Richard Madison?"

I used to know him, I thought, but that was before he started telling his patients they were crazy. That was before he started seducing his patients.

"We were roommates in college," I said.

"He's a good man," Dr. Stone said, dropping his hand easily, as if I had shaken it. "He's been doing some research on insomnia, I believe."

He's been taking advantage of one of his patients, I thought, and he could hardly tell his boss that, so maybe Richard wasn't the reason he was here after all.

"How well do you know Richard?" I asked.

"I've been in California for the past six months, working on a neurological dream-study project. I met him when I got back, but I haven't had a chance to discuss his work with him yet," he said, still smiling, and sat back down. "I'd only been back a few days when Mr. Broun asked me to come over and explain Lincoln's dreams to him. I was flattered to be asked, of course, but I'm afraid I haven't been much help. I don't know what Lincoln's dreams mean. Or what any dreams mean, for that matter. If they mean anything."

"He's had some very interesting things to say," Broun said. "Sit down, son. I want you to hear his ideas. I called on the way down from New York and left a message telling you Dr. Stone was coming over, but I guess you didn't get it." He motioned toward the only other chair in the study, a rickety wooden chair he used for reaching the top shelves. The seat was piled high with books, and his cat was on top of them, sound asleep.

"I was at the library doing research on dreams and getting nowhere," I said, relaxing a little, "so I don't know what Lincoln's dreams mean either." Or why you're here, I thought. Broun had been curious about Richard's odd behavior the night of the reception. I wondered if he had invited Dr. Stone over to try to find out why Richard had reacted so violently to his questions about Lincoln or whether he was simply trying to "run this dream thing to ground."

"Tell Jeff here what you were saying to me about Freud," Broun said eagerly.

Dr. Stone leaned back into the depths of the leather chair, his hands resting easily on the padded arms, and smiled. "As I was telling Mr. Broun, dream interpretation is not a science, although Freud attempted to make his colleagues believe it was one. He claimed that dreams were a stage on which people symbolically act out the traumas and emotions that were too frightening to deal with when they were awake. A Freudian would say Lincoln's dream was a symbolic enactment of Lincoln's secret wishes and fears, that not only the coffin but the stairs, the guard, everything in the dream was a symbol hiding the real meaning of the dream."

I went over to the chair, shooed the cat off, and started stacking the books on the floor beside the chair. The cat went over to the leather chair, looked speculatively at Dr. Stone's lap, and then went over by the fire to sulk.

"Which is?" I asked.

"I'm a scientist, not a psychiatrist. I don't believe dreams have a 'real' meaning. They're a physical process, and any 'reality' they have lies in the physical. Freud made no attempt to understand the physical. He felt the key to understanding dreams lay in content, and came up with an elaborate system of symbols to explain the images in dreams. In Lincoln's dream, for instance, the stairs represent the descent into the subconscious, of which Lincoln is both curious and afraid, symbolized by the crying that he hears. The guard and the cloth over the corpse's face are both symbols of Lincoln's unwillingness to find out the secret his unconscious holds."

I thought of Annie standing in the snow saying, "Richard says the blank paper pinned to the soldier's sleeve is a symbol for the message my subconscious is trying to send me only I'm too afraid to read it."

"What about the corpse?" I asked. "And the coffin."

"Oh, the coffin is the womb, of course. The entire dream's about Lincoln's desire to return to the safety of the womb." He smiled. "According to the Freudians."

"But that's not your interpretation," Broun said.

"No," Dr. Stone said. "In my opinion, dream interpretation as practiced by most Freudian psychiatrists, including some of mine at the Institute, is nothing more than a fancy system of guessing. I think trying to understand the 'real' meaning of a dream without reference to the physical state of the dreamer is as pointless as trying to understand what a fever 'means' without studying the body."

In spite of the fact that I still thought Richard might have sent him, I found myself liking Dr. Stone. He said things like "I think" and "in my opinion" and didn't seem to think he automatically knew all the answers where dreams were concerned. If Annie told him her dream, at least he wouldn't tell her she was crazy, and he might be able to help her. She was supposed to have seen him anyway. Maybe if I called her and told her he was back from California, she could change doctors and get out of Richard's clutches.

"Dreams are a symptom of physical processes," Dr. Stone was saying. "They don't 'mean' anything. Lincoln could have dreamed what he did for any number of reasons. He could have been to a funeral that day, or seen a hearse. Or he could have been reminded of someone who had died recently."

"Willie," Broun said. "Lincoln's son. He died in the White House. His coffin was in the East Room, too."

"Exactly," Dr. Stone said, looking pleased. "He could have been dreaming about Willie. The person in the coffin could have represented both Willie's and Lincoln's own fears of assassination. The combining of two people into one is very common in dreams. It's called condensation."

I thought of Annie and the way she had combined the two generals, A. P. Hill and D. H. Hill, into one.

"Or," he leaned back into the chair, "it could have been something he ate."

"So you couldn't tell if someone was emotionally disturbed just from the dreams they were having?" I asked.

"Hardly," Dr. Stone said. "If that were true, we'd all be certifiable. I remember a dream I had where I was using a cattle prod on my patients." He laughed. "No, dreams by themselves can't offer adequate evidence of emotional illness. Why?"

I realized, too late, that we shouldn't have gotten into this. "Somebody told Broun that Lincoln's dreams indicated that he was heading for a nervous breakdown."

"Really? A layman, I assume. A psychiatrist would never try to diagnose on the basis of a dream."

Well, a psychiatrist—one of his psychiatrists, as a matter of fact—had done just that, and I would have liked to tell him that Dr. Richard Madison, that good man doing research on insomnia, had done more than that, but telling him about Richard meant telling him about Annie, and I wasn't ready to do that just yet, not until I knew a little more about Dr. Stone.

"You said dreams can be caused by something you ate?" I said before Broun had a chance to tell him who had diagnosed Lincoln as crazy. "Is that really true? Can you get nightmares by eating Mexican food before you go to bed?"

"Oh, yes. Eating causes certain enzymes to be released into the dreamer's system, and those trigger . . ."

The phone rang. I turned and looked at the answering machine. Broun put his pen down. Dr. Stone leaned forward in his chair watching both of us.

"Do you want to get that?" Broun asked.

"No," I said. I pushed the message button. "It's probably only the librarian. She promised to get me some information on Lincoln's dreams. I'll call her back."

The phone rang a second time, finally, and the message light came on. I could hear the click as the recorder started its spiel, telling whoever it was that there was no one here and would they leave a message at the sound of the tone. And who was it? Annie, saying, "I had another dream"? Or Richard, calling to tell me to stop interfering with his treatment? The message light went out.

I turned back to Dr. Stone. "You were saying?"

"Digestion can have an effect on dreaming because the digestive enzymes in the bloodstream trigger chemical changes in the brain."

"What about drugs?" I said. "Drugs cause chemical changes

in the blood, too, don't they? Could Lincoln's dreams have been the effect of some drug he was taking?"

"Yes, certainly. Laudanum was known to cause—"

"What about Elavil? Could it cause dreams?"

He frowned. "No, actually Elavil represses the dream cycle. All the antidepressants do, and of course the barbiturates: Seconal, phenobarbital, Nembutal. The patient usually doesn't dream at all when he's on those drugs. Of course, when he's taken off them, the number and vividness increase dramatically, so I suppose you could say in that respect they cause dreams. But of course those are modern drugs," he said, looking at Broun. "Lincoln wouldn't have taken any of them."

"What do you mean, increase in vividness?" I asked.

"The drugs produce a dream deficit that is compensated for by a dream rebound as soon as the patient is taken off the drugs. The patient experiences what we call a 'storm of dreams,' for several days, powerful, frightening nightmares that rapidly succeed each other. It's the same thing that happens when a patient's been deprived of sleep for several days. We usually advise against abrupt discontinuation of antidepressants and sedatives to avoid triggering a storm of dreams." He gave me a look almost as sharp as one of Broun's. "Are you on Elavil?"

"No," I said. "Lincoln had insomnia after Willie died. I thought maybe his doctor might have prescribed something to make him sleep that gave him bad dreams, so I looked up 'insomnia,' and it said Elavil was a recommended treatment, but obviously I was in the wrong century." I stood up. "Speaking of sleep and drugs and digestion, would anybody like some coffee? Or does coffee give you bad dreams, too?"

"As a matter of fact, caffeine has been shown to have marked effects on dreaming."

"I'll make it decaffeinated," I said, and went downstairs to the kitchen.

Broun had another phone there, a separate line. I called the number of the phone in the upstairs study, and before it could ring, punched in the remote code that would play back the message. The only message on the machine was Broun's. "I'm on my way down from New York, Jeff. I should be there around ten. I'm meeting with a Dr. Stone from the Sleep

Institute at eleven. He's been doing dream research in California, and I thought I'd see what he had to say about Lincoln's dreams."

I put the coffee on and tried to call Annie. There was no answer. I found a tray and put Styrofoam cups and the cream pitcher and sugar bowl on it. I tried Annie's number again. Still no answer.

She's sleeping, I told myself. Her subconscious is trying to make up for the REM sleep she lost when she was on the Elavil. It was a logical enough explanation. When Richard took her off the Elavil, she had had a "storm of dreams," that was all. The dead Union soldiers and the horse with its legs shot off were nothing more than her subconscious trying to make up for lost time. When her dream deficit got caught up, she would stop dreaming about lost dispatches and Springfield rifles, and there was nothing to worry about.

But I had asked her, "When did Richard take you off the Elavil?" and she had told me it was *after* the dreams got suddenly clearer and more frightening, not before. Besides, the "storm of dreams" was only supposed to last a few days. Annie had had the dream about Antietam at least two weeks after Richard had taken her off the Elavil. And she had been dreaming about the dead Union soldiers for over a year.

Broun's cat had followed me downstairs. I looked in the refrigerator to see what the caterers had left behind and found half a plate of soggy crackers with shrimp salad on them. I set it on the floor and tried to call Annie again, and then went back upstairs with the tray.

They were talking about prodromic dreams. "A Dr. Gordon did a study on prodromic dreams a couple of years ago at Stanford on tuberculosis patients," Dr. Stone said, "but I don't think he found anything conclusive. The study I was working on in California . . ."

Dr. Stone stopped talking when I came into the study. Broun stood up and began heaping papers and books on one side of his desk to clear a space for the tray. I set it down.

"Dr. Stone was just going to tell me about his project," Broun said.

"Yes," Dr. Stone said. "The project I headed up in Califor-

50

nia involved using a probe on different parts of the brain. The probe produces an electrical charge that provides a stimulus to a localized region of the brain, and the patient, who's under local anesthetic only, tells us what he's thinking. Sometimes it's a memory, sometimes a smell or a taste, sometimes an emotion.

"The probe is used randomly, touching a large number of areas in a very short time, too short a time for the patient to respond individually to the stimuli. Then the patient is asked to describe everything that he's seen, and we compare the transcript of his account with transcripts of dream accounts obtained by traditional methods. We've come up with a statistically significant correspondence. And the most interesting aspect of it is that even though we know there's no connection between the images in the account, the patient connects them all into a coherent, narrative dream."

Well, so much for suggesting Annie change doctors. Dr. Stone might not tell her she was crazy, but what if he decided the best way to get at the "real" meaning of the dreams was to put her on an operating table and open up her head? What Annie needed was a doctor who would listen to her dreams and try to find out what was causing them instead of trying to force his own theories on her, and I was beginning to think there wasn't any such thing.

"You mean there was some kind of electrical shock in Lincoln's brain and he saw a coffin and then made up the rest of the dream?" Broun said.

"*Made up* is the wrong word," Dr. Stone said. "We have to remember that although the dream occurs in the subconscious, the memory of it occurs in the conscious mind. The dream is translated into the conscious mind, and it may be in that translation process that the dreams take on their narrative aspect. It may be the same kind of process that takes place when we watch film. We're seeing individual frames, but it looks like they've moving. Persistence of vision, it's called. Maybe there's a corresponding persistence that translates unrelated impulses into the dream we remember."

Broun poured a cup of coffee and handed it to me. "These impulses," he said, "where do they come from?"

"The initial results of our study indicate that the brain is processing the factual material of the day for storage."

Broun handed him a Styrofoam cup full of coffee. "Do you take anything in your coffee?" he asked.

Dr. Stone leaned forward a little, making the leather in the chair creak, and took the cup. "Just black," he said. "We're also getting indications that external stimuli have a marked effect on dream content. Everybody's had their alarm clock show up in a dream as a scream or a cat meowing or the sound of someone crying."

Broun poured himself a cup of coffee and stirred cream into it. "What about recurring dreams?" he asked. "After Willie died, Lincoln dreamed about him for months."

"The same dream?"

"I don't know," Broun said. He set down his cup and scrabbled in his notes. " 'Willie's death had staggered him, haunting his sleep until the little boy's face came in dreams to soothe him,' " he read aloud. "That's from Lewis. And Randall says he dreamed Willie was alive again."

"Our study has shown that most recurring dreams aren't the same dream at all. We used the probe randomly, repeatedly stimulating one selected region of the brain in each test. After each session, the patient would report that he had had the same dream as before, but when questioned about individual details he told an entirely different dream, though he persisted in his belief that the dreams were identical. Persistence of dreams again. Lincoln would naturally have many images of the living Willie stored in his memory that could be stimulated."

"What about Lincoln's dream of his own assassination?" I asked. "That couldn't just be Lincoln putting all the day's junk in some kind of mental file cabinet, could it? All the details fit—the coffin in the East Room, the guard, the black cloth over the corpse's face."

"Because his conscious mind *made* them fit. Remember, we have no idea of what the dream was really like." He turned and smiled crookedly at Broun, then turned back to me. "What we have is Lincoln's account of the dream, which is something completely different."

"Secondary elaboration," I said.

"Yes," he said, looking pleased. "You *have* been doing a lot of research, haven't you? Lincoln's real dream would have been a sequence of unrelated images, a stairway, a memory of Willie Lincoln in his coffin, a cloth of some kind, a napkin or a handkerchief or something. It wouldn't have to be black or even cloth, for that matter. It could have been a scrap of paper."

A scrap of paper, a cat, a Springfield rifle. It won't wash, Dr. Stone.

". . . and in the process of bringing the dream up to the subconscious and then telling it, the dream took on a coherence and an emotional importance it simply didn't have." He put both hands on the arms of the chair. "I'm afraid I'm going to have to get back to the Institute."

"What if *I* dreamed I was upstairs in the White House and heard crying but couldn't see anyone?" I asked. "What if when I went downstairs there was a coffin in the East Room?"

Broun reached for his cup. Coffee slopped onto his notes.

"I'd say you'd spent the whole day doing research on Lincoln's dreams," Dr. Stone said.

"Did you dream that?" Broun said, still holding the cup at an angle. More coffee spilled out.

"No," I said. "So you don't think Lincoln's assassination dream means anything, even though everything in it happened two weeks later? You think it's all just a matter of what he did that day and what he had for dinner?"

"I'm afraid so." Dr. Stone stood up and set his cup on the tray. "I know this probably isn't the sort of thing you wanted to hear, especially when you're trying to write a novel. One of the greatest difficulties I encounter in my reasearch is that people want to believe that their dreams mean something, but all the research I'm doing seems to indicate just the opposite."

You didn't see her standing there in the snow, I thought. You didn't see the look on her face. I don't know what's causing her dreams, but it's not random impulses and it's not indigestion. Annie's dreams do mean something. There's a reason she's having them, and I'm going to find out what it is.

"You've been a great deal of help, Dr. Stone," Broun said.

"I appreciate your giving us so much of your time. I know you're very busy."

He walked Dr. Stone downstairs. I waited till they were almost at the bottom of the steps and then went over and hit the play button on Broun's answering machine. There still wasn't any message.

I tried to call Annie. She didn't answer. Broun's cat jumped up on the desk and dipped its head into Broun's Styrofoam cup and began lapping delicately at the coffee. I put down the phone and picked him up by the back of the neck to throw him off.

"I take it you didn't think too much of Dr. Stone's theories," Broun said from the door.

"No," I said, depositing the cat on the floor. "Did you?"

"I thought he had some interesting things to say."

"About Lincoln's indigestion or about taking a cattle prod to his patients?"

"About the real meaning of Lincoln's dreams being physical." He sat down heavily in the leather chair. "And about the persistence of dreaming, how we take a lot of unconnected images and make them into one continuous dream."

Unconnected images. A carpet slipper, a red wool shirt, a horse with its legs shot off. "I thought it was all a lot of hogwash," I said.

"Jeff, are you all right? You've seemed upset about something ever since you got back from West Virginia."

"I'm just tired. I haven't caught up from the trip yet," I said, and then wondered why I didn't say, No, I'm not all right. I'm worried sick. That young woman you met at the reception is dreaming things she couldn't possibly know about. I might not be able to tell Dr. Stone, but I could surely tell Broun.

"Have you been sleeping all right?" He was sitting the way Dr. Stone had sat, his feet flat on the floor and his hands resting on the leather arms of the chair, watching me.

"Sure. Why?"

"I thought maybe you . . . when Richard called from the Institute and wanted to talk to you, I got the idea that maybe you were a patient of his, and then you asked Dr. Stone all those questions about Elavil causing bad dreams. I thought maybe he'd put you on some kind of tranquilizer."

"No," I said. "I'm not taking anything. And I'm not having bad dreams." But Annie was. And now was the time to tell him, to explain my behavior and Richard's and tell him about Annie's dreams. The cat made a flying leap onto the desk and right into Broun's coffee. I dived for the cup and Broun's notes at the same time. Broun pushed himself up out of the chair and came over to get the cat. I moved the notes out of the way.

"Broun," I said, but he had the cat by the scruff of the neck and was putting it out the door. He shut it on its indignant yowl and sat down in the chair again.

"I'm glad you're all right," he said. "I was worried about you. Did you know Lincoln had trouble sleeping? After Willie died? I think he must have almost gone crazy." He was looking past me now, as if I wasn't even there. "He had Willie's body disinterred twice so he could look at Willie's face, did you know that?"

"No," I said.

"Poor man. I was thinking about what you said, about dreaming Lincoln's dreams. That would be wonderful, wouldn't it?"

"No, it wouldn't," I said, thinking of Annie. "It would be terrible," but it was obvious he didn't hear me.

"When you were asking all those questions about having Lincoln's dreams, all I could think of was how wonderful for the book it would be if you were having them," he said, still not looking at anything.

"For the *book*?"

"Imagine, if you were having Lincoln's dreams, we'd finally know what he really thought, what he really felt. It's what every writer dreams about." He slapped the arms of the chair and stood up. "Jeff, I want you to go to California for me."

"No."

He was finally looking at me, and his sharp eyes were taking in everything the way they had the night of the reception. "Why not?"

The phone rang. I snatched it up, knocking the cup of

coffee flying, wanting it to be Annie and hoping against hope it wasn't. I didn't want to talk to her in front of Broun. A minute ago I had wanted to tell him. I still wanted to tell him, but I couldn't. He thought Dr. Stone had had "some interesting things to say" about how dreams were only unconnected images. He thought it would be wonderful "for the book" if I were having Lincoln's dreams.

He's not like Dr. Stone, I told myself, or Richard. He's never been anything but kind to you. If you tell him about Annie, he'll be as worried as you are, he'll do anything he can to help her. Maybe, I thought, and maybe he'll look at her with his bright little eyes and say, "This is what every writer dreams about." I couldn't risk it. Not with Annie.

"Hello," I said cautiously into the phone.

"Hi, this is Kate from the library. How do you spell 'prodromic'? I've looked through our stuff, and we don't have a thing on it, so I'm going to call over to the Library of Congress, but I wanted to make sure I was spelling it right. Is it ..." She spelled it for me, and I held the phone, hardly listening.

I couldn't tell him about Annie, but I would have to tell him something. I had to talk him out of sending me three thousand miles away from Annie when she might call anytime, when she might need me.

"That's the way it's spelled," I said to Kate, not knowing whether it was or not. "Thanks." I hung up and started wiping up the spilled coffee with one of the paper napkins on the tray.

"I'm determined to find out what caused Lincoln's dreams," Broun said, still watching me. "There's a man in San Diego who's been working on prophetic dreams."

Broun's notes were soaked. I blotted them with the napkin.

"I want you to fly out tomorrow and talk to him about Lincoln's dreams."

"What about the weather? They said on the radio this morning that the airport was closed."

"Then you can go the next day."

"Look, I really don't see the point of all this running around. I mean, can't you just call the guy? There's nothing he can tell me in person that he can't tell you over the phone, is there?"

"You can watch him while he says it," Broun said, watching me dab at the sodden notes. "You can tell whether he's telling the truth or not."

"And what difference will it make if he is?" I said angrily. "Lincoln's dead, and this guy won't know what caused his dreams any more than Dr. Stone or Richard did. No matter how many experts you ask, you're never going to find out what really caused the dreams. You've already got plenty of explanations. Pick the one you like the best. What difference does it make?"

"It made a difference to Lincoln," he said slowly. "It makes a difference to me."

"The way it made a difference to you when Lee bought Traveller? You didn't need to know that. No matter when he bought him, it was before Antietam. But you sent me chasing all over West Virginia looking for bills of sale, and now you want to send me to California on another wild goose chase."

"Never mind," he said. "I'll go myself."

I looked down at Broun's notes, afraid my relief would show in my face. The sodden pages were matted together. I tried to peel the top sheet off, and half the page came off in my hand. I looked at it. The ink was blurred so badly I couldn't read what he had written.

"Look, I just think you should keep a little perspective on things. You got totally wrapped up in *The Duty Bound,* and look what happened. And now you're getting obsessed with this."

"I said I'd go myself, damn it." He stood up. "Give me the damned notes before you ruin them. And call McLaws and Herndon. Tell them to wait on the galleys. I'm changing another scene."

"You can't do that," I said. "They've already set the type. What am I supposed to tell them?"

"I don't care what you tell them. Tell them I'm obsessed with *The Duty Bound.*" He grabbed for the notes, and they tore across without any sound. He yanked the torn pieces out of my hand. "Tell them you think I'm a little tetched in the head like Lincoln was after Willie died. Tell them I want to dig up the body to have one last look at it before it goes to press. Like that crazy Lincoln."

When I went downstairs to the kitchen to call McLaws and Herndon, he shut the door of his study, and I could hear the uneven stutter of his typing like sniper fire from across the river.

CHAPTER FIVE

Around Christmas of 1861, during the Carolina campaign, Robert E. Lee bought Traveller for a hundred and seventy-five dollars, adding an extra twenty-five dollars to counteract the falling value of Confederate money. "He has been my patient follower ever since," he wrote Markie. "He carried me through the Seven Days battle around Richmond, Sharpsburg, Fredericksburg, the last day at Chancellorsville, to Pennsylvania, at Gettysburg, and back to the Rappahannock ... to the final days at Appomattox Court House."

Broun didn't ask me to call in the scene this time. He called it in himself the next morning and then left to talk to a Lincoln expert in Georgetown. "I'm leaving for California tomorrow," he said belligerently. "Did you find out where Willie Lincoln was buried?"

"No," I said. "I'm going over to the library right now. Do you want me to go get the ticket first?"

"You can pick it up this afternoon," he said.

"Fine," I said, wishing I could say something that would make him less angry with me. I couldn't apologize because an apology meant an explanation, and I couldn't explain. Maybe it was just as well he wasn't talking to me because then there wouldn't be any questions either. "What about the galleys?"

"What about them?"

"McLaws and Herndon called this morning before you were up. They said they were sending them down Federal Express, they want them back in two weeks at the latest, and no major changes."

"You can give them the first reading, and I'll finish them when I get back."

"Which will be when?"

"I don't know. A week maybe."

I waited till he had left for Georgetown and then went upstairs and made sure the answering machine was set on "message." I drove over and picked up Broun's ticket from the travel agency and then went to the library.

Kate didn't have the bibliography ready, and I told her I wasn't in any hurry, I was going to be there awhile. I spent the rest of the day there, looking up information about Willie Lincoln and thinking about Annie.

She hadn't called last night. Broun had gone out for dinner, and I had spent the whole evening in his study waiting for her to call, but the phone hadn't rung even once. By ten o'clock I had come to the conclusion that Richard was somehow keeping her from using the phone, but this morning I didn't really believe that.

Richard had made it plain he didn't want me talking to her, but he was hardly going to have the phone disconnected or tie her up to keep her from answering it. She was his patient, not his prisoner, and she had disobeyed him before. He hadn't been able to keep her from going out to Arlington. He wouldn't be able to keep her from calling me either, if she really wanted to.

If she really wanted to. Maybe she didn't want to. She had seemed almost uninterested when I called her and offered her my services. What made me think she wanted to hear about Special Order 191 any more than she wanted to hear about traumas in the subconscious? She hung up on you, I told myself, and she's still at Richard's. You don't need Freud's *Interpretation of Dreams* to tell you what that means. She doesn't

want to talk to you. So stop calling her and find out what the
hell they did with Willie Lincoln.

I didn't believe that either, but I pulled out every book
on Lincoln and tried to concentrate on the research. I couldn't
find a word about Willie's burial. I found out what had happened to the pony he'd been riding "in bad weather" when he
came down with whatever it was that killed him, though. Several months after Willie's death, the White House stables caught
fire. Lincoln ran across the lawn and leaped a boxwood hedge
to save it, but he was too late. The guards hurried him back
into the White House, afraid the fire had been started by an
assassin to lure him out. Willie's pony was burned alive.

Every hour or so I went outside to the pay phone and
called the answering machine, but there weren't any messages.
By two o'clock I had run out of change and had to ask Kate
for a dollar's worth of quarters. "I'll have the bibliography
ready for you in a few minutes," she said.

I went out and called the answering machine. Broun's
agent had called, wanting to know why in the hell Broun was
still making changes. She'd just talked to McLaws and Herndon and they'd had to reset the type for the galleys. They were
talking about charging Broun for the extra plates.

I called Annie.

"I'm glad you called," Richard said. "I wanted to apologize
for my outburst the other day."

"I want to talk to Annie."

"She's asleep right now," he said, "and I don't want to
wake her up. I know I was out of line the day before yesterday.
I was just so upset about her condition. She was obsessed with
the idea that she could obtain factual verification for her dream."

He sounded completely different from the man who had
warned me to keep away from Annie. His voice was calm and
professional. "It's a common phenomenon, but a dangerous
one. The patient attempts to distance threatening dream images in his dreams by believing they have an objective reality of
their own."

I recognized the voice now. He had worked on it all
through medical school. The voice was one of the psychiatrist's
most important tools, he had told me when he was study-

ing psychoanalysis. The proper voice could be used to obtain the patient's trust, inspire confidence, and convince the patient that the psychiatrist had his own best interests at heart. I had told him I didn't care what it could do, just not to use it on me.

He was using it now.

"By convincing herself that the house in her dream is Arlington House," he said, "she is trying to protect herself from the latent material in the dream. The half-buried dead man becomes a Union soldier instead of the image of her own personal trauma, the cat becomes a real cat instead of the symbol of her need to uncover the repressed memory that's causing the dreams."

"The cat *is* a real cat. His name's Tom Tita. He got left behind when Lee moved out of Arlington."

"You're confusing manifest content with latent content," he said, inspiringly, compassionately. "We all dream real things, objects and people we've seen, things we've read about or seen in the movies, memories. They make up the visible content of our dreams. But the subconscious puts those real people and objects and memories to its own uses. It's a process called dream precipitant conversion. Let's say Annie had a cat as a child."

"She never had a cat. And she didn't see this cat, either, or read about it someplace. It's Tom Tita."

"I'm sure she was convinced of that when she insisted on going to Arlington, and that was why I objected to the trip. But I was wrong. The trip produced a catharsis, a break-through. She realized the house in the dream was really her own house, and that the half-buried soldier was a symbol of her own repressed guilt."

"What's the cat a symbol for?" And what about her band-aged hands? I was about to say when I realized that Richard, calm and inspiring and compassionate, hadn't said a word about the second dream. And what did that mean? That she hadn't told him? Or that she didn't want to believe what I had told her and had chosen to accept Richard's explanations: repressive guilt and manifest content and dream precipitant conversion. Terms that meant no more than bilious fever and rheumatic excitement and were as much help to the patient.

"I want to talk to Annie," I said.

"I'll let her know you called as soon as she wakes up," the Good Shrink said. "I have to warn you that she may not want to talk to you. She identifies you with her rejection of her psychosis."

I hung up on him and went back inside to Lincoln, who had had terrible dreams, too. But nobody had tried to convince him the East Room wasn't the East Room. Nobody had told him the corpse with the black cloth over its face was a symbol for repressive guilt or a neural impulse chosen at random by his hormones. Nobody had asked him what he'd had to eat before he went to bed.

Kate brought the bibliography over to me. "I've starred the ones we have," she said, pointing at ink notations in the margin, "and marked the branches these are at. Do you want me to have the branches send them over here?"

"No, that's all right. I'll go get them tomorrow."

"What's Broun's new book about?"

"Abraham Lincoln," I said.

"Oh, I didn't know Lincoln was sick."

"What?"

"Prodromic dreams are dreams people have when they're sick and they don't know it yet. What disease was Lincoln suffering from?"

"Bad dreams," I said.

Broun was back when I got home, standing in the solarium looking at his African violets. I handed him the bibliography. "Did anybody call?" I asked.

"I don't know," he said stiffly. "I left the machine on so you wouldn't miss any of your messages. Did you find out where Willie Lincoln was buried?"

"No." I started up the stairs. "Was Lincoln sick when he was shot?"

"He was obsessed with the Civil War," he said bitterly.

I went on up the stairs and into the study and shut the door, but there were no messages on the answering machine, and Annie didn't call.

I spent most of the next day rounding up the books listed in the bibliography so Broun could take them with him. The galleys came Federal Express in the afternoon. It was overcast all day, and cold. Broun's plane didn't leave till five-thirty, and by the time we left for the airport it was getting foggy.

"I want you to go down to Virginia for me," Broun said stiffly as soon as we turned onto the Rock Creek Parkway. "I know you disapprove of these wild goose chases, but I need you to talk to a doctor in Fredericksburg."

Fredericksburg was only fifty miles away. If Annie called I could drive back in an hour and a half's time. If she called. "What's the doctor's name?"

He rummaged in his jacket pocket. "Barton. Dr. Barton. Here's the address." He had fished out a folded piece of paper. He unfolded it. "Dr. Stone gave me his name. This Dr. Barton has acromegaly. That's usually treated before there are any overt symptoms, but he's old enough that his wasn't. I want you to find out what kind of dreams he has." He paused as if waiting for me to object.

"When do you want me to go? Tomorrow?"

"Whenever it's convenient for you to go," he said.

I drove past the Lincoln Memorial and onto the bridge. "I had no business saying that about the wild goose chases," I said. "I know how important this book is to you."

"An obsession, I think you called it."

I could see Arlington House up ahead on its snow-covered hill. I thought of Richard telling Annie she was obsessed with war and killing. "I had no right to say that either."

We turned onto the parkway heading south. "Lincoln suffered from acromegaly," Broun said as if he were apologizing for his rudeness before when I had asked him if Lincoln was sick. "It's what made him so tall. It's a gland disorder. The bones grow too much. The hands and nose get wide and the feet get big. People with acromegaly get rheumatism and diabetes and suffer from melancholia. It can be fatal."

"And you think that's what killed him?" I said, sarcastically, and then was sorry.

"I thought it might explain the dreams," he said, and turned and looked out the side window at the foggy darkness.

I wondered if it had occurred to him, through all these theories of repressed guilt and neural impulses, that the dreams didn't need any explanation. Lincoln dreamed that he had been killed by an assassin, and two weeks later he lay dead in the East Room. He lost his son, and the little boy's face came to comfort him in dreams. And where in all this did a gland disorder figure?

I didn't ask him. I wanted some kind of truce before Broun went off to California. When we pulled into the airport, I said, "I'll go see this Dr. Barton tomorrow."

He turned and looked at me, and I knew he didn't want a battle either. "Just have Mrs. Betts next door take the cat and tell her to water the plants. I left the answering machine on 'message' and didn't say where you'd be in case you wanted to take some time off. I've been working you too hard. There's a nice inn in Fredericksburg. You could drive down and stay for a couple of days, take a little vacation. Stay till I get back from California if you feel like it."

"Somebody's got to do the galleys," I said, "and you won't have time in California. Listen, don't worry about me. I'll take it easy. I'll run down to Fredericksburg and then I'll come back and work on the galleys."

"Well, at least get somebody to help you with them. It takes so long the other way. Why don't you ask that girl to help you, the pretty little blonde at the reception the other night, what was her name?"

"Annie," I said. "But I doubt if she'd want to sit for hours reading a book out loud and checking for typos."

He scratched at the stubble on his chin. "I watched you two the other night. I got the idea she'd do about anything if you asked her. And vice versa."

"She's Richard's girlfriend."

"'Did you hear that from the horse's mouth? Or did Richard tell you?"

"You're going to miss your plane," I said. "Don't worry about the galleys. I'll get them done if I have to read them onto a tape recorder and listen to myself."

He got his suitcase out of the back and then reached forward to give me the piece of folded paper. "Take care of yourself, son," he said.

"You, too," I said. "If you find out what caused Lincoln's dreams, let me know."

I went home and started in on the galleys, a long chapter about Ben's brother, who was in Mansfield's doomed Twelfth Corps, another, even longer one about Colonel Fitzhugh, whose men called him Old Fancypants and who went on for pages about a gentleman's duty and the glorious South.

"I thought the book was about Antietam," I had told Broun the first time I'd read those chapters. "And here it is chapter two and still the spring of 1862. The battle of Antietam didn't happen till the middle of September."

"It's not about Antietam," Broun had thundered, the only time I've ever seen him angry at one of my criticisms. "It's about duty, damn it." He had refused to take any of it out then, and now I saw that, although he had made so many changes I hardly recognized the book, all the passages about duty had been left in. It was chapter nine before we made it to the morning of September seventeenth and back to Malachi and Toby and Ben:

It was still dark when Ben woke up. "I thought I heard something," he said, sitting up.

"Not yet," Malachi said. It was too dark to see him.

"What time is it?" Ben asked. "I thought I heard guns." It had stopped raining and there seemed to be a little light there to the east, but he couldn't be sure.

"No more'n three o'clock," Malachi said, and then Ben must have gone back to sleep because when he opened his eyes again, it was light enough to see Malachi. He was sitting by his little cookfire, stirring the cold ashes, trying to get a spark, but the fire was completely out. A cold fog was drifting through the cornfield they had camped next to, so low he couldn't see the tassels on the corn.

"How'll we see to fight if there's fog?" Ben said, huddling his blanket around his shoulders. His teeth were chattering.

"Fog'll burn off as soon as the sun comes up, and then it'll be hot," Malachi said, and he sounded as calm and wide awake as if he were back on the farm, up at three in the morning for a big day of planting.

"What would happen if we lit out beforehand?" Ben said. His teeth were chattering so hard he wouldn't be able to hear the guns. "Couldn't nobody see us in this fog."

"I thought you was the one just had to sign up. This here's what you signed up for."

"I know," he said. "I just hadn't figured on getting killed."

"How's a body supposed to get any sleep with you two clucking like hens?" Toby said. He yawned. "Should you run? Will you git kilt? Me, I can't get kilt. Not Toby Banks. No, sir, I promised my mama I wouldn't." He pushed his blanket down so it covered his feet and rolled over, and Ben lay down again and watched the fog drift across Malachi and the cold fire.

Toby poked him awake with his foot. "You set up all night worrying and then you sleep through the battle," he said. "Don't you let Old Fancypants see you sleeping."

Ben sat up. The sun was up and the fog was gone. Steam was rising like smoke over the cornfield. Malachi had another fire going. He was roasting ears of corn in the coals. "Me, I been up practicing my Rebel yell for close on an hour," Toby said.

Ben got up and folded his bedroll, trying to wake up. Toby was whistling something, a jig tune, but when Ben turned to look at him he stopped. He was writing something on a dirty white handkerchief. "I want them Yankees to know who's shooting at 'em," he said. He whittled a twig down to nothing and used it as a pin to stick the handkerchief to his shirt. "Not that I'm letting any of 'em get close enough to read it." He went over to the fire and plucked one of the roasting ears out of the coals. The husk was charred. It smelled wonderful.

She woke me out of a sound sleep. I had the idea that it was almost morning, and I couldn't think who would be calling at that hour. I answered the phone, and, as I did, it rang again, and I thought, "It's the answering machine," and punched what I thought was "play" and had time to be surprised that there was no message before it rang again and I recognized the sound finally as the doorbell.

Annie was standing on the front steps. She had her gray coat on and was carrying a duffel bag. There was a suitcase on the step beside her. It was dark and foggy out, and I thought, "That will burn off when the sun comes up, and it will be hot tomorrow."

"Can I stay here?" she said.

I still had the idea that the phone had rung. "Did you call?" I said.

"No," she said. "I know I should have given you some warning, but . . . if this is a problem, Jeff, I can go to a hotel."

"I thought I heard the phone," I said, rubbing at my face as if I expected a scraggly stubble of beard like Broun's. "What time is it?"

She had to transfer the duffel bag from one hand to the other to look at her watch. "Ten-thirty. I woke you up, didn't I?"

No, you didn't, I almost said. That was the problem. She had not, with all her ringing of the doorbell, managed to wake me up. I was still asleep and dreaming her, and they were not somebody else's dreams. She looked beautiful standing there in her gray coat, her light hair curling a little from the damp fog. She looked as if she had just awakened from a long and refreshing sleep, her eyes clear and bright, and healthy pink-ness in her cheeks.

"Of course you can stay," I said, still not awake enough to ask her why she was here, or even to wonder. I opened the door and leaned past her to pick up the suitcase. "You can stay as long as you want. Broun's not here. He's in California. You can stay as long as you want."

I led the way up the stairs to the study, still unable to shake the feeling that it was very late. The answering machine was blinking rapidly—I must have put it on "call return" in my sleepy fumblings. I wondered what poor soul I had been calling for the last ten minutes. I hit the "pause" button and yawned. I was still not awake. I'd better make some coffee.

"Do you want some coffee?" I said to Annie, who was standing in the door of the study looking rested and wide awake and beautiful.

"No," she said.

I still had my hand on the answering machine buttons. "I've been worried about you. I tried to call you. Did you have another dream?"

"No," she said. "The dreams have stopped."

"They've stopped?" I said. "Just like that?" I still wasn't awake.

The answering machine was still flashing. I stabbed at the buttons. The tape clicked. "Annie's gone," Richard said. "I think she'll come to you. You have to make her come back. She's sick. I only did it to help her. I didn't have any other choice."

"Did what?" I asked.

She pulled something out of the duffel bag. "He's been putting these in my food," she said, and handed me two capsules in a plastic bag. One of the capsules was cracked and there was a dusting of white powder along the bottom edge of the bag.

"What are they?" I said. "Elavil?"

"Thorazine," she said. "I found the bottle in his medical bag."

Thorazine. A drug strong enough to stop a horse in its tracks. "Richard gave you these?" I said, looking stupidly at the plastic bag.

"Yes," she said. She sat down in the club chair. "He started putting them in my food when I got back from Arlington."

When I called her I had asked her if she had been asleep, and she had said Richard had made her a cup of tea and sent her to bed. She had been so sleepy she could hardly answer my questions. Because Richard had put Thorazine in her tea. Thorazine. "They use Thorazine in mental hospitals. With uncontrollable patients."

"I know," she said.

"How many of these did he give you?"

"I don't know. He . . . I didn't eat anything last night and all day today."

I had taken her out to Arlington three days ago. She couldn't have been on the drug more than two and a half days, so there couldn't be that much in her system, but what kind of dose had Richard given her? Any dose was too much.

"Annie, listen, let me call the hospital. They'll know what to do. We've got to get this stuff out of your system."

"Jeff, tell me what happened to the horse," she said quietly. "The gray horse I saw in my dream. It didn't fall forward on its knees, did it?" I looked at her hands, expecting them to be gripping the arms of the chair, but they were lying quietly in her lap. "Please tell me."

I knelt down in front of her and took hold of her hands. "Annie, the dream's not important. What's important is that you've got a dangerous drug in your system. I don't know what symptoms it can cause, but we've got to find out. There might be withdrawal symptoms of some kind. We've got to get you to a hospital. They'll know what to do."

"No," she said, still quietly. "They'll give me something to stop the dreams."

"No, they won't. They'll try to get the Thorazine out of your system, and they'll run tests so we'll know exactly how much Richard's been giving you and for how long. What if he's been giving you drugs for weeks? What if Thorazine isn't the only thing he's been giving you?"

"You don't understand. They'll put me on medication."

"They can't give you anything without your consent."

"Richard did. I can't go to a hospital. The dreams are important. They're the most important thing."

"Annie . . ."

"No, you have to listen, Jeff. I figured out he was giving me something when you called me. When I got up to answer the phone I was so dizzy, and then when you asked me if Richard was giving me anything, I knew that must be it. But I didn't tell you."

"Why not?" I asked gently.

"Because it stopped the dreams." Her hands were ice cold. I chafed them gently between my hands. "When you'd called I'd been asleep all afternoon, and I hadn't had any dreams at all. Then you called and told me about Special Order 191 and I didn't even want to listen. I just wanted to go back to sleep. I wanted to sleep forever."

"That was the Thorazine," I said.

"I wanted to sleep forever, but I couldn't. Even under the Thorazine, even when I was asleep, I knew the dreams mattered, and that I had to have them. That's why I came here. Because I knew you could help me. I knew you could tell me what the dreams meant."

"Annie, listen." I looked anxiously into her blue-gray eyes, trying to see if they were dilated. They weren't. They looked clear and alert. Maybe she *had* only been on the Thorazine for a couple of days. "Will you at least let me call Broun's doctor? He's not a psychiatrist or anything. He's just a G.P."

"He'll call Richard."

"No, he won't," I said, and wished I could be sure of that. If I told him that Richard had given Thorazine to one of his patients without her knowledge, he would immediately think she was a mental patient. He would call Richard, and Richard would tell him that she was highly unstable, that she suffered from delusions of persecution. He would use his Good Shrink voice and Broun's doctor would believe him. And then what? Would he take Annie back to the Sleep Institute, or would he have Richard come and get her?

"At least let me make you some coffee," I said, patting her hands. "We need to get that junk out of your system."

She wrapped her fingers around mine. "Tell me about the horse. Please."

"It was D. H. Hill's horse. It was shot out from under him." I held on to her hands as if I expected her to pull away from me. "Its front legs were shot off."

"Did Lee see it happen?"

"Yes," I said.

"I didn't want to believe it when you told me about Tom Tita and Hill's red shirt and the lost order," she said, and her voice was still calm, but her grip tightened. "But I knew it was true, even under the Thorazine. I knew what the dreams were that night at the reception as soon as you told me about the house at Arlington, but I didn't want to believe it."

She bent her head so that it almost touched our hands. "That poor man!" she said. "The Thorazine made me sleep all the time, and even when I was awake it was as if I were asleep. It was wonderful. I hadn't been able to sleep before because I was so afraid I'd dream about the soldier in the orchard, and now I slept and slept and didn't dream anything. It was wonderful. I was so glad Richard had given it to me."

She looked up at me. "But even when I was asleep I kept thinking how terrible it was that they didn't have Thorazine in those days, that there wasn't anything to stop those awful dreams. He had to keep dreaming them over and over again till he was afraid to go to sleep, too." She was holding my hands so tightly they hurt. "That's why I have to have the dreams, that's why I came to you. You have to help me have the dreams. So he can get some sleep."

"Who?" I said, but I already knew the answer.

"Robert E. Lee. They're his dreams, aren't they?" she said, and it wasn't even a question. "I'm having Robert E. Lee's dreams."

I could almost smell the corn, hear it rustling in the still, hot steam of the morning, and I knew the guns were about to open up and the slaughter begin.

"Yes," I said.

I got Annie something to eat and made her drink some coffee. I wondered if I should walk her around to try to keep her from falling asleep the way you did for a drug overdose, but she had been asleep for days. I wished Broun had a medical book from later than 1865 so I could look up Thorazine's side effects.

The phone rang. "It's Richard, you know," she said, and took hold of my hands again. "He'll come and get me."

The answering machine clicked on. "He won't know where we are," I said. "The message on the answering machine says Broun's in California. He'll think I went with him."

"What if he comes over?"

"We won't be here," I said. "I have to go to Fredericksburg to do some research for Broun. You can come with me. He won't have any idea where we've gone."

Annie was asleep before I'd finished talking, still holding on to my hands, her head turned slightly against the back of the club chair, her cheeks as pink as a child's. I eased my hands out of hers and went and got a blanket from my room to put over her, and then, wide awake finally, I packed a bag and put it and Annie's things into the car and then came back to the study and read galleys.

Richard called every ten minutes for the next three hours and then stopped, and I turned off all the lights in the study and went downstairs and made sure all the doors were locked. I went into the dark solarium and stood at the window, watching Richard pull up and park across the street and thinking about how the Civil War started.

Lincoln had offered Lee the command of the Union army, but he couldn't take it, even though he was opposed to secession and hated the idea of war. "I have not been able to make up my mind to raise my hand against my relatives, my children, my home," he wrote his sister. "I know you will blame me; but you must think as kindly of me as you can, and believe that I have endeavored to do what I thought right."

"I could have taken no other course without dishonor," he wrote after the war, after he had killed two hundred and fifty thousand of his own men; and Lincoln, that other good man entrusted with mass murder, had said, "Let us have faith that right makes might, and in that faith let us do our duty as we understand it."

Our duty as we understand it. "I had to do it," Richard had said, and had slept with a patient, had given her a dangerous drug without her knowledge, and I had promised I'd take care of her, so I couldn't let him get away with it, even though he was my old roommate. "He just one day signed up," Broun's character Ben had said, "and I knew I had to, too." And there we were, enemies.

At seven o'clock I went back upstairs and woke Annie up. I called the woman next door and told her I'd changed my mind about going to California with Broun and would she watch the cat, I'd put its food by the door and she could come and get it and the cat anytime she wanted.

Then I said, "And would you tell the police we're gone? Broun doesn't usually bother with that kind of thing, but there's been a car parked across the street with a man sitting in it ever since I got back from taking Broun to the airport last night. I can't tell if he's watching the house or not, and I'm probably crazy to think it means anything. But Broun's got a lot of first editions."

When the police car pulled up next to Richard's, I took Annie out through the back door to the garage, and we fled south, into the land of dreams.

CHAPTER SIX

Traveller was a perfect horse for Lee. He could stand the bad weather and the parched corn, and he had incredible stamina. When Lee reviewed the troops, Traveller would start out at a long lope and never once change his stride. The men would be lined up for sometimes as much as ten miles, and Traveller would gallop the whole distance while the other officers' horses dropped out, one by one.

Fredericksburg was only fifty miles south of D.C., but it was an entirely different world. The redbud and forsythia were in bloom, and the martyred blossoms of the dogwood were everywhere.

I checked us in at the Fredericksburg Inn, a big old building with a wide porch. I asked for two adjoining rooms and then told the clerk I wanted to see them before we signed in. The clerk gave me a key and we went upstairs. The two rooms were really a suite on the second floor at one end of the building. I could see the parking lot from the window of one of the bedrooms and the Rappahannock from the other. There was a fire escape at the other end of the hall that went down to another, smaller parking lot that couldn't be seen from the front of the building.

I left Annie in the room and went down and signed us in as Mr. and Mrs. Jeff Davis. The clerk grinned when he read it. I debated telling him that an angry husband might show up and giving him twenty dollars to tell the husband we weren't there. Instead, I grinned back and said, "No, no relation. Everybody asks that," and went out to move the car around to the little parking lot by the stairs and get the bags.

When I got back up to the suite, I put my bag in the bedroom with the view of the big parking lot and Annie's in the other.

"You can relax," I told her. "Richard will have no way of knowing we're here. The only person who knew I was going to Fredericksburg is Broun, and he's in California. You can go ahead and unpack and then we'll go get some breakfast."

I went into the other bedroom, shut the door, and called Broun's answering machine to make sure Broun hadn't left the name of his hotel or the number on the machine. "I'm in sunny California doing research on my new book," Broun's voice said. "If you'll leave your name and number and any messages, I'll be picking my messages up remotely, and I'll try to return your call as soon as possible."

Good. He hadn't left a number, and he hadn't said anything about his research assistant picking up his calls. He had meant it when he said he wanted me to take some time off. I tried to think of anybody else he might have given his California number to. His agent probably, but she wouldn't give out information to a stranger, even if he claimed to be an old roommate of Jeff's. McLaws and Herndon maybe, though I doubted if he'd told them he was running off to California when he was supposed to be working on the galleys.

I punched in the remote code that would play me any messages left on the machine. There was a click and then a short whirring sound while the machine rewound, another click, and Broun said, "Jeff, I'm in California, and I must have brought the damned fog with me. I'm going to see the prodromic-dreams man tomorrow. Call me if you run into any trouble with the galleys. And get some rest. I'm worried about you."

I unpacked the bag I'd thrown together the night before

and opened the box I had brought the galleys in. There were books lying on top. I didn't remember packing any books. I picked the top one up. It was volume two of Freeman. I sat down on the bed and pulled out the other three hefty volumes, one after the other.

A soldier running from battle would sometimes find miles later that he was still clutching his rifle, or his hat, or a half-eaten square of hardtack, and had no more memory of doing it than he did of running away. And here we were fifty miles from the battle with a suite at the Fredericksburg Inn and Freeman's *R. E. Lee* and who knows what in Annie's duffel bag, two Johnny Rebs on the run. But sooner or later that soldier would stop running and decide what to do next, and I had no idea. I hadn't thought any farther than getting Annie safely away from Richard.

I had done that, and we could stay here for at least a week and maybe longer if Broun stayed in California, but sooner or later we were going to have to go back to D.C., and sooner or later we were going to have to talk about the dreams.

But not yet. There was no telling how much Thorazine Annie still had in her system or how long it would take to work its way out. Dr. Stone had said taking somebody off a sedative abruptly might cause a "storm of dreams." I wasn't going to insist on figuring out what was causing Robert E. Lee's dreams if she was having nightmares of her own. What she needed right now was breakfast and some rest and a vacation from the whole crazy mess.

There was a slick colored brochure lying on the oak chiffonier by the bed. I picked it up. Maybe we could take a walk around historic Fredericksburg, see some of the sights. "America's Battlefield," the brochure said. "Visit the Historic Civil War Battlefields. Where 100,000 fell! Stand in the shoes of the generals. Self-guided tour."

I thought of Annie standing halfway up the hill at Arlington, looking down at the snowy grass. Fredericksburg's battlefield had been made into a national cemetery, too, with twelve thousand unknown soldiers buried in it.

Maybe I shouldn't have brought her here, I thought. She hadn't dreamed about Fredericksburg yet, and I didn't want her to. The battle had been a complete slaughter, with the Union soldiers trying to cross a flat plain to the defended ridge called Marye's Heights. But Lee won, I thought. Maybe he doesn't dream about the battles he won.

The other attractions were minor, to say the least: James Monroe's law office, Mary Washington's cottage, and Kenmore, a southern plantation where George Washington's sister Betty Fielding Lewis lived, but when I checked the map, they weren't anywhere near the battlefield, which meant we could go sightseeing and read galleys and do what Broun had sent me to do, which was interview a doctor about his acromegaly.

I dug the number Broun had given me out of my wallet and called Dr. Barton. The number had been disconnected. I opened the drawers in the oak chiffonier till I found the phone book and looked him up under "Physicians" in the Yellow Pages. There wasn't any listing. There was a Barton listed in the white pages, but no "doctor" after his name. Broun had said he was old enough that his acromegaly hadn't been treated. Maybe he'd retired. I called the number.

"Dr. Barton's office," a woman's voice said.

"Good," I said. "This is Jeff Johnston. I'm Thomas Broun's researcher. I'd like to make an appointment with Dr. Barton."

"Is this about a horse?" she said.

"No," I said, squinting at the paper Broun had given me. "Is this Dr. Henry Barton's office?"

"Yes."

"Dr. Barton's name was given to my employer, Thomas Broun, by Dr. Stone in Washington, D.C. I'm doing research on Mr. Broun's new book, and I wanted to ask Dr. Barton a few questions."

"Oh, how interesting," she said. "I know my husband will want to see you. Let me look at the appointment book." There was a pause. "Could it be next week sometime? He's very busy. It's spring, you know."

I didn't know why spring was so busy, but I didn't say that. "What about in the evening?"

"Tomorrow's Sunday. Could you come out tomorrow?"

"Sure," I said.

"Do you know how to get here?" she said. "We're out of

town." While she gave me directions, I thumbed through the yellow pages again. Yep. There he was, Dr. Henry Barton, DVM. Practice Limited to Large Animals. No wonder his wife had wanted to know if it was about a horse.

I put the phone book back in the drawer, picked up the brochure of "Historic Fredericksburg," and took it into Annie's room. "Dr. Barton can't see me till tomorrow, so we've got the whole day. What do you want to see? Mary Washington lived here. We could go tour the house. There's a mirror in her bedroom that . . ."

"I shouldn't have come with you," she said. She was sitting on the four-poster bed. It had a green-and-white sprigged muslin coverlet with a ruffled flounce. Annie had her hands flat on either side of her, trying not to clutch at the muslin flowers the way she had Broun's African violet. "When I started having the dreams I was so scared I didn't know what to do. I was afraid to be alone at night, and Richard was trying to help me. . . ."

And it just happened.

"I'm not Richard," I said. "I don't know what kind of ideas you've got about me, but I didn't bring you down here for a fun weekend on Broun's expense account. I brought you down here because you were running away from Richard, and I thought this was a safe place for you to hide. That's it. I'm here to read the galleys for *The Duty Bound* and talk to some guy with long bones and big ears. I got a suite and registered us under a phony name because that way Richard couldn't call and find out you were here, but if you want a separate room, I can . . ."

"That's not it," she said, crushing the coverlet in her clenched hands. "I didn't think you . . . the suite is fine, Jeff. I'm glad you didn't get separate rooms because I need somebody in the room at night. And you shouldn't blame Richard for what happened. It was my fault. I shouldn't have gotten involved with him. It just made things worse." She let go of the coverlet and looked up at me. "The dreams scared Richard. He was afraid they were hurting me, and so he tried to stop them, but I couldn't let him. I have a duty to the dreams."

"And you're afraid I'll get scared, too, and start putting Thorazine in your food. I told you, I'm not Richard."

"I'm all right. The Thorazine's almost out of my system. I know. I'm feeling a lot better. There's no reason to go see a doctor. He'll try to stop the dreams. He'll put me on some other drug."

"I didn't say anything about going to see a doctor," I said helplessly, and then realized I had. "You mean Dr. Barton? That's the guy Broun asked me to interview. He's got acromegaly, the same growth disorder Lincoln had, and he's not even a doctor. He's a vet. When I called, his wife asked me if I wanted to see him about a horse." I tried to smile at her. "I know it's your duty to have the dreams. It's my duty to take care of you while you do. I promise I won't try to stop the dreams."

"Okay," she said. She smoothed out the coverlet where she had wrinkled it.

"Now how about some breakfast, and then we'll hit all the hot spots of Fredericksburg? Mary Washington's got this mirror that people flock from miles around to see."

"All right," she said, smiling. "Who was Mary Washington?"

"I don't know," I said, looking down at the brochure. I had twisted it into an unreadable wad of colored paper. "George Washington's mother? Or his daughter maybe? Did George Washington have any daughters?" She was staring at the brochure. "I'll pick up another one in the lobby." I dropped it in the wastebasket.

"Annie, it's going to be all right," I said. "I'll take care of you."

"I know."

Mary Washington was George's mother. We had breakfast in a coffee shop across from the inn and then walked downtown to see Mary's dressing glass and her sundial in a little house at the foot of the formal gardens of Kenmore.

I watched Annie anxiously all morning, but she looked fine. Better than fine. The warm spring air and exercise seemed to be doing her a world of good. She laughed at my comments on what sort of person Mary Washington had been, considering that her daughter had stuck her as far away from the house as possible, and said, "She probably talked as much about that awful dressing glass as the tour guide did."

She smiled, a beautiful, untroubled smile. Oddly, it made her look older, more like a woman and less like a ravaged child, and I thought, Good, I'm doing the right thing.

But after lunch, browsing through our third antique shop, she started to look tired. She picked up a china cat and started to say something, and then stopped in mid-sentence and went over to the window of the antique shop and looked anxiously out toward the south as though she were waiting for A. P. Hill's men to come up.

"Are you all right?" I said, worried that this was some side effect of the Thorazine.

She was still holding the china cat.

"Let's go get some coffee," I said. I'd been pouring coffee into her all day, in spite of Dr. Stone's theory that caffeine caused bad dreams. I couldn't think of any other way to get the Thorazine out of her system.

"I think I've had enough coffee," she said, smiling. "I'm fine. I just have a headache."

"Well, how about some aspirin then?"

"No, I'm fine. I'm just tired. Maybe we should go back to the inn."

"Sure thing. Do you want to walk? If you're tired, I can run back and get the car. Or we can call a taxi."

"I don't think Fredericksburg's got taxis," she said, putting the china cat down carefully on a drop-leaf table. "There isn't any reason to panic, Jeff. It's a sinus headache. I get hay fever. It's probably the apple blossoms."

She seemed fine on the walk home. A breeze had come up, and it blew the light hair back from her face and colored her cheeks. "This is a pretty town," she said, "all these old houses. Was there a battle here? In the Civil War?"

"Yes." I pointed at a dilapidated blue Ford sedan with a hand-lettered sign on its side. "I told you they had taxis in Fredericksburg."

We went up the outside staircase of the inn to our rooms. A black cat with white paws was sunning itself on the second step from the top. It made no effort at all to get out of our way.

"Hello, there," Annie said, reaching down to pet it. The cat closed its eyes and allowed itself to be petted as if it were doing Annie a favor. "I've always wished I could have a cat. My father was allergic to them."

"Your father?"

"Yes. They gave him hives."

"You know, I don't know anything about you. Your family, where you come from, what you were doing before you started having Lee's dreams. Where do you live?"

She straightened up, her smile gone. She looked the way she had that night when Richard had been ranting about Lincoln's psychological problems. "A little town. About the size of Fredericksburg."

"Broun has a cat," I said hastily. "It's a selfish brute. Like this one here." I chucked the cat under its black chin and walked on up the stairs to open the door for Annie, hating Richard at that moment more than I had ever hated anyone.

I didn't know anything at all about Annie. Correction: I knew she had a father who was allergic to cats, and that she came from a little town, and from the look on her face that was all she was going to tell me. I didn't blame her. Richard knew all about her. If it wasn't on the forms she had filled out at the Institute or the records her doctor had sent, Richard had found it out in his therapy sessions, and whatever he knew he had used: "I see your father died last year. Did you feel responsible for his death? What did he look like? Did he have a white beard? Like Robert E. Lee's? Isn't that what your dream is really all about?"

And as if that wasn't bad enough, he had probably spent the morning calling those numbers on the forms, Next of Kin Not Living at Above Address, and demanding to know where she was. No wonder she didn't want to tell me anything. I might turn out to be another Richard, and when she ran from me, she would want to make sure I couldn't follow.

"Broun's really going to be mad when he gets back," I said, opening the door to my room and smiling reassuringly. "I gave his cat the leftover shrimp doodads."

She followed me into the room. "What did they taste like?"

"Well, I wouldn't want Broun to find out, but I think they're awful. I was afraid that night of the reception he was actually going to force us to eat some of them. Now you go ahead and take a nap if you're tired. Is there anything I can get you?"

She rubbed her hand across her forehead. "Jeff, I think I could use some aspirin after all."

"I'll see if I've got any," I said, knowing full well I hadn't packed any in the mad dash down here, and went into my room. I had almost offered to go get some for her, but there was something I had to do first. I shut the door and called Broun's answering machine.

Broun's California-fog message repeated itself, and Richard had called.

"I'm calling to tell you that I'm not angry about your getting me hauled in for questioning by the police this morning," the Good Shrink said. "I know you felt threatened, and I know Annie feels threatened, but I want to reassure you that my only concern is my patient and her welfare."

The psychiatrist must convince the patient he has her own best interests at heart.

"Running away isn't the answer, Jeff. You have to bring Annie back so she can get the proper treatment. I know you choose not to believe me, but this neurotic fantasy of hers is dangerous. She's completely dissociated herself from her dreams. She told me they're Robert E. Lee's dreams. She's on the edge of a complete psychotic break, and taking her to California is only going to precipitate it."

Good. He thought we were in California. That meant he wasn't going to show up here while I was gone. I didn't want to leave Annie alone, but I had to find out about the Thorazine Richard had given her. I hung up and went back into Annie's room. She was standing by the window, looking out at the trees that lined the river.

"I didn't bring any aspirin. I'll run get you some. I saw a drugstore on the way back here."

"You don't have to. . . ."

"I've got to go anyway. I forgot to pack my razor, too, and, unlike Broun, I have no desire to grow a beard. Is there anything else I can get you?"

"No." She managed a fair smile. She was looking flushed again.

"You're sure you'll be okay here? I'll just be a few minutes."

"I'll be fine," she said. She tried for a better smile. A truck rumbled past the front of the inn, and Annie raised her head and gazed out over the trees as if what she had heard was the low thunder of artillery fire.

I took the car, bought the razor and some aspirin at a convenience store, and then drove downtown to the library. I'd seen it on our way back to the inn, a three-story brick building that looked like it had been a school.

The reference books were in a drab basement room lit by fluorescent lights. The only drug compendium they had was badly out-of-date, and it didn't say anything about how to get Thorazine out of a person's system, but it said abrupt withdrawal from a high dosage could cause nausea and dizziness.

It didn't say what a high dosage was, and it didn't particularly matter anyway since I didn't have any idea how much Richard had given her, but how could he have given her any at all? The compendium described it as being just as dangerous as I thought it was.

Dozens of contraindications and warnings were listed, drowsiness and jaundice and fainting spells, and there was a note set off in double borders that read, "Sudden death, apparently due to cardiac arrest, has been reported, but there is not sufficient evidence to establish a relationship between such deaths and the administration of the drug." I wondered if in the ten years since the book had been published they had managed to establish a relationship, and if Richard cared.

He had to have known exactly what Thorazine could do to Annie, and yet he had given it to her anyway. Why? It wasn't used to cure mental patients. It was used to keep them under control.

I couldn't find anything about headaches or fever in the list of side effects, although it said infections could result after the fourth week. All of the side effects and warnings seemed to be related to long-term use of the drug, and the last page reassured me. In spite of all the warnings, it was recommended in the treatment of everything from hiccups to lockjaw.

I went back to the inn and found Annie sitting on the outside steps, playing with the black cat. "My headache's gone," she said when I handed her the aspirin. "I feel much better."

We ate dinner at the coffee shop where we'd had breakfast. "How are you feeling now?" I asked her when the waitress brought our check. "Have you been dizzy at all today?"

"No."

"Nauseated?"

"No. Why?"

"You still may have some Thorazine in your system."

"I don't see how," she said. "Between you and the waitress I've drunk enough coffee today to get anything out of my system. You don't have to worry about the Thorazine."

"Okay," I said, picking up the check. "Then I won't."

She stood up and looked across at the inn as if she were afraid of it. "Now all we have to worry about is the dreams."

I went back to the table to leave the tip. Her paper napkin was lying on the seat of the booth. She had shredded it into tiny pieces.

When we got back to the room, I said, "I thought I'd read galleys in here for a while." I pulled a green chair over near the foot of the bed, and went to my room to get the galleys, taking a while to gather up Broun's copyedited manuscript and a couple of blue pencils so Annie could get ready for bed, and whistling the whole time so she'd know I was there.

When I came back in, she was already in bed, in a long-sleeved white nightgown, sitting up against the pillows, her hands clenched together.

"Is that Broun's book about Antietam?" Annie asked.

"More or less," I said. "He keeps making changes. That's why I need to get these done before he comes back from California, so he'll quit fooling with it."

"What do you have to do with them?"

"Read them over. Look for mistakes, typos, missing lines, punctuation, that kind of thing." I moved the chair closer to the bed so I could prop my feet on the end of it.

"Can I help?" She said it calmly enough, but the knuckles

of her clenched hands were white. "Please. I don't want to just sit here and wait to go to sleep."

I put the galleys down. "Look, I don't have to work on these right now. We could watch some TV or something."

"Really, I'd like to help with the galleys. I think reading would take my mind off the dreams. Do we take different parts or do we read it out loud to each other?"

"Annie, I just don't think it's a good idea."

"Because it's about Antietam?"

Because it's about Lee's bandaged hands and a horse with its legs shot off and dead soldiers everywhere. "Yes."

"You read those out loud, don't you?" she said. "That's exactly the reason I should help you. I can see if Broun made any mistakes. After all, I was there."

There was nothing I could say to that. I handed her the galleys and a blue proofreader's pencil. "I'll read from the copyedited manuscript and you follow along to make sure everything's there and they haven't left out a line. You can check for typos, too. Just mark an X in the margin, and I'll go back and put in the proofreader's marks." I handed her a pencil and put my feet up on the footboard and began to read:

"What time is it, do you reckon?" Ben said. They were crouched in a cornfield a little behind the sunken road where all the fighting was. They had fired over the heads of the men in the road until they ran out of cartridges and then had begun working their way backwards between the rows of shredded corn, taking rifles away from dead and wounded men and firing them. It seemed like they had been doing it for hours, but there was so much smoke Ben couldn't even see the sun. He wondered if maybe they had been here all day and the sun had gone down.

"It ain't noon yet," Malachi said. He had his hand under a soldier whose left shoulder had been shot off and who was lying face down in the broken corn stalks. He had yellow hair. His arm was lying on the ground beside him, still holding on to his Springfield. There was a scrap of cloth pinned to his sleeve with a stick. Ben put down his rifle and unpinned the cloth. It was a handkerchief.

Malachi turned him over and rummaged in his pockets. It was Toby.

"Come on," Malachi said. "Looks like he ran out of minnies, too,

before they got him." He thrust Ben's rifle at him and yanked him backwards. "Listen. They're bringing the guns up," Malachi said, and Ben could feel the rough dirt shake under his feet.

"I have to . . ." Ben said and started forward again.

Malachi stood up and grabbed him by the back of his shirt. "What in tarnation do you think you're doin'?"

He showed the handkerchief to Malachi. "I gotta pin this back on Toby. How will they know who he is? How will his kin know what happened to him?"

"They'll have a right good idea, but they won't find out from that," he said, and jerked his finger at the handkerchief. Ben looked at it. It was covered with soot from the powder so badly he couldn't even make the letters out. "Now come on! What the hell you doin' now?"

"I know him," Ben said, scrabbling in his pockets. "I know where he's from. Do you got some paper?"

A bullet hit Toby's arm and gouged out another red hole. "Come on," Malachi shouted, "or that gal back home's gonta be findin' out about you." He took hold of Ben's coat and yanked him back through the corn till they couldn't see Toby anymore.

After a while the shooting let up a little and Malachi said, "Me, I stick my pertinents in my boots."

"They can shoot you in the foot, too," Ben said.

"They can," Malachi said, "but most likely you won't get kilt straight off and you kin tell 'em who you are before you die."

"I'm sorry," I said. "We had no business reading that."

She was asleep. I took the galleys back from her and put in the proofreader's marks till I began to feel sleepy myself, and then went and looked out the window a while at the Rappahannock. Union troops had camped on the far side of the river, no more than half a mile from here, their campfires hidden by the fog along the river, waiting for the battle to start. Everyone who had written about the Civil War, generals, platoon historians, journalists, said the waiting was the worst part. Once you were in the battle, they said, it wasn't so bad. You did what you had to do without even thinking about it, but beforehand, waiting for the fog to lift and the signal to be given, was almost unbearable.

"It's so cold," Annie said. She sat up and tugged at the blankets with both hands, trying to pull them free of the foot of the bed.

"I'll get a blanket," I said, and then realized she was still asleep. She yanked hard on the coverlet and it came free.

"Get Hill up here," she said, wrapping the flounced muslin around her shoulders and holding it together with one hand at her neck, as if it were a cape. "I want him to see this." Her cheeks were flushed almost red. I wondered if she would be feverish if I touched her.

She let go of the coverlet and leaned forward as if looking at something. The coverlet slipped off her shoulders. "Bring me a lantern," she said, and fumbled with the satin edge of the blanket.

I wondered if I should try to wake her up. She was breathing fast and shallowly, and her cheeks were as red as fire. She clutched the edge of the blanket in a desperate pantomime of something.

I moved forward to take the blanket away from her before she tore it, and as I did she looked directly at me with the unseeing gaze of the sleeping, and let go of it.

"Annie?" I said softly, and she sighed and lay down. The coverlet was bunched behind her neck, and her head was at an awkward angle, and I gently eased the coverlet out from under and pulled the blanket up over her shoulders.

"I had a dream," Annie said. She was looking at me and this time she saw me. Her cheeks were still flushed, though not as red as they had been.

"I know," I said. I hung the coverlet over the end of the bed and sat down beside her. "Do you want to tell me about it?"

She sat up, tucking the pillow up against the headboard and pulling the muslin coverlet up over her bent knees. "I was standing on the porch of my house at night, looking down at the lawn. It was winter, I think, because it was cold, but there wasn't any snow, and the house was different. It was on a steep hill, and the lawn was a long way below me, at the bottom of the hill. I was looking down at the lawn, but I couldn't see it because it was too dark, but I could hear the sound of someone crying. It was a long way off, so I couldn't really be sure what I heard, and I kept squinting down at the lawn, trying to make out what was down there.

"I turned on the porch light, and that just made it worse. I couldn't see anything. So I turned it off again and stood there in the dark and just then somebody crashed into me and it was a Union soldier. He had a message for me, and I knew it would be good news, but I was afraid if I turned on the porch light to read it by, I wouldn't be able to see what was on the lawn.

"Then I saw a light in the sky, a long way off, and I thought, Oh, good, somebody on their side has turned a porch light on, but it wasn't like that, it bobbed and danced, and I thought, Somebody is bringing me a lantern to read the message by, and then the whole sky lit up with red and green, and I could see the bodies on the lawn."

"Were they Union soldiers?" I asked.

"Yes," she said, "only they weren't wearing blue uniforms. Some of them were wearing long underwear, red and white, and some of them were naked, and I thought how cold they must be lying there without any clothes on. Do you know where we are?"

Oh, yes, I thought, I know where we are. I hadn't taken her anywhere near the battlefield all day, but she had been there anyway. And why had I thought the battles Lee had won would haunt him any less than the ones he had lost?

"They weren't wearing uniforms because the Confederates came down from Marye's Heights in the middle of the night and stole them off the dead bodies. After the battle of Fredericksburg."

She leaned back against the pillows as if I had said something comforting. "Tell me about the battle."

"After Antietam, Lee retreated back into Virginia. It took forever for the Union army to make up its mind to follow him, and when they did it was at the worst possible place. In December, the Union army crossed the Rappahannock at Fredericksburg and tried to march across the plain southwest of town, but the Confederate army held Marye's Heights above the plain. They proved beyond a shadow of a doubt that you can't attack a defended ridge from an open plain."

"And after the battle the wounded soldiers lay there crying for help on the plain?"

"Yes. It froze that night."

"And the Confederate soldiers stole their clothes," she said softly. "What about the message?"

"A Union courier got lost in the dark the night before the battle and wandered up to a Confederate picket line. He was captured and the orders he was carrying were taken to Lee. That same night the aurora borealis shone, lighting up the whole sky with red and green. Both sides took it as a good omen."

She sat a long time huddled under the coverlet. "What time is it?" she asked.

"Eleven forty-five."

She lay down. "If this time is anything like the others, I shouldn't have any more dreams tonight. I usually don't have them after midnight."

"Was this dream like the others, Annie?" I asked, thinking of the "storm of dreams" Dr. Stone had said followed abrupt discontinuation of a sedative.

"No," she said. She had propped herself up on one elbow, and she was smiling. "It was easier. Because you were here to tell me what it meant." She yawned. "Can I sleep late tomorrow?"

"Of course. The morning after a battle the soldiers always get to sleep late," I said, which was a lie. The morning after the battle the soldiers were marched off to the next battle, and the next, till they came to the one that killed them.

I sat down in the green chair and picked up the galleys.

"You don't have to stay up, Jeff," she said. "I won't have any more dreams. You can go to bed."

"I just thought I'd finish reading the chapter we were on," I said. "Don't worry about me. Go back to sleep."

She was asleep almost instantly, but I kept on reading. Ben and Malachi made it out of their cornfield and into the dubious safety of the West Wood. Hooker opened fire on another cornfield with every battery he had, and nobody made it out of there. Ben's brother and the rest of Mansfield's Twelfth Corps got the order to hold the East Wood and, in the smoke and confusion, began firing at their own Union troops.

When Mansfield tried to stop them he was hit in the chest by Confederate fire. It was a mortal wound, but he managed to dismount and lead his wounded horse to safety before he died.

CHAPTER SEVEN

$\mathbf{D}$.H. Hill had three horses shot out from under him at Antietam. Lee rode Traveller through the whole battle, though he had trouble controlling him with his bandaged hands. When General Walker brought the last of his men across the ford into Virginia the following night, Lee was sitting on Traveller in midstream. "How many divisions are left?" Lee asked, and when Walker told him he was the last except for some wagonloads of wounded that were right behind him, Lee said, "Thank God!" It was Walker's impression that he had been sitting there all night.

Annie didn't have any more dreams. I dozed in the green chair until it was light outside and then went to bed and slept until after nine. Annie was still dead to the world, but Richard was up. He had already called Broun's house and left another message for me.

"It's obvious that you're projecting your hostility onto me as an authority figure, but of course Broun is the real object of your anger. You're superimposing your own revenge fantasy on Annie's emotional illness, but it's Broun who's your real enemy."

He stopped long enough for me to say, "You're the enemy, you bastard."

"Your conscious mind can't acknowledge the rage you feel toward Broun for getting his name on the books you've researched, so your subconscious cloaks that rage by distorting Annie's neurotic dreams into Robert E. Lee's dreams. By so doing, your subconscious can declare war on Broun, as Lee declared war on Lincoln. It's a common phenomenon in neurotic patients."

"How about drugging patients? Is that a common phenomenon in neurotic psychiatrists?"

Annie was standing in the doorway in her nightgown. She looked frightened. "Who were you talking to, Jeff? Richard?"

"I wasn't talking to anybody," I said, and held the phone out to her so she could listen. "It's the answering machine. Richard doesn't know where we are, so he's trying to get you back this way, by remote psychoanalysis. You'll be glad to know I'm the one who's crazy today." I put the phone back up to my ear. "This may take a while. Broun's answering machine can hold three hours of messages. Why don't you get dressed and we'll go have breakfast. We've got to go see the vet at eleven."

She nodded and disappeared into the other room. I listened to the rest of Richard's harangue, made sure Broun hadn't called in another message, and erased everything on the machine. Broun usually didn't call in to pick up his messages when he was out of town. He left messages for me as to where he could be reached and then let me get back to him with a list of the things that couldn't wait. I didn't think he'd pick up his messages this trip, especially when he thought I was there to do it, but I thought I'd better call the machine once a day to collect them and erase the tape just in case. I didn't want Broun hearing Richard's ravings.

Annie came and stood in the doorway again. "You were friends, weren't you?" she said. "Before all this?"

"We were roommates. I guess we were friends, but we were headed in different directions all along." I picked up my jacket. "He thought I should study something useful instead of history."

"I'm sorry," Annie said.

"About what? My studying history?" I grinned at her. "It hasn't turned out to be all that useless."

We went over to the coffee shop. It was crowded with people who looked like they were on their way to church. We had a different waitress from the one who had drenched us in coffee the night before, a pretty redhead not much older than Annie, but she came over immediately with the coffeepot, too. "You two must be tourists," she said when she saw the map of Virginia I'd brought along. She pulled two menus out from under her arm and handed them to us. "Have you been out to the battlefield?"

"No," Annie said. "We haven't been out there yet."

"Well, you've got to go. It's the only thing Fredericksburg's famous for." She set the coffeepot down and fished an order pad out of her pocket. "The National Park Service has it fixed up real nice. They've got an electric map and everything. Now, what'll you have? Eggs? Hotcakes?"

The waitress took our order, gave our still-full cups what she called a warmup, and went off to the kitchen.

"Did you say the appointment with the vet was at eleven?" Annie said.

"Yeah, but it's out of town so we'd better allow a little time to find it. You didn't have any other dreams last night, did you?"

She shook her head.

"Was the dream different from the other dreams? I mean, I know it was about Fredericksburg, but was it the same kind of dream as the others?"

She thought about it a minute. "It was clearer than the other dreams. I don't know how to describe it exactly, but they make more sense." She shook her head again. "That's not it, exactly. I still don't have any idea where I am or what the things in the dream are until you tell me afterward, but it's as if I'm getting closer to understanding the dreams."

"You mean what's causing them?"

"I don't know. It's . . . I can't explain it. They're getting clearer." And more frightening, I thought, watching her face. Whatever it is that she thinks she's starting to understand is terrifying her.

The waitress brought our breakfast and more coffee. I waited till Annie was done with her eggs and then asked her,

"When do you usually have the dreams? You said last night you usually don't have them after midnight."

"Between nine and midnight. That was why Richard was so worried that night at the reception, because it was after nine. I think he thought I might fall asleep on the loveseat or something, but I don't have narcolepsy. I just have bad dreams."

"You said the Thorazine kept you from dreaming that afternoon after I took you home from Arlington. Do you have the dreams during the day, too?"

"When the dreams first got bad I thought maybe if I could stay awake past midnight, the dreams would leave me alone, and it worked for a while, but then I started dreaming as soon as I went to sleep, so then I tried staying up all night and sleeping during the day, but that didn't work either."

"And that was two weeks ago?"

"Yes."

"And you were on the Elavil then?"

"Yes. I'd been on it for a month and a half."

"Did Richard think that was odd, that you were dreaming? Antidepressants are supposed to repress the dream cycle. Did Richard say anything about that?"

"He was a little worried at first, but he said it took the Elavil a while to work and my sleep record was better. I wasn't waking up so often, and I was getting a lot more rest."

"What about when the dreams got worse . . . clearer?"

"He said that was a good sign, that whatever was causing the dreams was trying to break through, that my subconscious was determined to make itself heard."

I had assumed that he had taken her off the Elavil because it wasn't working or was even making the dreams worse. If that wasn't the reason, what was? According to Annie, he hadn't even been worried about the dreams, but something had happened to frighten him so badly that he had given her Thorazine to try to stop them.

The waitress made a frontal assault on our coffee cups again, and Annie and I both tried unsuccessfully to hold her off. "Maybe we'd better retreat before she drowns us in this stuff." I looked at my watch. "It's ten-fifteen. Why don't we go ahead and see if we can find this Dr. Barton?"

"All right," Annie said. She folded her napkin and laid it on the table.

"Were you on anything before you came to the Institute? You said your doctor sent you to the Institute. Did he have you on any sedatives or anything?"

We stood up. "Phenobarbital," she said, reaching for her coat.

"Did Richard know that?"

"Yes, he was upset about it. He said that nobody used barbiturates anymore, certainly not in cases of pleisomnia, that my treatment had been all wrong."

"You didn't keep taking the phenobarbital, did you?"

"No."

I handed Annie the map and got the directions the vet's wife had given me out of my wallet. South of town, she had said, past Hazel Run on the Massaponax road. A house with a porch.

All the houses had porches, and we meandered along at least three roads marked Massaponax before we found it. Dr. Barton was back from rounds but just barely and he still had a few animals to look at, his wife told us. She was much younger than she had sounded on the phone, not much older than Annie. She told us we were welcome to go around back to the stable and talk to him there.

The vet was young, too, with a thin, boyish mustache, and he obviously had never had acromegaly. He was only about five foot eight. He was wearing a pocketed blue shirt, jeans, and a pair of high boots that made him look like a Union army officer.

"What can I do for you?" he said, looking at a sorrel mare with a bad foot.

"I doubt if you can do anything for me," I said. "I've made a mistake. I was looking for a Dr. Barton who has acromegaly."

"That was my father," he said, picking up the mare's left hind foot. "I told Mary I bet that was who you wanted to see when she told me you'd mentioned Dr. Stone's name." He put the foot down. "Dad died of a heart attack this fall. What did you want to talk to him about?"

"I work for Thomas Broun." The vet nodded as if he'd

heard of him. "He's doing a book on Abraham Lincoln. Lincoln had acromegaly."

"I know," he said. "Dad was always interested in other people who'd had acromegaly, especially famous people. Edward the First, the pharaoh Akhenaten, but especially Lincoln. I think because late years he got to look like Lincoln. That happens, you know, with the acromegaly. They all get the big ears and nose and the splayed hands."

He picked up each of the mare's feet one by one, laid his hand flat against the sole of it, and then set the foot back down so the mare would put her weight on it. When he got to the right forefoot, the mare held the foot above the ground for a minute and then set it down carefully. Annie sat down on a bale of hay and watched him.

"What Broun's really interested in is Lincoln's dreams," I said.

"The boat dream, huh?" He picked up the forefoot, looked at it, and set it down again. This time the mare put it firmly on the ground. "Dad was always fascinated by that."

"Boat dream?"

"Yeah. Lincoln had this recurring dream." He started on the mare's feet again, picking them up, setting them down. When he let go of the right forefoot, the mare put it down and then picked it up again and held it just above the ground. "In the dream he was in a boat drifting toward a dark, hazy shore. He dreamed it before battles: Bull Run, Antietam, Gettysburg. He dreamed it the night before he was assassinated, too."

I looked at Annie, worried about what effect all this talk about dreams might be having on her, but she looked more interested in the mare than in our conversation.

"Did your father ever mention having any dreams?"

He pulled a small curved knife out of his shirt pocket. "About boats? I don't think so. Why?"

"Broun thinks Lincoln's dreams may have had something to do with his acromegaly. Did he ever mention the acromegaly causing him to dream a lot?"

"That's an interesting theory." He thought a minute. "I don't remember Dad ever mentioning any dreams. If you know anything about acromegaly, you know it produces headaches and depression. My father was a very unhappy man. He didn't talk much, especially about his acromegaly. He told me as much about his symptoms as this mare does. The only time I ever heard him talk about it was in connection with famous people like Lincoln or Akhenaten. Toward the end it became almost an obsession with him."

He picked up the right front foot and began scraping away at the bottom of the hoof with the knife. "Speaking of Akhenaten, the Egyptians were big on dreams," he said. "They wrote them down, hired soothsayers to interpret them, believed their dreams could predict the future. There might be something . . ." He brushed away the shavings and peered at the bottom of the foot. "No, I doubt if there'd be anything on Akhenaten's dreams. The next pharaoh who came along, Ramses, wiped out just about every trace of him. Knocked down all his statues, scratched out his name wherever he could find it, burned everything."

"Then how do they know he had acromegaly?"

"They don't," he said. He poked at something on the hoof with the top of the knife and frowned. He let go of the foot and watched as the mare put her foot down. She put her weight on it with no hesitation. "It was just a pet theory of Dad's. There are a couple of wall paintings and statues that Ramses missed. They show him as having elongated ears and a wide, flat nose, and what records there are comment on his height. One of the hieroglyphics also called him melancholy, which, like I said, is one of the symptoms of acromegaly."

"Or of knowing the next pharaoh's going to do his best to make everybody forget you," I said.

He grinned. "Right. It's all just a game, guessing what diseases people back in history had. Or guessing what diseases people have now, for that matter." He took hold of the mare's bridle and began walking her up and down past us, watching carefully to see which foot she favored.

"With animals it's really a guessing game. They can't tell you where it hurts or what they think they have. Like this mare here," he said, still parading her in a slow circle. "She's got a sore foot, probably a bruised sole or a prick from a horseshoe nail, but it could be laminitis or corns or something else al-

97

together. I can't find the infection, so I can't tell. The only sure way of finding out is to let her alone till it's gotten really serious. Then the infection will be easy to find—the hoof will be hot to the touch, she won't be able to put any weight on it, and she'll have developed a lot of other symptoms. Only problem is, by then it could be too late to do her any good, especially if she's picked up a nail. I need to find it now."

"What if you can't find it?" Annie said.

"Then I'll give her a tetanus shot and wait till I can, but I'll find it. The clues to what's going on are there. You just have to look a little harder to find them at this stage." He stopped the mare and tied her bridle securely to a rail and picked up the right front foot again. "With animals you either have too many symptoms or not enough, and one's as bad as the other. I had a bay in here last week had every symptom in the book and then some. Had to sort through a dozen diseases before I got the right one. But I love a good mystery, don't you?"

He scraped away at the caked dirt on the hoof, turning the knife blade on edge to get in close to the shoe. We weren't getting anywhere with all this, but the barn was warm and smelled of dry hay, and Annie looked as if she was thinking about the mare's sore foot and not about that other horse with its legs shot off. Dr. Barton dug in with the knife, and the mare began to shake her head as if telling him to stop. Annie stood up and went over to her, taking hold of the bridle just under her chin, and stroking her neck.

"Your father never talked about his dreams, not even in connection with Lincoln's boat dream?"

"Not to me. He moved to Georgia last year when he started having heart problems. Did you know high blood pressure and heart disease were connected to acromegaly?"

"No, I didn't."

He stopped scraping and put the horse's foot down. "Dad might have told my sister his dreams. She was always his favorite, and he used to talk to her more than to the rest of us. Would you like me to call her?"

"I'd appreciate it if you would," I said, and wrote out our phone number at the inn. "Ask her if he had any dreams. They don't have to be about boats."

"Boats," he said thoughtfully, folding up the piece of paper and sticking it in his pocket. The mare had tangled her mane in the bridle when she tossed her head. Annie pulled the forelock out from under it, smoothed it, and patted the mare's forehead. "The Egyptians dreamed a lot about boats. Symbol of the passage to the world of the dead."

We left the vet to the mystery of the sore foot and drove back to the inn. We had lunch at a McDonald's on the way back into town, and when we got back to the inn, Annie took a nap.

I called the answering machine. There was a jumble of messages from people who hadn't figured out Broun was gone yet, and Richard had left another message on the machine.

"I've been looking at the results of Annie's blood tests, and I think I've found the key to what's happening here," he said in his Good Shrink voice. "Her L-tryptophan levels are indicative of cryptomnesia." He waited long enough for me to ask what cryptomnesia was. "It occurs when the patient presents early memories as reality, something the patient saw or read in a book and the conscious mind has forgotten. The subconscious mind then reintegrates the material as reality. Bridey Murphy. Her memories of an earlier life in Ireland were stories her nurse had told her in a preverbal stage, and under hypnosis she presented them as a previous life."

"Annie wasn't hypnotized," I said. "She was drugged."

"She obviously had preverbal contact with someone who told her stories about the Civil War, or there's a possibility of more recent reading of Civil War novels. Maybe she read one of Broun's books. That would account for her immediate neurotic attachment to you. She's experiencing schizophrenic dissociation, and you represent Broun."

So now it was cryptomnesia, and I represented Broun. This morning it had been a revenge fantasy and Broun had represented Annie's dreams. And before that it had been a psychotic break and a half-buried trauma and a murder in the orchard with a cap pistol, and who knew what it would be the next time Richard called, and never in all these calls a word about the Thorazine he had given her.

Did he honestly think he could talk me into bringing

Annie back with all this psychiatric gibberish? Maybe he was the crazy one and all this talk about Annie's repressed guilt and my obsession and Lincoln's impending nervous breakdown was nothing but—what was the proper psychiatric term?—projection.

I called Broun at the number he had given me before he left for California. "How's it going?" I asked. "Did you get in to see your prophetic-dreams expert?"

"This morning. He told me time and space aren't real, that they only exist in the conscious part of our brain, and down in the subconscious there's no such thing as a space-time continuum. He said everything that's ever happened or is going to happen is already in our subconscious, and it comes out in dreams." He talked the way he always had, as if we had never had that fight about California. "Then he says most people have to wait for dreams to tell them what's going to happen, but *he* can tell me my future right now just by putting me to sleep and watching my rapid eye movements."

"And what did you say?"

"I said I'd already dreamed I didn't give money to phony fortune-tellers, and since it had already happened there wasn't any way I could change it."

"And what did he say?"

"I didn't wait to find out. I wish I could dream what was going to happen. Then I wouldn't get stuck listening to cock-and-bull stories like that. Where are you, at home?"

"No," I said. "I'm in Fredericksburg. The phone rang off the hook yesterday, and I decided I wasn't going to get any work done, so I came down here. I think I might stay awhile. At least until McLaws and Herndon figure out where I am. There isn't any snow here."

"I won't tell a soul where you are, son. Let McLaws and Herndon talk to the answering machine. That's what the damned thing's for. How're you coming on the galleys?"

"Fine. I looked up your Dr. Barton. He died last fall, but I talked to his son. He couldn't remember his father talking about any unusual dreams. He's going to call his sister and ask her. Oh, by the way, I've got another dream for your collection. Lincoln had a dream the night before he died. He told his Cabinet about it. He dreamed he was in a boat."

" 'A singular and indescribable vessel,' " Broun said. "I know."

"You knew about the boat dream?" I said. "Then why didn't you tell me?"

There was a silence at the other end so long that I had plenty of time to think of all the things we hadn't told each other in the last week. I wondered what would happen if I told him I thought the fortune-teller was right, and down in Annie's subconscious Lee was fighting the Civil War. Would he call that a cock-and-bull story, too?

"Are you all right?" he asked. "Are you taking care of yourself?"

"I'm sleeping till noon every day," I said, "and don't worry about the galleys. I'm over halfway through the book already."

"I'm not worried about the galleys," he said.

After I hung up I went and woke Annie up. We drove down to Bowling Green for dinner. Annie didn't show any of the tension I'd seen the day before, and the color in her cheeks was back to normal. Even after we got back to the inn and were reading galleys up in her room, me in the green chair and she sitting cross-legged on the bed, she was relaxed and interested.

"Why don't you go ahead and go to bed, Jeff?" she said at a little after eleven. "You didn't get much sleep last night. I don't think I'll have a dream."

"Okay," I said. "Call me if you need me."

I left the door of the room open and the light beside the bed on. I took off my shoes and settled down with the book I'd bought in Bowling Green. It was a pop history moment-by-moment account of the day Lincoln died, but it had a long description of the Cabinet meeting.

Lincoln had told his boat dream before the meeting started, while they were still waiting for Stanton. Grant said he was worried about Sherman, and Lincoln said not to worry, that he had had a sign, and told them his dream. He said he had had the same dream before every victory in the war and named Antietam and Gettysburg and Stone River.

Grant, who didn't believe in dreams, said Stone River wasn't his idea of a victory and a few more victories like that would have lost the war, and Lincoln said, "It must relate to Sherman. I know of no other important event which is likely just now to occur."

I looked at my watch. It was a quarter to twelve. I turned off the light. What if Grant had believed in dreams? Would he have been able to figure out where the danger lay in time to bring up reinforcements, to set up a line of defenses that would have stopped John Wilkes Booth?

He didn't believe in dreams. He knew a cock-and-bull story when he heard one, even when Lincoln was the one telling it. But I wondered if, afterwards, he ever dreamed that Cabinet meeting?

"My house is on fire," Annie said.

I turned on the light. She was standing in the door in her white nightgown, holding the galleys. She came over to the bed and handed them to me. "He's dead, isn't he?" she said, and the tears streamed down her unseeing face. "Isn't he?"

CHAPTER EIGHT

Lee and Traveller were well matched. If Lee demanded more stamina and spirit than the average horse could give, Traveller had too much stamina and spirit for the average rider. He chafed at being reined in, had to be exercised strenuously, and had an uncomfortable, high trot. When Rob Lee had to ride him down to Fredericksburg for his father in 1862, he complained, "I think I am safe in saying that I could have walked the distance with much less discomfort and fatigue."

It took me almost an hour to get her back to bed and sleeping more or less peacefully. I had tried to wake her up, even though I had read someplace that you weren't supposed to wake sleepwalkers—or maybe that was one of Richard's theories—but I couldn't.

"Annie!" I said, and took hold of her hands. They were hot. "Wake up, Annie!"

"Is he dead?" she said, the tears running down her face and under her chin.

Is he dead? Who? General Cobb? He had died at Fredericksburg, but I wasn't convinced we were still there. We could be anywhere. Armistead and Garnett had died at Gettysburg,

A. P. Hill at Petersburg two weeks before the surrender. It could even be Lincoln.

"Who, Annie?"

Her nose was running from all the tears, but she didn't make any effort to wipe it. I led her gently by the hand into the bathroom and got a Kleenex. "Tell me what's happening," I said gently and wiped her reddened nose. "Can you tell me, Annie?"

"My house is on fire."

I dabbed clumsily at her cheeks with the wadded-up Kleenex. "What does the house look like, Annie?" I asked, and wiped her nose again.

She stared at our reflections in the mirror. "He's dead, isn't he?"

I walked her back to her own bed and covered her up. She had stopped crying, but her lashes were matted with tears. The Kleenex was a sodden wad, but I wiped her nose again with it and tucked her in.

I stood beside the bed for a while, thinking she would wake up, but she didn't. I reached for Freeman on the floor next to the green chair and tried to find a burning house. During the battle of Antietam, Longstreet had helped some women and children get their belongings out of a burning house in Sharpsburg, but Lee hadn't been there. In the weeks before the battle of Fredericksburg, most of the town had been burned down, but no one had been killed except for seventeen thousand soldiers.

"I had another dream," Annie said, without any trace of tears in her voice. She sat up in the bed. "My house was on fire." She shook her head as if to contradict what she was saying. "It was the same house as in the other dreams, but it wasn't my house, and it wasn't Arlington."

"Whose house was it?"

"I don't know. We were standing under the apple tree watching it burn, and a rider handed me a message. I couldn't open it because I was wearing gloves, so I handed it to somebody who was standing beside me. It was the clerk here at the inn. He opened the message with one hand. There was something wrong with his other arm. When he opened the message, I saw it was a box of candles."

I shut Freeman. I knew whose house was on fire now. "One of Lee's aides risked his life to bring Lee a box of candles because he was having trouble reading the dispatches by the light of the campfire," I said. "It's the Chancellor house that's on fire. We're at Chancellorsville."

"It isn't a box of candles, though," Annie said, looking at me the way she had looked at her own reflection in the mirror. "It's a message."

"The message is about Stonewall Jackson," I said. "Lee's right-hand man. He was injured at the battle of Chancellorsville. He had his arm amputated."

"I sent a message back to Jackson, didn't I?"

"Yes," I said. I knew what was in that message, too. "Give Jackson my affectionate regards," Lee had written. "Tell him to make haste and get well and come back to me as soon as he can. He has lost his left arm, but I have lost my right."

Annie leaned back against the pillows, rubbing her wrist as if it hurt. "But he's not going to get well, is he? He's going to die."

"Yes," I said.

She lay down immediately, docilely, as if she were a child who had promised to go to sleep after a bedtime story, and I went back into my room and got a blanket and brought it into Annie's room so I could spend the night in the green chair.

Jackson's doctors had predicted a speedy recovery, but he developed pneumonia and died nine days later. Toward the end he was delirious much of the time. "Order A. P. Hill to prepare for action!" Jackson had said once. Lee had called out for Hill, too, when he lay dying of a heart attack seven years later. "Tell Hill he must come up!" he had said clearly. I wondered if they had dreamed of the same battle and which one it was, and if Annie was doomed to dream it, too.

At five I gave up trying to sleep and went into my room and read galleys, leaving the door open in case Annie woke up again. Ben and Malachi spent the rest of the morning and most of a chapter trying to find their regiment, and Robert E. Lee found his son Rob. He was standing on a little knoll by the road when Rob's artillery unit came straggling past with the only gun they had left. They were filthy and exhausted, and Rob stopped in front of his father and said, "General, are you going to send us in again?"

Robert E. Lee had his arm in a sling. A courier was holding Traveller because Lee's hands were too swollen for him to hang on to the reins, and all around them cornfields and woods were on fire, and Antietam Creek ran a rusty red.

"Yes, my son," Lee said. "You all must do what you can to help drive these people back." He told them to take the best horses and sent them back into battle.

I had left Freeman on Annie's bed. I went in to get it. She was asleep on her stomach, one hand under her cheek, the other flung out across the book. I eased the book gently out from under her, and then went on sitting there, as if my presence could somehow protect her from the dreams.

She had made me promise to help her have the dreams. Well, I was helping, all right. She'd already had more dreams since she met me than she had ever had with Richard, drugs or no drugs, and there didn't seem to be anything I could do for her while she was having them. I couldn't even wake her up.

Sitting here wasn't helping her either. I needed to be awake and alert when she had the next dream, and I hadn't had any real sleep since we got to Fredericksburg. But I didn't want to get up and go in to bed. I don't know what I wanted. Maybe for Annie to wake up, to open her blue-gray eyes and look at me. Not at smoke and horses and fallen boys, but at me. To look at me and smile and say sleepily, "You don't have to stay here with me," so I could say, "I want to." And what did I want her to say to that? "I'm glad you're here. I never have the dreams when you're here"?

Annie murmured something and turned her face ever so slightly against the pillow. There weren't any traces of tears left, though her nose was still red. Her hair had stuck to her cheek when the tears dried, and I brushed it back off her face. Her cheek felt warm to the touch. I laid my hand against it.

She frowned as if she were disturbed. I took my hand away. Her face softened at once. She sighed and turned onto

her side, pulling her knees up, drawing into herself. Her
breathing steadied.

I stood up, carefully, so as not to disturb her, and took
Freeman into the other room and looked up Lee's insomnia.
He had had trouble sleeping throughout the war. "I fear I
shall not sleep for thinking of the poor men," he had written
to his wife a week after Antietam. If he was ever able to get to
sleep before midnight, his aides were under strict orders not to
wake him up unless it was absolutely necessary. He had told
them that to him one hour's sleep before midnight was worth
two hours' after that time.

I fell asleep with the volume of Freeman still open on my
chest and slept till after noon, and even though my sleep
hadn't come before midnight, it was still worth its weight in
gold. I felt better than I had since before the trip to West
Virginia, and able to think clearly for the first time about this
whole mess. I had promised I would help Annie have the
dreams. There was only one way to do that, and that was to
figure out what was causing them.

I checked on Annie, who was still asleep. I shaved and got
dressed, took a sheet of Fredericksburg Inn stationery out of
the chiffonier, and started making a list of the dreams. Arlington first, and then Antietam, Fredericksburg, Chancellorsville.
The Lees had evacuated Arlington in May of 1861. I wasn't
sure of the date of the letter from Markie Williams that told
what had happened to Tom Tita the cat, but it was sometime
in 1861. Antietam was September 1862, Fredericksburg December of the same year, and Chancellorsville May of 1863.
That meant the dreams were in chronological order, though
they were telescoped in some way. Annie had dreamed almost
a year of the war in one week, though she had dreamed about
Arlington for over a year, with it only gradually becoming
clearer. And there were important battles during that period
of time that Annie hadn't dreamed about at all.

I started another list on a second sheet of stationery,
writing the dates of the dreams in one column and the drugs
she had been taking when she had the dreams in a second
column. The drugs had some connection with the dreams,
though I didn't know what it was. They had not suppressed

REM sleep or kept her from dreaming at all, even though they were supposed to.

It was when Annie was on the Elavil that her dreams had suddenly become clearer, and the phenobarbital her family doctor had had her on apparently hadn't worked at all to stop the Arlington dream. Thorazine had stopped the dreams, but she hadn't had the storm of dreams Dr. Stone had predicted when she stopped taking it, and none of the dreams seemed to have any particular correlation with the drugs she was or wasn't taking, so maybe there wasn't a connection after all, and the timing of the dreams had more to do with when Lee managed to get a few hours of sleep than with the tranquilizers.

Annie was awake. I could hear her moving around. I folded up the lists and put them into my jeans pocket. I knocked on the half-open door and she opened it the rest of the way immediately.

"Have you been up forever?" she said, looking at her watch. She looked tired in spite of all the sleep. "I couldn't believe it when I saw how late it was."

"I could. I woke up starving to death. It's a good thing they serve breakfast all day at the coffee shop. What say we go get some?" I pulled on my coat. "I want to go to the library this afternoon. I think I've got an idea of what's causing the dreams."

I told her about Lee's insomnia at breakfast, and then we walked down to the library. I bought a notebook at the convenience store on the way. "I should probably be doing research on Lincoln's dreams, too, in case the vet doesn't find anything out," I said.

"I'll do that for you," Annie said. "What do you want me to look for?"

"Anything on his acromegaly, which won't be in the indexes because nobody knew what he had. Any references to his having headaches or bouts of depression. And anything you can find out about Willie's death."

"Willie. That was his son that died during the war?" she asked.

I nodded. "Yeah. He was Lincoln's favorite child. Lincoln could hardly stand it after he died."

We went into the library and looked around for the biographies. I hadn't paid much attention to the library when I'd come here to look up Thorazine the day before yesterday, except to notice that it had been a school before it was a library, one of those square three-story buildings built in the early 1900s.

It could have been beautiful, with its high, sashed windows and oiled wooden floors, but it seemed almost determinedly drab. The hardwood floors had been covered with speckled tile and a carpet that looked like the Union army had marched over it. Stiff, patched shades had been pulled down over the windows so that the only light of any use was the sharp fluorescent light from tubes in the ceiling.

I'd spent a lot of time in libraries, and I usually preferred the old-fashioned ones with their dusty stacks to the modern plastic-and-plants "multimedia resource centers," but I would have been glad to see a little updating in here.

The room the biographies were in was off to the side and up a few steps, an old classroom probably, though the blackboards had been replaced by bookshelves. I put my notebook down on the scratched wooden table and went to see what they had in the Ls. There were exactly two books on Lincoln: Thomas's *Abraham Lincoln* and an ancient leather-bound book by someone whose name I didn't even recognize.

I handed them to Annie. "We're in the South now. We're lucky they've got any books on him at all."

She took the books back to the table, and I got down on all fours to see what they had on Lee. It might have been the South, but I didn't do much better. I went out to the desk, asked where the history section was, and got directed to a little alcove located a half-flight up from the reference section where I had found the drug compendium.

Since I was already there and I knew where Annie was, I took the opportunity to look up phenobarbital in the dated drug compendium. It said about what I expected it to, that it was a tranquilizer and worked by suppressing REM sleep. Barbiturates were addictive, especially when used over a long period of time, and maybe that was why Richard had been so upset about Annie's family doctor prescribing it, but phenobarbital was comparatively mild, and it didn't have nearly the number of contraindications and warnings that Elavil had had, let alone Thorazine.

I went up into the alcove. It was labeled "Virginiana," and was about as sparse as the biographies had been, which didn't make any sense. Fredericksburg was a major battle, and we were within shooting distance of Spotsylvania, Chancellorsville, and the Wilderness. This should be a main source library for those battles, at least, and, since researchers would inevitably come here, for the rest of the Civil War as well.

I gathered up what I could find on the three battles Annie had dreamed so far and took them back up to the biography room. The librarian, a sharpish-looking woman who would have been at home teaching school there in the old ruler-rapping days, gave me a suspicious glance but made no attempt to stop me.

Annie had the books open and had torn some pages out of my notebook to take notes on. She looked up and smiled when I came in and then bent back over the book, her light hair swinging forward across her cheeks. I sat down opposite her and tried to find out Lee's sleeping habits.

Lee's "precious hours" of sleep between nine and midnight couldn't account for the dreams Annie had had late at night or during the day, but she had said that she'd started having those only after she began staying awake to avoid the dreams. And maybe Lee had tried to grab a few hours here and there to compensate for his sleepless nights.

Lee had "slept little" the night before Antietam, and, according to General Walker, who had seen him sitting on Traveller in midstream when he took his division across, Lee had been there all night, supervising the retreat across the Potomac.

On the night before Fredericksburg, that same night that the aurora borealis lit up the sky and the Union messenger stumbled into Confederate lines, Lee had kept his staff up working all night. At dawn he had ridden out to inspect the pits dug by the work parties overnight. None of the books mentioned whether Lee had gotten some rest after the battle was over, though it was obvious from these accounts that he must have been ready to collapse with fatigue.

Dr. Stone had said that when the body was deprived of

REM sleep, it made it up with a vengeance. Was that what the dreams were? Had Lee, worn out from the strain of battle and a lack of sleep, experienced a storm of dreams?

I couldn't find the same clear-cut pattern with Chancellorsville. Jackson had been wounded on May 2, and as soon as Lee found out about it, he wrote him, "I would I were wounded in your stead." The message of the amputation of his arm arrived on the night of the fourth. There was no mention of Lee's having insomnia that night, though it was hard to imagine him getting a good night's sleep after news like that. On the fifth, word came that Jackson was recovering, and he definitely slept well that night, under a fly-tent at Fairview.

On the morning of the seventh, Jackson began to get worse, and by afternoon he was lost in delirious dreams, calling out for A. P. Hill and telling the infantry to move up. "Do your duty," he told the doctor who was dosing him with mercury and opium. "Prepare for action." On Sunday he said clearly, out of the final dream of some battle, "Let us cross over the river and rest under the trees," and died.

Annie closed both the Lincoln books. "Would they have anything else on Lincoln?" she asked.

"I don't know," I said. "They might have something in the reference section. It's downstairs."

She nodded and left, taking her notes with her.

I started through the biographies of Lee, wishing I had brought Freeman with me. The first book was arranged so hopelessly I never even found Chancellorsville, let alone any references to Lee's insomnia, but the second one, so old the pages were edged in gilt, and written in indecipherably flowery language, said, "When Lee received the dreadful news that the doctors' ministrations were to no avail and that Jackson was sinking fast, he turned to that last, best source of hope in times of trouble. All night he prayed fervently on his knees for Jackson's recovery."

He had been up all one night praying and probably had slept badly three or four nights before that because of worrying about Jackson. There was definitely a pattern. During each of the events Annie had dreamed about, Lee had gone without sleep for several days in a row. Maybe when he did finally sleep, he experienced the storm of dreams that Dr. Stone had described. Dr. Stone had called them powerful, frightening dreams. Could they have been powerful enough to have blasted their way across a hundred years to Annie? And if they had, why was she having them one right after the other? Jackson had died five months after the battle of Fredericksburg.

I looked at my watch. It was four-thirty. I piled the books up and took them back downstairs. Annie was in the reference section with a large book spread open in front of her. They must have had something after all. I went up into the alcove and put the books back on the shelves where they belonged so they would be there if I needed them again and not on a cart guarded by that fierce-looking librarian, and found a book on Gettysburg.

It weighed a ton. I didn't try to carry it back up to the biographies room or even get it up onto a table. I just laid it open on the floor and bent over it, trying to see if the same pattern of lack of sleep persisted with Gettysburg. Gettysburg was the next big battle after Chancellorsville, but Annie wasn't dreaming all the battles. I needed to see if the same conditions for dreaming had occurred during that battle.

There was a full page of references to Lee in the index. I tried looking them up, keeping one hand in the index page and going down the two-column pages with a finger of my other hand, hoping Lee's name or the word *sleep* would jump out at me. At five-fifteen I gave up. It was in there, every word ever written about Gettysburg had to be in there, which was the whole problem. There was too much stuff to sort through, the way the vet's bay had had too many symptoms. Lee's insomnia was lost in the sheer volume of facts. I hefted the book back onto its shelf and went to look for Annie.

She wasn't in the magazine section. I looked along the stacks and found her finally back in the biographies room. She had let up one of the shades and was looking out the window in the direction of the Rappahannock.

"I think I've figured out what's causing the dreams," I said.

She turned around. She looked tired, as if she had been up all night instead of a few hours.

"I think you were right when you said you were helping Lee sleep," I said. "I think that may be exactly what you're doing."

We went out the arched green doors and down the cement steps. It must have rained while we were inside because the library's asphalt parking lot was covered with puddles, but the sky was as clear as when we went inside, paling to lavender with the evening. The air smelled like apple blossoms.

"You said he couldn't sleep," I said. "You were right. He apparently suffered from insomnia through the whole war, and during the battles he didn't sleep at all." I explained my theory to her as we walked back to the inn, telling her about Dr. Stone's storm of dreams and the pattern I'd discovered in her dreams.

"I still think the drugs you took are somehow connected to all this, but I haven't figured out how yet," I said. "You said your family doctor put you on phenobarbital. Did you notice any change in the dreams while you were on it?"

"No," Annie said, looking in the direction of the inn two blocks away. The black cat was coming out to meet us, highstepping its way along the wet sidewalk.

"How long were you on the phenobarbital?" I asked.

The cat meowed a greeting that sounded like a complaint. Annie knelt to pick it up. "Did you know that when Willie Lincoln had pneumonia he kept calling for the boy across the street?" she said. "His name was Bud Taft. He came and held Willie's hand and sat with him the whole time, did you know that?"

"No, I didn't."

"One night while Bud was with Willie, Lincoln came in and said, 'Better go to bed, Bud,' and Bud said, 'If I go, he will call for me.' "

The cat struggled to be let down. Annie put it back on the sidewalk, and it stalked off, offended. Half a block away, it sat down on the sidewalk and began to lick its white paws.

"You didn't happen to find out where Willie Lincoln was buried, did you?" I said.

"I thought he was buried at Arlington."

"Nope. And I don't know where he *was* buried."

Annie looked at the cat. "Maybe nobody knows," she said.

When we came up even with the cat, it stood up and walked alongside us all the way back to the inn.

CHAPTER NINE

Lee's affection for Traveller was obvious. "If I were an artist like you," he wrote his cousin Markie Williams, "I would draw a true picture of Traveller.... Such a picture would inspire a poet, whose genius could then depict his worth and describe his endurance of toil, hunger, thirst, heat, cold, and the dangers and sufferings through which he has passed. He could dilate on his sagacity and affection, and his invariable response to every wish of his rider. He might even imagine his thoughts through the long night marches and days of battle through which he has passed. But I am no artist."

When Michael Miley took Lee's photograph, Lee insisted that he be mounted on Traveller, "just as we went through the four years of war together."

We went back to the inn after dinner and waited for Lee's aides to deliver some last message so that he could take off his boots and settle onto his camp cot and go to sleep.

Annie rechecked the galleys that I had read the night before, and I got out my trusty Freeman and started in on Gettysburg. It was impossible for me to believe that Lee wouldn't dream about this, the worst battle of the war, the end of the war really for the Confederacy, though Broun would fight me on that.

He claimed that Antietam was the decisive battle, that with the failure of Lee's push into Maryland the war was effectively over for the Confederacy, even though there were three more years of killing left and Lee knew it.

Whether it was or not, and, more important, whether Lee was aware of it, he certainly knew it at Gettysburg a year later, and if anything would have given him bad dreams, it was that misbegotten battle. The high-water mark of the Confederacy. Lee made it all the way into Pennsylvania before the Union army stopped him, and then for three days he unleashed one assault after another that made it look like he could win after all.

On the morning of the third day, Lee met with Longstreet outside a schoolhouse. Longstreet didn't like Lee's plan of attack. Later Longstreet claimed he had said, "It is my opinion that no fifteen thousand men ever arrayed for battle can take that position," and had considered the matter settled. Lee never blamed anybody but himself for the failure of Pickett's Charge, but when his aide Colonel Venable said bitterly that he'd distinctly heard Lee direct Longstreet to send up Hood's division in support, Lee had said, "I know! I know!"

Lee's plan was to send Pickett's men directly on a frontal assault at the Union center, and it almost worked. Pickett's men made it up to the famous bloody angle of a stone wall and held it for almost twenty minutes, without any support at all, in spite of the fact that this time it was Fredericksburg in reverse, Lee's men in an open field marching toward a defended ridge. But Longstreet didn't send up the supporting divisions, and they couldn't hold the wall. When the soldiers began to fall back, Lee rode down to meet them and send them back to Seminary Ridge, speaking encouragingly to nearly every man who passed.

"Try to reform your division in the rear of this hill," he had told Pickett, and Pickett had said, "General Lee, I have no division."

Annie went to sleep around ten, the covers pulled up over her shoulders as if she were cold. I called the answering machine, and Richard gave me his new theory, this one about sexual guilt and repressed Oedipal attachments.

I had felt all along that these calls, these theories, were leading somewhere, that they were all part of a pitch to persuade me to bring Annie back, but now I was not so sure. The theories didn't fit together. Sometimes they even contradicted each other, and he jumped from one to another with the same quiet urgency of a man recounting a dream. He still used his Good Shrink voice, but, listening to him, I had the feeling that it was not me he was trying to convince, but himself.

"I talked to a Jungian psychiatrist today," Broun said after Richard ran down. He pronounced Jung to rhyme with "hung." "He's got a theory that our subconscious is really a storage bin for everything that's ever happened in the past. Jung's collective unconscious, only he says it's not just common racial memories, it's everything."

He sounded excited, agitated. Maybe he *was* getting obsessed with Lincoln's dreams. "Dates, people, places. It's all down there, but people only dream bits and pieces of it, and even then something has to trigger the memories. That's where Lincoln's acromegaly comes in. He says a hormonal imbalance can unlock the collective unconscious. I know, I know, this sounds like the fortune-teller, but I think he's on to something."

I erased the messages, thinking about what he'd said. If a hormonal imbalance could unlock the collective unconscious, maybe a chemical imbalance could, too, and that was where the drugs came in. It would explain why the dreams had suddenly gotten clearer when Annie was on the Elavil. Maybe the phenobarbital had started to let down some kind of guard in the subconscious, and then the Elavil had completed the process, so that Lee's dreams came through loud and clear.

If that was the case, then the dreams would gradually lose their power and clarity now that Annie was off the drugs, and the best thing to do was to wait them out till the chemical balance in her brain was restored and the dreams faded away.

I shut off the lights and went back into Annie's room to wait it out with her, and was asleep in the chair within minutes. When I woke up it was three-thirty by the lighted dial of my watch. Annie was still sleeping peacefully, though she had flung most of the covers off. I thought, with the confused logic of the half-awake, that I must somehow have slept through her dream, but her breathing wasn't the heavy, almost drugged-sounding breathing she had after the dreams, and my next thought, even more confused, was that I had stopped the dreams simply by telling her what caused them, and went back to sleep.

I must have heard the door slam because when I woke up again I was already halfway to it, only barely glancing at the bed because I knew she wasn't there. I had it open and was out in the hall in time to hear the outside door close. The outside door that opened on the fire escape.

I ran to the end of the hall and pushed down on the metal bar. The bar gave, but the door wouldn't open. Annie must be pushing on it from the outside. Or be lying crumpled against it. "Annie!" I shouted through the door, and then stopped. You weren't supposed to startle a sleepwalker. If they were somewhere dangerous, on a cliff or something, they might fall. I tore back down the hall, down the front stairs, and through the empty lobby to the front door. It was locked, but from the inside. I got it open and raced around to the side of the building.

Annie was standing at the top of the stairs in her white nightgown, looking like a ghost in the gray, indistinct light of dawn. The cat was sitting on the top step, watching her.

"Annie," I said quietly from the bottom of the stairs, "you're having another dream."

She was looking toward the Rappahannock. Fog lay along the line of trees like a gray blanket. "Goodbye, Katie," she said with a catch in her voice. "Promise you'll come back."

"Stay there," I said, "I'm coming." I started up the stairs, one hand on the railing and the other held out to catch her if she fell. "What are you dreaming, Annie?"

She half-raised her hand in its full white sleeve as if to wave. "I wish you didn't have to go," she said, and then buried her face in her hand and began to cry. The cat watched her incuriously.

I stepped onto the landing and put my hand gently on her

shoulder. "Annie, can you wake up? You're having a bad dream."

She took her hand away from her face and turned to me, her face alight. "No tears at Arlington!" she said brightly, "no tears," and flung her arms around my neck and sobbed.

"Annie, don't cry!" I put my arms around her. Sobs shuddered through her. "Honey, oh, don't cry!"

She clung tighter to me, shivering in the thin nightgown. I patted her back and reached behind me for the door with one hand. I was afraid it would be locked from the outside, and how would I ever get her down these narrow stairs and back inside the inn? The metal bar gave under the pressure of my hand and opened. "Let's go inside, Annie," I said. "It's cold out here, honey. Let's go back to the room."

She tightened her arms around me and pressed her face against my neck. "I don't want you to leave," she said, and lifted her tear-stained face up to mine, her face full of love and sorrow. Her eyes were wide open, but she wasn't looking at me. Whoever she was clinging to, begging them not to go, it wasn't me.

Her nightgown had come unbuttoned at the neck and was pulled away from the long curve of her throat. I could feel the uneven catch of her sobs through the thin cotton of the nightgown. "Annie," I said, and the pain in my voice brought her awake.

Her eyes focused on me, frightened or surprised. "Where am I?" she said, and looked bewilderedly at the stairs and the fog-shrouded Rappahannock. "Did I have another dream?"

"Yes," I said, disengaging her hands gently from my neck. I stepped back and down a step, almost onto the cat. "Do you remember it?"

"I was at Arlington," she said. She looked down at her unbuttoned nightgown. "What did I do?—when I was asleep?"

I shoved down the bar of the door and it opened. "You did a little sleepwalking, that's all." I motioned her through the door, standing back, not touching her. The cat stood up and sauntered after her, and I shut the door in its face and then jammed the door down into its lock position and followed Annie into the room.

She was standing with her head bent, buttoning up her nightgown. I locked the door and put the chain on, which was what I should have done in the first place. If I had, none of this would have happened.

"You said you were at Arlington in the dream," I said. "Was it the same dream as before?"

"No." She took her blue robe off the bedpost and put it on. "I was standing on the porch with the waitress from the coffee shop, the one with the red hair, and she was getting ready to leave." She cinched the tie belt of the robe and sat down on the bed, holding the robe closed at the neck with one hand. "We were waiting for the carriage. There were a lot of suitcases piled up on the porch. I didn't want her to go."

"I got that much," I said, thinking of her arms around my neck, of the beautiful curve of her throat. "Why did you say, 'No tears at Arlington'?"

"I didn't. He . . ." She frowned and looked past me. "We were standing on the porch and then . . ." She leaned forward as if she were trying to reach something, though her hand remained fastened on the collar of her robe.

"Why don't we talk about this in the morning," I said. I stood up and pushed the green chair over against the door. "This probably won't stop you if you sleepwalk again, but it'll slow you down long enough for me to hear you." I balanced the volume of Freeman on the arm. It would fall off if she tried to move the chair.

"Jeff," she said, clutching the blue robe tight against her neck. "I'm sorry I . . . about all this."

I wanted to shout at her, "I'm not Richard. I'd never take advantage of you while you were asleep, for God's sake," but I wasn't sure that was the truth.

"There's nothing to be sorry about. You were dreaming," I said, and went into my room and shut the door.

My collar was wet from Annie's tears. I took off my shirt and put on another one and then went over and stood by the window, waiting for it to get light and thinking about Richard. "I wasn't trying to hit on her, it just happened," he had said when I accused him of taking advantage of Annie. "I was trying to help her."

"That's no excuse," I said out loud, and didn't know if I was talking to Richard or myself.

When it was light enough to read, I picked up volume one. I had left volume four, the one with the index in it, out on the chair for a sleepwalking alarm, but I didn't know what to look for anyway, except for the reference to Arlington. If the dream had really taken place there, then this dream was from before the war, which meant my carefully worked-out theory was shot to pieces and I could start over, and volume one was as good a place to start as any.

I read till eight-thirty and then went out my bedroom door and over to the coffee shop and had breakfast. The redheaded waitress was there. "Your name wouldn't be Katie, would it?" I asked her when she refilled my coffee cup.

"No," she said disapprovingly, as if she thought I was trying to flirt with her in Annie's absence. "It's Margaret. Did you guys make it out to the battlefield yesterday?"

"No," I said. Maybe we should have, I thought. Maybe then Annie would have dreamed about Fredericksburg again, and I would have known what to tell her when she woke up.

"We were standing on the porch at Arlington," Annie had said. "The waitress was leaving and I didn't want her to go." Who could Lee have had visit that he wouldn't want to go home? I didn't know much about Lee's life outside the war. All the research I had done for Broun had been about specific battles, and I was not even sure what family and friends Lee had outside of his son Rob, whom he had sent back into battle at Antietam, and the cousin, Markie Williams, who had gone back through enemy lines to fetch the Lees' belongings from Arlington and found the cat.

Who would Lee have flung his arms around, have cried over? The answer was nobody. The men who had been in the war with Lee described him almost uniformly as "grave and kind" and "showing no sign of his emotions." One of his biographers had nicknamed him "the marble man," and all of them said he was devoted solely to his duty. He never talked about what was troubling him, never wept, not even over Stonewall Jackson. When the war was over, he never spoke of it.

He had paid dearly for that self-control. He had died of a heart attack, the controlled man's disease, and he had had bad dreams about the war up to the very end. He had told Hill to come up when he was dying, and then, at the very end, said, "Strike the tent." But he hadn't cried or clung to his family, even on his deathbed.

What if this wasn't one of Lee's dreams at all? What if now that the barriers to the collective unconscious were down, Annie would start dreaming other people's dreams?

Annie came over at a little before ten, looking like she hadn't slept either. She was wearing a high-necked blouse buttoned all the way up.

"I don't have any idea what your dream was," I said. I dog-eared the page I was on and shut the book. "You're sure it was at Arlington?"

"Yes. I was standing on the porch. The cat was there, and the apple tree. Its leaves had turned. It must have been in the fall. I'm sure it was Arlington. I mean, it's always my house, the house I grew up in, but it stands for other houses." She shook her head as if that weren't the right word. "It feels like other houses. I think Lee must have to use the images I have in my mind to make the dreams out of, and then he makes them stand for other things. It's the same with the people. I think he must choose the person who's most like the person he knew. . . ."

The redheaded waitress bustled over and took Annie's order, apologizing for not having seen her right away and filling both our coffee cups to the very brim.

"Like the waitress?" I said after she left.

"Yes. It was the waitress, but it wasn't her really."

"You called her Katie. Do you know her last name or what her relationship to Lee was? Was she a friend of his, a relative?"

"No, she was a friend of . . ." She picked up her spoon and stirred her coffee. "I just remembered something about the dream," she said. "That never happened before."

"What?"

"The waitress . . . Katie and I were standing on the porch saying goodbye, and I didn't want her to go. We were both crying, and laughing at the same time because neither of us had a handkerchief, and then all of a sudden I was out by the

apple tree and walking up to the house. You know how sometimes in a dream you're one person and then you're somebody
else, only you're still the first person, too? That's how this was.
I was walking up from the apple orchard, too, and I was still
on the porch saying goodbye to Katie. I had on my white
nightgown, and she was in her waitress uniform, and we were
both crying, and I went up on the porch and said to them, 'No
tears at Arlington!' and laughed, and gave Katie my big handkerchief to blow her nose on."

"Do you know who the girl on the porch was?" I asked.
"The girl who was you?"

"No. But coming up from the apple orchard I was Lee."

Well, at least the Pandora's box of the whole world's dreams
hadn't been opened yet, and she was still dreaming Lee's
dreams, even if I couldn't place this one. "And so then this
girl, whoever she is, flung her arms around Lee's neck and
started to cry?"

"No." She put her coffee cup down and stared into it. "He
. . . I . . . Lee came up on the porch," she said slowly, "and
said, 'No tears,' and all of a sudden I felt that I knew what was
causing the dreams." She looked up at me. "I was myself in the
dream right then, not Lee or the girl in the white nightgown. I
was myself. And I knew what was causing them. I knew why I
was having the dreams." She put her hand up to her mouth.
Her eyes filled with tears. "Poor man," she said softly. "Poor
man."

It had been Annie with her arms twined around my neck,
after all, even though it wasn't me she clung to. "Do you still
know?" I said, wanting to reach across the table and comfort
her, but not daring to even touch her. "Do you remember
what it was that was causing the dreams?"

She wiped her eyes with her paper napkin. "No. I woke
up and found myself hanging all over you. I was so ashamed
that I'd been sleepwalking and that my nightgown was half off.
I was afraid I'd tried to kiss you or something."

You didn't try to kiss me, Annie, I thought. I wasn't even
there. "You didn't try to kiss me," I said.

"And then when I tried to remember the dream, I
couldn't . . ." Her voice trailed off again the way it had the

night before. After a minute she shook her head. "Jeff, I think we should go back to Arlington."

That one had come right out of left field. "We can't go back," I said, stammering in my surprise. "Richard's there."

"I know, but when I went there before, it helped."

Helped her to dream the horrors of Antietam and Fredericksburg and Chancellorsville, I thought. I could see the look of terror on her face as she stood there in the snow, looking down at the bodies on the lawn. I didn't want to subject her to that again, even to solve the puzzle of the dreams.

"We're only going to be here a couple more days. I need to see the vet again and finish up my research at the library for Broun." These were useless excuses. I could obviously call the vet from D.C., and the only research I'd done since I'd been here had been on Lee, not Lincoln, but Annie wasn't listening to me. She was leaning forward, as if she could almost reach out and touch the meaning of the dreams.

"The dreams have something to do with Arlington," she said in that inflectionless voice she used to recite the dreams. "And the yellow-haired soldier. And the cat. Nobody knows what happened to them." She looked up at me. "Did Lee have a daughter?"

"He had several, I think," I said, relieved that she had changed the subject. "I know he had at least one. Agnes, I think her name was." I stood up. "Go ahead and finish your breakfast. I'm going to go get my notebook and then we'll go to the library and see what we can find out about Agnes."

I went back to the room and gathered up the two volumes of Freeman that were by my bed. Annie had left the chair close to the door. Volume four was on the seat. I pushed the chair back where it belonged so the maid wouldn't think we were trying to steal the furniture and picked up the book.

Annie was standing at the cash register talking to the redheaded waitress when I got back. I hoped she wasn't pitching the battlefield again.

"The weather's supposed to turn this afternoon," the waitress said. "Big cold front moving in."

Good, I thought. Maybe we'll be snowed in here.

We walked down to the library. The librarian glared at me

when I came in carrying my stack of books, as if she thought I'd taken them the day before without checking them out. Annie borrowed a piece of paper and a pen from me and said she was going back down to the reference section.

"I'll be in biographies, where we were yesterday," I said.

I looked up "Lee, daughters of." He had had three other daughters besides Agnes: Mary, Ann, and Mildred. Since I had no way of knowing which one was in this dream, I used the only other clue I had. An hour into the index references under Arlington, I found what I was looking for.

In the fall of 1858, Katherine Stiles, a friend from Georgia, had come for a visit. When she got ready to leave, Lee had found her and his daughter Annie weeping together. "No tears at Arlington!" he had told them. "No tears!" His daughter Annie.

I looked up "Lee, Annie Carter (Robert E. Lee, daughter of)" in the index and started going through the page references. On March second, 1862, Lee had written her: "My Precious Annie, I think of you all, separately and collectively, in the busy hours of the night, and the recollection of each and every one whiles away the long night, in which my anxious thoughts drive away sleep. But I always feel that you and Agnes at those times are sound asleep, and that it is immaterial to either where the blockades are or what their progress is in the river."

There it was, the connection I'd been looking for. I had tried to come up with all kinds of complicated rationales for why Annie was having the dreams—Richard's drugs and chemical imbalances and Dr. Stone's storm of dreams. It had never occurred to me that Annie might simply be having the dreams because Lee had called out her name in his sleep.

The sharp-faced librarian was leaning over me. "I see you brought your own books with you today," she said in a voice with a surprisingly gentle tone and a marked Virginia accent. "I'm afraid our Civil War materials are very limited. Most people do their research out at the National Park Service Library."

"The Park Service?" I said.

"Yes. It's out at the Fredericksburg battlefield. When I saw you in here yesterday I wondered if you knew about it, but I didn't like to interrupt your work. All the main source materials are out there. Do you know how to get there?"

Yes. March across an open plain to a defended ridge. "Yes. Thank you." I gathered up my stack of Freeman. "Do you happen to know when they're open?"

"Nine to five," she said in that impossible Southern belle voice. "The battlefield itself is open until dark, I believe."

I went and found Annie, who was in the encyclopedias, surrounded by the *L*s. "I found what I needed. Let's get out of here," I said.

The librarian was standing at the front desk looking as forbidding as ever. I hustled Annie past without even telling her thank you, for fear she would say something to Annie about the battlefield, and suggested we walk downtown and get something to eat. "I saw a drugstore on the way up that had a soda fountain, believe it or not," I said.

"I'm not very hungry," Annie said.

"Well, then something to drink. A lemonade or something."

The drugstore did have a fountain, though it was pretty decrepit-looking. The faded pictures of ice cream and grilled cheese sandwiches and root beer floats looked like they'd been up since the Civil War, and there was nobody behind the counter. A balding pharmacist was filling prescriptions in a booth at the back, but he didn't look up, even when we sat down on two of the plastic stools.

"I'll go ask if the fountain's open," I said and started toward the back, but before I got there the phone rang and he answered it. I waited for him to look up, reading the labels on the medicines. Half the rack was devoted to sleeping pills: Sominex, Nytol, Sleep-Eze. Richard would have felt right at home.

The pharmacist cupped his hand over the mouthpiece of the phone and whispered, "Be right with you."

I nodded and went back up to the front. Annie was looking at the rack of postcards next to the counter. I hoped to God they didn't have one of Arlington.

"The pharmacist said he'll wait on us as soon as he gets off the phone." I leaned over her shoulder to see the postcard she was holding. It was a photograph of Lee's tomb at Lexington. The marble statue was of Lee asleep on his camp cot in his dress uniform and boots, with a blanket draped over him. One arm lay at his side, the other was folded across his chest. "I think I know what's causing the dreams," I said. "The girls on the porch were Katherine Stiles and Annie Lee."

She put the postcard back in the rack with infinite care. "Annie Lee?"

"Lee's daughter. You were right about it being one of his daughters. Annie didn't want her friend to leave. Both girls were crying, and Lee told them, 'No tears at Arlington.' "

Annie sat down at the counter. "No tears," she said and put her hands on the volume of Freeman, one over the other.

"Don't you see what this means? The dreams aren't meant for you. Lee was thinking of his daughter, and through some freak of time, the message got sent to you by mistake. I don't know how. Maybe you heard your name being called down in the collective unconscious or something."

"Mistake," Annie said, and shook her head. "He's trying to tell me something. That's what the paper on the soldier's sleeve is, only I can't read it. It's a message of some kind."

"But not to you," I said. "You were right in more ways than one when you said they weren't your dreams. They belong to Annie Lee. Her father was sending them to her."

"There are messages in all the dreams except this last one," Annie said. "There's the message that the Union soldier was carrying when he got captured at Fredericksburg, and the message about Jackson's arm being amputated. And Special Order 191."

"And the reason you can't make out the messages is because they weren't meant for you. They were meant for Annie Lee. She'd recognize Katherine Stiles and she'd remember that day at Arlington and Tom Tita. She'd know what all of it meant. They're her dreams, Annie, not yours."

The pharmacist came bustling up to wait on us and tell us a long and involved story about Lila who usually took care of the front for him but who had broken her foot. "Messing around with horses at her age," he said without explaining what she'd been doing. He stuck two paper cones into metal bases. "She should have known better." He squeezed lemons into the paper glasses. "You folks tourists?"

"Sort of," I said. "We're here for a few days."

He held the glasses under the soda water siphon one at a time, stirring the lemonades with a long-handled spoon. "You been out to the cemetery yet?"

"Cemetery?" Annie said.

"The battlefield. It's a national cemetery now. Union soldiers. Confederates are buried over on Washington Avenue." He scooped ice into the glasses.

"How far is it from here?" Annie said.

"Two miles maybe. You go down Caroline, that's this street, till you come to Lafayette Boulevard," he said, drawing a map on the damp counter with his finger. "That's US 3. Turn right on Lafayette and follow it all the way out to Sunken Road. You can't miss it." The phone rang. The pharmacist plopped two lemon slices into the glasses, shoved them across the counter at us, and hurried back to answer it.

I peeled the paper off a straw and jabbed the ice in my lemonade with it. Did everybody in this whole damned town own stock in Fredericksburg battlefield? It's a great place to visit. Seventeen thousand dead. There's even an electric map, red lights for the mortally wounded soldiers, blue for the ones who froze to death. You can't miss it. Take US 3 to Sunken Road, where the bodies are lying ten deep in front of the stone wall.

Annie was still looking at the counter where the pharmacist had drawn the map. In a minute she would say, "I want to go out to the battlefield, Jeff," or worse, "I think we should go to Arlington," and what excuse was I going to come up with this time?

"Do you think they'd have any aspirin in those little tins?" Annie said. "I didn't bring any with me today, and I've got kind of a headache."

"Sure," I said. I slid off the stool and went to the back to ask the pharmacist. He was still on the phone. "You of all people should know I can't prescribe without a doctor's orders, Lila," he said loudly. There was a long, frustrated pause, during which he stared at the phone.

I searched along the rack of medicine but didn't find any tins. I grabbed a bottle of a hundred and took it back up to Annie. "Are you all right?" I broke the seal, dug out the wad of cotton, and shook two into her hand. She took them with a sip of lemonade. "Do you want to go back to the inn?"

"Yes," she said.

I went back to the pharmacist and handed him three ones, holding up the bottle of aspirin where he could see it. "Especially not for you!" he shouted at Lila. "With your heart condition?" I waited some more. He looked up, finally, and nodded at me.

Annie was standing by the door waiting for me, the four volumes of Freeman in her arms. "Here. Let me take those," I said, tucking them under my arm. I opened the door for her. "Do you want me to go back to the inn and get the car?"

"No, I'm fine, Jeff, really." She smiled wearily. "I think Lee must be thinking about his daughter again."

"I can go get the car," I said, and then saw the blue Ford sedan let an elderly black woman out a block down and start toward us.

"Taxi!" I shouted, jumping out into the street as if I were trying to stop a runaway horse. "Taxi!"

The taxi driver pulled over and opened the back door for us. He was at least sixty, with a huge cigar and a stubbly beard that looked even sharper and more disreputable than Broun's. I gave him the inn's address, and he pulled out into the street.

"You two tourists?" he said over his shoulder. "You been out to the battlefield yet?"

CHAPTER TEN

Pickett's Charge was the worst moment of the war for Lee. In spite of his telling his men, "Don't be discouraged," he had to have known the war was lost with it. Generals Garnett and Armistead were dead, General Kemper was mortally wounded, and there had been over twenty thousand casualties in three days. Even if the army managed to retreat safely into Virginia, it would never have the strength again for a major offensive. The long retreat to the apple orchard was beginning.

That night, worn out, Lee had tried to dismount and been unable to. A cavalryman leaned forward to assist him, but before he could reach him, Lee had gotten down by himself and stood leaning against Traveller. "Too bad!" he said. "Too bad! Oh, too bad!"

Annie slept fitfully all afternoon, not dreaming but not getting any rest either. At six I drove to McDonald's and got hamburgers. She got up then, but she ate hardly anything, and afterwards she couldn't get back to sleep. She walked the length of the room, back and forth, like a penned animal.

"Do you want to read galleys?" I asked, remembering that she'd said they helped keep her mind off the dreams, but she shook her head and went on pacing, stopping now and then to lean against the window. She looked dead on her feet. Her eyes were shadowed with fatigue, and there was hardly any color in her face.

"Do you think the library would be open tonight?" she asked.

"It closed at six," I said. "We could go take in a movie. I could go get a paper and we could see what's on."

"No, I . . ." She went over to the bed and lay down. After a while she said sleepily, "When does it open in the morning?"

"The library? Nine," I said, wanting to ask her what she wanted at the library but afraid I'd wake her up. She seemed to be asleep already.

I read Freeman awhile. I didn't try to find out anything else about Annie Lee. There was no point. I had thought Annie would be glad we had finally found out why she was having the dreams, but she hadn't even acted like she cared. And the information hadn't helped her sleep.

When I got bored with Freeman, I picked up the galleys. Ben and Malachi ran into some of their own artillery and took cover behind it. I didn't remember that. In the last version I'd read, they'd gotten separated, with Ben ending up on an ambulance detail, but in this version they were clear across the valley from where they should have been. I wondered if this was the scene Broun had written that afternoon after I'd accused him of being obsessed with the Lincoln book.

"Shouldn't we ask somebody where our regiment is?" Ben asked.

Malachi pointed back across the cornfield to a road and a fence full of men. It wasn't so smoky down there, and Ben could see the sun glinting off their bayonets. "They're clear the hell over there, mebbe, and how do you conjure we get to 'em? We got ourselves separated and we're gonna stay that way."

Malachi shouted the whole speech, but toward the end of it Ben could only tell what he was saying by reading his lips. The noise of the guns was getting louder every minute, and the firings and the shells landing had stopped making separate sounds and were roaring, like thunder. Ben could only tell when the guns fired by the smoke.

"Come on!" Malachi said. Ben didn't hear that either, but they started to run, keeping their heads down as if to protect them from the noise.

They ran straight into one of the guns. Its barrel had exploded and there were men lying on their backs in a circle around it. A man wearing a straw hat, and a boy were trying to free the horses from the caisson. A lieutenant rode up and shouted, "Pull those horses back!" and Ben wondered how he was able to make himself heard. "You two there! Help him!" he said, pointing his sword at the boy, who was struggling with the reins.

The man wearing the straw hat had unbuckled the harnesses, but the horses had gotten themselves tangled in it. One of the girth straps was wrapped around the nearer horse's hind leg. The harder he strained the tighter it pulled.

Ben grabbed hold of the horse's dragging reins and tried to steady him. Malachi got alongside the horse and began to push him back against the caisson. The man in the straw hat reached under to cut the strap. The horse whinnied and reared up.

"Dang your hide, you crazy fool," Malachi shouted at the horse. "Do you want to get kilt?"

Ben stepped back out of the reach of the hoofs, grabbing for the reins. "Hold still, dang ya!" Malachi shouted.

There was a terrible roar. It surprised Ben that he could hear it. Dirt and grass and pieces of metal flew up in front of the caisson, and the horse came down on its front feet, hard, and pitched sideways onto Malachi. Ben ran over to him. The horse's full weight was on his chest. "Dang your hide, you ugly plug!" Malachi said. "Get off 'n me."

Ben got his hands under Malachi's shoulders and tried to pull him out, but he couldn't budge him. He stood up and called to the boy to come and help, but he couldn't see him anywhere. The man with the straw hat was bending over the tongue of the caisson, his arms swinging lazily back and forth.

"I allus hated horses," Malachi said in a strong, clear voice that Ben didn't have any trouble hearing. "Danged gray gelding bit me in the backside when I was a young 'un, and I never trusted them since."

Ben was still holding on to the reins. He stepped back and pulled on them, and the horse's head moved a little. Its neck looked impossibly long, lying there on the ground, like he had stretched it with his pulling. Ben tried again.

"Dang horse throwed a shoe and I got off to look at his hoof. No way he'd let me pick it up to look at it, so I bend over to see if mebbe he's split the hoof," he said. A bubble of blood and mucus showed in his *nose. He sniffed and went on talking. "He takes a piece out of my britches and what's under 'em. I stood up to supper for two weeks."*

Ben dropped the reins and knelt down beside Malachi. He worked his hands under the horse's flank and tried to lift it up a little. "Can you ease yourself out a ways?" he asked.

"You are allus lookin' behind you after a thing like that, but I never expected a durn horse to come at me from the side." A larger bubble of blood came out of the corner of his mouth and trickled into his beard.

"Malachi?" Ben said, even though he knew he was dead. He stood up. The fighting had moved farther south, toward Sharpsburg. Ben could hear the individual guns easily now. He looked back down at Malachi. One of his boots was sticking out from under the horse's tail, and the other one was half under its leg. Ben knelt down and pulled the boot off. Malachi wasn't wearing socks, and there was a blue-black blister on the heel. Ben turned the boot upside down. He set the boot down next to Malachi and started to pull the other one off.

"You there!" a man on a horse said. It was the same lieutenant who'd told them to help pull the horses back. He waved his sword at Ben. "Come away from there! What's your regiment?"

The boot came free, and Ben straightened up, holding it. "I was looking . . ."

"You were looking to get a new pair of boots. Get back to your regiment before I have you shot for looting!" He waved the sword close to Ben's middle.

Ben felt around the inside of the boot and pulled out a damp square of paper. "You got no call to talk to me thataway," he said. "I was just trying to help." He knelt down and tucked the paper in the pocket of Malachi's shirt and started down the hill toward the sound of shooting.

In the original version Ben had never found out what happened to Malachi. He had simply dropped out of sight, like how many soldiers at Antietam and Fredericksburg and Chancellorsville? "Did he die?" I had asked Broun after reading the first draft.

"Die? Hell, no, an old vet like Malachi was too tough to die. He hightailed it to California after Gettysburg."

Broun had rewritten the scene because he was furious with me, but what was he trying to communicate? Was he supposed to be Malachi, struggling with a recalcitrant research assistant who wouldn't cooperate even when it was for his own good, or was he supposed to be Ben, who was only trying to help and who got threatened with being shot as a looter for his pains? Broun had been angry with me that afternoon, but he'd been worried, too. He had asked me that afternoon if I was Richard's patient, if I was taking any medication. Maybe he had written this chapter to show me he was worried about me, that he only wanted to help.

I looked at my watch. It was eleven-thirty, eight-thirty in California, and God only knew what time it was in northern Virginia or Pennsylvania or wherever the hell Lee was tonight. Annie sighed in her sleep and turned over. I put the chain on the door and moved the chair over between it and the bed. I stood there awhile, watching her sleep, wishing I could help, and then went on reading.

Ben carried wounded soldiers off the field all afternoon. Ben's Union brother made it out of the East Wood and away from the Sunken Road before he was hit in the side. He lay still for a while in the hot sun and then crawled under a haystack and passed out. Around two-thirty an artillery shell set the haystack on fire, and he was burned alive.

"They can't possibly hold that position," Annie said. She sat up and swung her feet over the side of the bed. "I told him . . ." She stood up.

I glanced at the door, even though I had just fastened the chain, and took a protective step toward it, but she sat down on the side of the bed and put her arms around the wooden poster at the head of the bed. "My fault," she said, so softly it was almost a sigh.

I tried to sit down next to her, but she pulled away, so I sat in the green chair and leaned forward, my hands between my knees. "Annie!"

"I know! I know!" she said bitterly. She stood up again, one arm still wrapped around the bedpost. "Where is he?" she asked, and turned to look at someone behind her. "He was supposed to tell Hood to bring up his division."

She took a stiff, sleepwalker's step toward the door to my

room. "Try to reform your men among the trees," she said kindly, as if she were speaking to a child.

"Annie?" I said quietly, moving so I was between her and the door, wishing I had chained the outside door of my room, too. "I know where we are. It's Pickett's Charge. Longstreet didn't send the reinforcements up."

She looked straight at me. "Don't be discouraged," she said. There was no emotion in her voice at all, but the look on her face was the look she had had at Arlington, looking down the hill at the bodies on the lawn. "It was my fault this time. Form your ranks again when you get under cover."

It went on for half an hour like that. Sometimes she reached down, her hand almost touching the floor, and I thought she must be helping lift up a soldier who had fallen. Then I remembered that Lee had been on horseback. He had ridden Traveller down from his command post to meet the survivors and send them back to the safety of the woods. He must be reaching down to rest his hand on a private's shoulder, to give his soldiers some encouragement as they limped past. "My fault," Annie said softly, over and over. "My fault."

And I had wanted her to dream Gettysburg to prove my theory. "It's not your fault," I said.

I took her arm, gently, and led her back to the bed, and she sat down and put her arms around the post again. "Too bad," she said despairingly. "Oh, too bad."

She wouldn't let go of the post even after she was awake. "I was under the apple tree watching the house," she said calmly, but her arms were still wrapped around the turned wood. "Only this time it wasn't an apple orchard. It was a forest."

"The point of woods," I said. "At Gettysburg."

"I knew it wasn't really an apple orchard and that they weren't really apple trees even though there were green apples on them. It was summer. It was so hot it was like an oven. I was wearing my gray coat, and I kept thinking I should take it off, but I couldn't because I had to tell all the soldiers who kept coming past to get under the trees. They were trying to get up over the railing onto the front porch and it wasn't a railing, it was more like a wall, but they couldn't and I couldn't see why they couldn't get onto the porch because of all the smoke and then they'd come back into the apple orchard, all bloody. I said, over and over, 'This is my fault, this is my fault,' to all of them as they came past."

I sat beside her on the bed and told her what the dream meant, even though I was past believing I was helping her with my explanations any more than Richard had helped her with his theories and his sleeping pills.

She had told me that my explaining the dreams made them easier, but I had been doing that for a week, and the dreams had gotten steadily worse. Taking her to Arlington wasn't going to help, either, and I wasn't about to take her back within reach of Richard, but keeping her here in Fredericksburg wasn't much better. Sooner or later she would decide she wanted to go out to the battlefield. To find what? A whole new batch of dreams? Spotsylvania? Petersburg? The Wilderness, where the wounded were burned alive? There were all sorts of wonderful possibilities. The war was only half over.

"Promise me you won't try to stop me from having the dreams," she had said that first day in Fredericksburg. And I had promised. Lee had made promises, too. "I could have taken no other course," he had written Markie Williams. But when he saw boys of sixteen cut down like stalks of corn, when he saw them barefoot and bleeding and dead on their feet, didn't he ever consider breaking his promise?

I felt suddenly too tired to even stand. I went back into my room, pushed the galleys off my bed onto the floor, and went to bed.

I slept till six-thirty. Three-thirty in California. Too early to call Broun. I went over to the coffee shop and read galleys, letting the redheaded waitress fill my coffee cup whenever it got halfway down, till it was a uniform, undrinkable temperature.

D. H. Hill's horse got its legs shot off. Ben found his regiment, and they marched south and east toward Sharpsburg. Lee tried to look through a lieutenant's telescope but couldn't because his hands were bandaged. A. P. Hill came riding up in a red wool shirt to save the day, and Ben got shot in the foot. At nine I called Broun's hotel from the pay phone in the coffee shop. He had checked out.

I went back to the room and let myself in through my door. Annie was asleep, clutching her pillow the way she had the bedpost. I called the answering machine. "You're probably wondering where I went," Broun said. "I'm in San Diego. At the Westgate. I came here to see an endocrinologist. The psychiatrist put me onto him. He's an expert on hormonal imbalances in the brain. Call me if you need anything, son."

"I'm trying to," I said. I called the Westgate in San Diego. A recorded voice asked who I was trying to call, and when I told it, it rang Broun's room. He wasn't there.

I wondered where he really was. He could be meeting with the endocrinologist, or standing in line at LAX, or be someplace else altogether, and his kind, gruff voice would still say, "I'm in San Diego at the Westgate." The plane to San Diego could have crashed and it still wouldn't have made any difference. That voice would still have talked to me. I wondered if that was what was happening here, if the dreams were some kind of prerecorded message left by Lee, and he wasn't there at all.

I went and got the car. Take Lafayette Boulevard to Sunken Road. You can't miss it. The pharmacist had been right about that. There were signs everywhere: highway signs for US 3, small brown National Park Service signs every block or so on Lafayette Boulevard, a big brown sign at the entrance, a "Closed After Dark" sign next to the iron gates, Fredericksburg Historic Tour marker Number 24, a white "National Cemetery" sign. Sunken Road was marked with a regular green-and-white street sign. I pulled into Sunken Road and parked across from the Visitors' Center. It was after nine, which meant the Visitors' Center and, presumably, the library were open, but I didn't go in. I went up the hill to see the graves.

It wasn't as bad as I had thought it would be. The hill was terraced into grassy shelves just wide enough for a row of graves, and at the top the carved headstones sloped down and away in neat rows toward a flag anchored with pyramids of decorative solid shot, but the hill wasn't even half as high as the hill at Arlington, hardly high enough to be called a ridge.

The plain below, where all the bodies had lain, was covered with grass and trees and criss-crossed with brick paths.

Azaleas and ivy had been planted around the Visitors' Center. It looked like somebody's backyard.

Well, that was the kind of war the Civil War had been, wasn't it? A backyard war, fought in cornfields and on front porches and across rutted country lanes, a homey little war that had killed two hundred and four thousand boys and men outright and four hundred thousand more with dysentery and amputated arms and bilious fever. But in spite of the neat rows of graves stretching away like points on a radius, it didn't look like anybody had ever been killed here. And it didn't look like Arlington.

At the top of the hill I took the brick path that led along its edge to a large sign that turned out to be a painting of Lee looking through binoculars out over the battlefield. Next to it was a brick pillar with a speaker in it. I pushed the button for the know-nothing tourist's guided tour.

"At this spot on Marye's Heights," the deep, authoritative voice said, "General Robert E. Lee stood, commanding the Battle of Fredericksburg." It sounded like Richard on the answering machine. I let the voice ramble on while I looked at the graves on the edge.

They were marked with granite squares maybe six inches across. There were two numbers on each square. The one nearest me read 243, and then a line, and below that the number 4. I scribbled the numbers down on a piece of paper so I could ask what they meant.

"Good morning," a brown-hatted ranger said. He came up beside me, carrying a plastic trash sack. "Did you need in the Visitors' Center? I was out checking the grounds, so I locked it up, but I can go open it. We've been having problems with kids getting in at night." He pulled a beer can out of the sack to show me and then dropped it back in. "The first tour's at eleven. Are you looking for a particular grave?"

"No," I said. "I just wanted to see the battlefield from up here."

"It's hard to imagine there was ever a battle here, isn't it? The artillery were all along this ridge, and there were sharp-shooters down behind that stone wall, where the road is. It's not the original wall, by the way. General Robert E. Lee commanded the battle from up here," he said with the enthusiasm of someone who's never been in a war. "He watched the Union army coming up from the river there," he pointed across the trees and roofs of Fredericksburg toward the Rappahannock, "and he said, 'It is well that war is so terrible, or we should grow too fond of it.' "

"What do the numbers on the unmarked graves mean?"

"Those are the graves' registration numbers. After the war there were bodies buried all over this area from the battles of Fredericksburg and Spotsylvania and the Wilderness. When the battlefield was made into a national cemetery, quartermaster teams were sent around to disinter the bodies and rebury them here. The numbers tell where the bodies were found."

I took out the piece of paper I'd written the numbers on and unfolded it. "Can you tell me about this one?" I said. "Two hundred forty-three, and under that there's a line and the number four."

"Two hundred forty-three is the registration number. The four is the number of bodies."

"The number of bodies?"

"That were found in the original grave. Or parts of bodies. It was hard to tell, sometimes, how many soldiers there really were. Some of the bodies had been buried for three years."

Like Willie Lincoln, I thought irrelevantly. Maybe he had been buried in a field somewhere, and then a quartermaster's team had dug him up and sent him home with his father's body to Springfield.

"At Chancellorsville they found a grave full of arms and legs. They figured it must have been near a field hospital where they were doing amputations. And lots of times they'd buried horses along with the bodies."

"How did they arrive at these numbers, then?"

"Skulls. It was a grisly business," he said cheerfully. "If you'd like to come down to the Visitors' Center, I can look up that grave number for you."

"No," I said. "I think I'll stay up here awhile."

"It is beautiful up here, isn't it?" he said. He tipped his broad-brimmed hat to me and went back along the brick path and down the hill, stopping once to pick up a scrap of paper by one of the graves.

It was beautiful up here. The spreading town with its blue and gray roofs and blossoming trees hid where the plain had been, and below, where the infantry had been cut down by the rifles behind the stone wall, there was a line of ragtag souvenir shops selling postcards and Confederate flags. There was no sign of the dead horses that had littered the field, the wounded Union soldiers taking cover behind them because there was no other cover. "It is well that war is so terrible," Lee had said, watching it, "or we should grow too fond of it."

Too fond of it. Was that what the dreams were all about? Was Lee so fond of it he couldn't let go of it, even in dreams? No, of course not. He had said that in the morning, when the plain was full of flags and bugle calls and sunlight glinting off the barrels of Springfield rifles.

That night the wounded had lain there where the souvenir shops and the Visitors' Center were now, freezing to death, and Lee's barefoot, threadbare soldiers had gone down the hill and over the stone wall that would have been black with blood and icy to the touch. Of course they had to put up a new one. The Confederates had gone down the hill and over the wall and taken their uniforms, with the names pinned to the sleeves, their boots with the names stuffed in the toes. And nobody, not even Lee, could have been fond of war at that point.

I could not possibly let Annie come out here. She had been here already in her dreams, had seen the bodies lying there on the cold ground, had seen the aurora borealis do its bloody dance in the northern sky, but she hadn't seen the rows of granite markers, and she hadn't seen the Roll of Honor or heard the ranger read the entries cheerfully, enthusiastically, not even aware of the horror of what he was saying. A lot of times they'd buried horses along with the bodies.

Maybe I couldn't stop the dreams, but I could protect her from this. And that meant getting her out of Fredericksburg, where well-meant waitresses and pharmacists and taxi drivers drew maps on drugstore counters in their eagerness to get us out here. I went down the hill and into the Visitors' Center.

The ranger was behind the information desk, emptying a metal wastebasket into the trash can. "I found that grave number for you," he said, brushing his hands together. He opened a thick, leather-bound book to a page he had marked with a scrap of paper. "They're listed alphabetically by quartermaster team."

He turned the book toward me, and I read down the fine-printed page. "Found Wilderness battlefield. Three bodies. Found Charis farm, in cornfield. Two skulls. Found Chancellorsville battlefield. Two bodies."

"Here it is," the ranger said, twisting his body around so he could read the numbers. "Two forty-three." He pointed to a line near the bottom of the page. "Found Lacey's farm, in apple orchard. Four skulls and parts."

Found in apple orchard. Four skulls and parts. "It has something to do with the soldier with his name pinned to his sleeve," Annie had said, trying to get at the meaning of the dreams. But it wasn't one yellow-haired boy with his name too blurred to read. It was so many it took them years to dig up all the bodies buried in cornfields and under apple trees and put them here, so many they couldn't bury them separately, they had to bury them all together under one marker.

"Do you know of any good tourist attractions away from Fredericksburg?" I said. "Someplace we could go today? Say within a hundred miles of here."

He pulled a brochure out from under the desk. "The Wilderness battlefield is only . . ."

"Not the Wilderness. Not anything to do with the Civil War."

He reached under the counter again, looking bewildered, and came up with a road map of Virginia. "Well, there's Williamsburg, of course. It's about a hundred miles." He spread out the map on the counter. "Shenandoah National Park is about a hundred and twenty." He pointed. "It's got a lot of beautiful views and hiking trails. I don't know what the weather's like to the west, though. There's supposed to be a big front coming in."

I leaned over the map. There was no way out of Fredericksburg. To the south, Sayler's Creek blocked our way to

Richmond; to the north we would have to cross the Antietam. Chancellorsville and the Wilderness were between us and Shenandoah on US 3. But if we went south, not so far that we would run into Spotsylvania, and kept to the back roads till we were west of Culpepper, where the battle of Cedar Mountain had been fought, we might be able to do it.

"Is there anything else I can do for you?" the ranger asked eagerly. "There's a guided tour at eleven."

"No, thanks." I folded up the map. "How many unknown soldiers were there altogether?"

"Here, you mean? There are twelve thousand seven hundred and seventy buried in Fredericksburg National Cemetery," he said as if it were a point of pride. "They're all Union soldiers, of course."

"How many altogether? In the whole war?"

"The whole war? Oh, I have no idea. I'm not even sure there's any way . . ." He took a pencil out of his pocket and began writing on the battlefield brochure. "All right. We have twelve thousand seven hundred seventy here, and there are eleven hundred and seventy Confederate unknowns in the Confederate Cemetery, and then Spotsylvania." He wrote down a figure and then reached under the counter again and brought up a stack of brochures. "The Unknowns of the Civil War Memorial at Arlington has two thousand one hundred and eleven. . . ." He shuffled through the brochures, turned one over. "There are four thousand, a hundred and ten at Petersburg. Gettysburg has nine hundred and seventy-nine unknowns in the cemetery proper, but of course there are more graves on the battlefield. Most of the Confederate dead were moved to Richmond and Savannah and Charleston after the war and buried in mass graves there."

He riffled through the brochures again. "It all depended on who won the battles, of course. For the loser, over eighty percent would be unknown at any one battle." He started adding up the figures. "I'd say between a hundred and two hundred and fifty thousand unknown dead altogether, but if you want a more accurate number . . ."

"Never mind," I said, and got in the car and went to get Annie.

CHAPTER ELEVEN

Traveller only let Lee down once. It was on the march into Maryland, right before Antietam. Lee had been sitting on a log, holding Traveller's reins loosely in his hands. It was raining, and Lee was wearing a poncho and rubber overalls. Someone shouted, "Yankee cavalry!" and Traveller started. Lee stood up to grab his bridle and tripped over the poncho. He caught himself on his hands. One of his wrists was broken and the other was severely sprained. At Antietam his hands were still in splints.

Annie wasn't at the inn or the coffee shop. The redheaded waitress, still disapproving, said she had told her to tell me she was at the library, and I thanked her with such obvious relief that she was probably convinced we had had some kind of lovers' quarrel.

Annie was in the reference section, the *L* encyclopedias spread out around her in a half-circle, most of them open to a picture of Lincoln's care-worn face, but she wasn't looking at them. She was staring at the orange-painted bookcases across from her and not seeing them, thinking hard about something. I hoped the something wasn't Gettysburg.

"Good morning," I said, sounding like the inanely cheerful park ranger. "I didn't think you'd be up this early."

She made a reflexively protective gesture toward the book in front of her, and then shut it before I could see the page it was open to.

"I want to go out and see the vet," I said. "Maybe he's heard from his sister."

"All right." She closed the other books and stacked them on top of the book in front of her. "Let me just put these away."

"I'll help you," I said, and grabbed for the bottom three books before she could pile the others on top of them. The top two were encyclopedias. The bottom one was the drug compendium I had used to find out about Thorazine. "What are you looking up in here?" I asked. "Are you all right? You're not having any side effects from the Thorazine, are you?"

"I'm fine," she said, turning away to put the other encyclopedias back on the shelves. "I wanted to know if the Thorazine was causing the headaches I've been having, but it isn't. Did you go out to the battlefield this morning?"

"Yes," I said, trying to keep my voice as casual as hers. "They've got a reference library out there. That's why this library's so skimpy on Civil War-iana. Ready? Maybe we can catch the vet before he makes his rounds."

We drove out and saw the vet. He was in the stable again, feeding some horses he was boarding. "I'm afraid I don't have any information for you," he said, forking a bundle of hay into one of the stalls. "I haven't been able to get in touch with my sister yet, but I'm going to a conference on horse diseases in Richmond tomorrow, and I should be able to run down and see her then."

I had been counting on his having already talked to her, so that I could say to Annie, "Well, we've done what we came to do. There's no point in sticking around here."

"When will you be back?" I asked.

He stopped and leaned on the pitchfork. "It lasts through the weekend. I'll probably come back Monday. Will you still be here?"

"If I'm not, I'll call you on Monday." Annie was looking at me. "We'll still be at the inn. You've got the number, don't you?"

"Yeah. Sorry you had to come all this way out here for nothing." He filled a washtub with a hose. "I looked through some of my dad's stuff on Akhenaten. There was nothing about him having dreams. Dad did have this one book on dreams and what the Egyptians believed about them, though. It was pretty interesting. They believed that dreams were messages from the gods or from the dead."

"Messages?" Annie said. "What kind of messages?"

"All kinds. Advice, warnings, blessings. The gods could tell you who you were going to marry, whether you should take a trip, if you were getting sick and with what. If you were getting a fever you dreamed about one thing, if you were catching cold you dreamed about something else. They had it all written down in this dream book, what everything meant."

The vet's wife came to the door to tell him he was wanted on the phone.

"I'll call you when you get back from your conference," I said.

"Is the horse all right?" Annie said. "She didn't get lockjaw, did she?"

"What horse? Oh, the mare that was out here the other day? She's fine. Bruised sole, just like I thought."

"Good," Annie said. "I'm glad."

I headed back toward town the way we had come until the first fork in the road and then took the left-hand turn. Annie didn't seem to notice. She had rolled her window halfway down and was leaning back, her head against the seat. The breeze from the moving car ruffled her hair. Her face had the serious, almost wistful expression it had had in the library.

This road wasn't as pretty as the one we'd taken down to the vet's. It was lined with the debris that towns always have on their outskirts: storage units, car junkyards, old trailers with porches and dog kennels tacked on and a horse tethered out back.

"It's beautiful out here, isn't it?" I said to be saying something, anything to get her mind off whatever battlefield she was thinking about. "The waitress said a cold front was supposed to be coming in, but I don't see any signs of it."

I turned again, to the south, and ran right into the interstate.

"Is this the way we came?" Annie said when the six-lane road loomed up ahead.

"I thought I'd take the scenic route back," I said, ignoring the I-95 sign and cutting over to US 1. "I saw the cat this morning. It was sitting in front of the coffee shop. I think it was waiting for you. Have you been feeding it?"

"I gave it one of those little cream containers this morning," she said. "And some bacon. It looked hungry," she added defensively.

"All cats look hungry," I said, looking for road signs. I didn't want to turn west until we were past Spotsylvania. "You realize you're stuck with him for life. Or at least until something better comes along. He'd desert you in a minute for somebody with a sardine."

"Desert," she said, looking out the window. We were passing a field with a haystack in it. "They shot deserters, didn't they? In the war."

And there we were, right back in it, in a war she didn't even call the Civil War anymore because it was so familiar to her, because she fought its battles every night.

"Not always," I said. "A lot of deserters got clean away. To California. Speaking of California, Broun's gone down to San Diego, so he'll be in California a few more days, and the vet won't have any information for us till Monday. Why don't we drive over to Shenandoah this afternoon? See the Blue Ridge Mountains? There's supposed to be a great place for fried chicken in Luray, be a nice change from the coffee shop. There's really no reason to stick around Fredericksburg."

We were going to run into the interstate again if we went much farther north. I turned left at the next road. It was State Highway 208. The road to Spotsylvania. I turned north onto a gravel road, then made three more turns, going north and west, trying to get as far from Fredericksburg as I could.

"What about *The Duty Bound*?" she asked.

"The galleys? Broun and I can finish them after he comes home from California."

"I think we should finish them," she said. "I'd like to know how it ends."

"Fine. We'll finish them when we get back." The road we

were on jogged north and ran into a four-lane highway. I hoped I hadn't managed to run into the interstate again. I hadn't. It was US 3, and the towns in both directions were clearly marked with arrows. The Wilderness was that way, Chancellorsville the other. Take your pick.

"Maybe it is a good idea," Annie said, looking at the signs. "To get away."

"Great," I said. I crossed the highway and went west at the next turn. "We'll get some fresh air and some southern fried chicken, a little exercise. There are all kinds of hiking trails."

"And no battlefields," she said softly.

"You know what else is in that neck of the woods? Monticello. Thomas Jefferson's plantation. We could spend the night in Luray and then drive down the Skyline Drive tomorrow and see Monticello."

We could drive down to Monticello, and while we were there that big front would come in, and we would have to go south to avoid it, into North Carolina and then Georgia and finally Florida, where there hadn't been any war.

"Monticello's a great place," I said, turning again onto what looked like a paved road. After the first mile, the asphalt gave way to gravel. "Jefferson made this great clock out of cannonballs. And curtains," I added hastily. "Jefferson made his own curtains." The gravel turned into dirt, and the road became so deeply rutted I was going to high-center the car if I didn't turn around. I put the car in reverse.

There was barely room to turn in the narrow lane. On one side of the road the weeds grew up knee-high next to a ditch, and on the other was a thin stand of pines that had been planted almost to the edge of the road. I stretched my arm out over the back of Annie's seat and started to back carefully so I wouldn't end up in the ditch.

"The dreams all have messages," Annie said.

"What?" I said, angry that something in this rutted lane, this pine woods, had made her think of the dreams again. I could no more get her out of the Civil War than I could get her out of the grave-filled circuit of Fredericksburg. I shifted into first again and killed the engine.

"I was thinking about what Dr. Barton said about the

Egyptians. He said they believed that dreams were messages from the dead."

"I thought we weren't going to talk about the dreams again," I said. I tried to start the car again and flooded it.

"Did you know that Abraham Lincoln dreamed about Willie after he died?" she said. I turned the ignition again, but Annie reached out to stop me. "Willie's face came to comfort him in dreams, the book said. I think he's dead, Jeff. I think the dreams are messages from the dead."

I took my hand away from the keys. So it hadn't been the sunken lane, the west wood after all.

"I thought you were right, that Lee was having the dreams during the Civil War and they were coming across time somehow, but yesterday, when I saw that postcard of his tomb at Lexington, I knew he was dead." She was looking at me earnestly, her hand still on my arm. "Richard told me that dreams help you work through the things that happened to you, that they're kind of a healing mechanism to help you get over grief and come to terms with the guilt you couldn't deal with any other way, only if there's too much guilt the dreams can't handle it. That's what he said was happening with me, but what if you had so much guilt and grief that you went on dreaming after you were dead?"

How many dreams would it take to heal Lee of Fredericksburg? Twelve thousand seven hundred and seventy? Lee's dreams weren't a "healing mechanism." They were a burial detail, and how many dreams would it take to bury all those boys at Gettysburg who staggered back from Pickett's Charge to collapse at Lee's feet, how many dreams to bury all the boys in the bloody angles and sunken roads of Lee's mind? Two hundred and fifty-eight thousand? A hundred years' worth?

"You told me Lee was a good man," Annie said, "and he is, Jeff, but he had to send all those boys back into battle, and they didn't have any shoes and no ammunition. He knew they'd be killed, but he had to send them in anyway. He had to send his own son Rob back in. How could he stand it, all those boys killed and nobody even knowing what happened to them? I think they still haunt him, after all these years, even though he's dead."

"And so he haunts you."

"No. It isn't like that. I think he's trying to atone."

"By inflicting his nightmares on you?"

"He's not inflicting them on me. It isn't like that. I'm helping him sleep somehow. Even though he's dead."

"And in the meantime, what are the dreams doing to you?"

She didn't answer.

"I'll tell you what they're doing. The dreams are getting worse, and they're going to go on getting worse until we do something." She started to protest. "Look, maybe you're right. Lee's dreaming in his tomb, and you're letting him get some sleep by having the dreams, in which case it won't matter where we go, the dreams will go right along with us. Only maybe not. Maybe it's the battlefield that's aggravating the dreams, and if we get away from it, the dreams will let up. The point is, you're not getting any sleep, you're not eating anything, and what good are you going to be to Lee if you pitch headlong down a flight of stairs some night?"

I started the car. "I think we should go to Shenandoah, get some rest, eat some fried chicken, get away from the dreams for a while, and if we can't get away from them, try to ignore them. You're not deserting. You're just getting away for a little while. On furlough." I was lying. If I managed to get her out of here I would never let her come back.

"Clean away," Annie said, and I wondered if she knew I was lying, if she wanted to get away, too.

"We won't talk about the dreams, we won't think about the dreams, we'll go hiking and eat fried chicken and look at the Blue Ridge Mountains. All right?"

She sighed, a long, surrendering sigh. "All right," she said.

I drove back onto gravel, onto pavement, and out onto the road we had come up on. A mile up it turned into a county road, and a few miles after that onto a two-lane highway with a long, straight stretch of road.

It could have been summer. Some of the trees were already in full leaf, and it was unbelievably warm. There weren't any clouds at all in the sky, not even above the line of blue in the west where we could already see the Blue Ridge Mountains. I speeded up, anxious to put as much distance as I could between us and Fredericksburg. It was past lunchtime, but we would eat later, when we were closer to Shenandoah.

"This is more like it," I said, resting my arm on the open window. "I thought for a while there we were never going to see a highway again." I had told Annie we weren't going to talk about the dreams, but that was easier said than done. The dreams were all we'd thought about for days. I couldn't talk about the battlefield, or Lee, or Lincoln either, who had been afflicted with bad dreams, too. And I could hardly tell her carefree college-days stories about my old roomie Richard.

"This is pretty country, isn't it?" I said, sounding more than ever like the park ranger. "Broun and I got lost on a back road like that one time when I first came to work for him. He wanted me to take some pictures of the country around Antietam, but he was convinced I'd get lost, so he came with me and got us both stuck in a mud puddle. We had to walk out and get a tow truck. He wouldn't even let me do that by myself. He was like that the whole first year I worked for him."

"Not letting you do anything?" Annie said. "Why not?"

"I don't know. He'd never had a research assistant before, and I guess he was used to doing everything himself. He was just starting *The Duty Bound,* and there was tons of research to do on Antietam, but he insisted on doing it all, especially the stuff at the battlefield. I thought when we got there he'd let me do at least some of the legwork for him, but he wouldn't. He traipsed around the battlefield, taking notes like crazy, snapping pictures, stretching out flat on his back so he could get what he called 'the soldier's eye view—' "

I stopped and glanced anxiously at Annie, but she was watching the scenery, still smiling. Her blonde hair was blowing in the wind, and she brushed it out of her face.

"He cut his foot wading across Antietam Creek," I went on. "On an old tin lid. It bled like crazy. His foot, not the lid. He had to have a tetanus shot and twelve stitches, and he still wouldn't let me take over."

Outside of Remington, the two-lane highway connected with the state highway to Culpepper. I cut south again.

"So here he is, hobbling around, trying to run things—"

"Like Longstreet," Annie said.

"And he announces he's going to Springfield. His publishers called and they want him to check the epigraph he used on the last book, so he's going all the way to Springfield to see what's written on Lincoln's tomb or some damn thing, and I blew up. I said, 'What in the hell did you hire me for? You won't let me do anything, not even go look at some damned dead bodies.' "

Oh, Richard would have a heyday with this conversation. "Those are obviously Freudian slips," he would say in his Good Shrink voice. "The subconscious is speaking, bringing up subjects the conscious mind wants to avoid."

"So did he let you go to Springfield for him?" Annie asked, looking like she was unaware of the slips, Freudian or otherwise. She had taken my advice to heart. She was relaxing, getting away, even though I didn't seem able to.

"He let me go to Springfield, but he kept calling me on the car phone on the trip out, reminding me to look at this and remember to ask that. He left messages at my motel and made me call every night and dictate my notes onto that damned answering machine of his. He just about drove me crazy. And then I don't know what happened. Maybe he decided he hadn't hired an incompetent idiot or something. He quit pestering me and let me do the research he'd sent me to do and from then on he let me do what he'd hired me to, which was to help him."

I didn't know till I got to the end of that instructive little story that that was what it was. My subconscious was calling for attention, all right, banging on the door to be let out. "He still does a lot of his own research," I said, as if to convince myself that I hadn't just been lecturing Annie on the subject of letting me take over, letting me help her. I have your best interests at heart.

"Maybe he had trouble giving up the research because he loved it," Annie said.

"Maybe," I said, thinking of how excited he had sounded about Lincoln's dreams. "He loves Lincoln anyway."

"And you."

"Yeah."

151

"I came to see Broun the night of the reception," she said. "I made Richard come. I knew Broun knew all about the Civil War. I thought he might be able to tell me what the dreams meant."

"Only Richard wouldn't let you near him, and you got stuck with me."

"Not stuck," she said, and smiled at me the way she had that night in the solarium, that sweet, sad smile. "It's you that got stuck with me."

"We're stuck with each other," I said lightly. "And with Lee. But not today. Today we're on leave. Are you hungry?"

"A little."

"We'll stop for lunch the next town we come to. We just came through Remington. There's a map in the glove compartment. You can see if there's a town coming up—"

"Stop the car," Annie said. She had her hands on the edge of the half-open window and was looking back at what we had just passed. "Stop the car!"

She was out of the car before I had even pulled halfway onto the shoulder. She grabbed for the door handle and was out of the car and running toward the road.

"Annie!" I shouted, fumbling with the door. I leaped out after her.

She was standing on the edge of the shoulder, looking at nothing in particular, a rail fence and a plowed field, off in the distance a house with a wide porch. Her hands were balled into fists at her sides. "What is this place?" she demanded. "I know this place."

Damn it. Damn it. I had thought we would be safe coming this way, away from Chancellorsville and the Spotsylvania Courthouse and the Wilderness. I had brought her this way on purpose because I thought it was safe.

"Did you dream it?" I said, dreading the answer.

"I don't know," she said. "I have the feeling that I've been here before. Where are we?"

"I don't know," I said. "We just went through Remington." I opened the car door and reached in for the map. The engine was still running. I switched it off. It couldn't be Culpepper. I had seen a sign for Culpepper in Remington. We were still at least ten miles east of it. I grabbed the map out of the glove compartment, snapped it open, and scanned the map, unable to find Remington.

We were only a few miles past Remington. The next town . . . The next town was Brandy Station, two miles away. We were north of Brandy Station. There wasn't a monument symbol next to it on the map, or a cross, though there should have been. The whole damned state was a graveyard. That plowed field was probably full of yellow-haired boys and grizzled veterans and horses.

"I feel like I've been here before," she said, and walked across the road. She didn't look in either direction, and I was not sure that for her there was even a road there. A blue car whipped around the curve and between us. It missed Annie by inches, lifting her skirt in the wind it made when it zoomed by. She didn't jump or step away from it, startled. She didn't even know it had been there.

I ran across the road to her. "It's Brandy Station," I said. "There was a cavalry battle near here. Lee's son Rooney was wounded. Lee saw him being carried off the field. I'm sorry." I took hold of her arm. "I shouldn't have brought you here. Let's go back to the car and get out of here."

She didn't move. She didn't resist me, either. She simply stood there, stock-still, in the middle of the road. "Did he die?" she said.

"Rooney? I don't know. I don't think so. It was a leg injury." I tugged at her arm. "We can find out when we get to Luray."

She shook her head. "I want to go back to Fredericksburg."

"Why? They'll have a library in Luray. We can look up Rooney there. He didn't die. I know he didn't die. He was at his father's funeral."

Annie was staring at the plowed field as if she could see it all, Rooney on a litter, his leg torn open, the bandage soaked through with blood. "None of Lee's sons were killed in the war," I said.

"I have to go back," she said. "I can't desert him like that."

I could hear a car coming, the low roar rising in pitch as it started to round the curve. "Desert him?" I said angrily, and practically pushed her back across the road and into the car. "You're not one of his soldiers, Annie. You didn't sign up for this war."

A jeep roared past, straddling the center line. I came around and got in. I started the car and roared off the shoulder and onto the road, whipping around the rest of the curve at the same speed as the jeep, wanting us out of sight of the plowed field, out of sight of Rooney on a stretcher. "I had no business bringing you here!"

"It's not your fault," Annie said.

"Then whose fault is it? I take you to Fredericksburg. Fredericksburg, for God's sake, where they've got so many bodies they've got to bury them in groups! I read you a book about Antietam out loud! And then, just to make sure you dream about Brandy Station tonight, I bring you out here so you can see the battle for yourself. And I wonder why the dreams are getting worse!"

There was a billboard up ahead. VISIT MANASSAS NATIONAL BATTLEFIELD PARK. I pushed my foot down hard on the accelerator. "Why don't we drive up to Manassas? And then tomorrow we'll run down to Richmond so you can dream the Seven Days battle. I was trying to get you the hell out of there to someplace that wasn't a goddamned battlefield!"

The truck in front of me put on its brake lights. I jammed on the brakes. Annie's hands came up hard against the dashboard.

"I was trying to help."

"I know," Annie said. "I know you were trying to help."

I slowed the car down to a sane speed. "I was taking the back roads because I didn't want to run into the Wilderness. Did I hurt your hand?" I asked anxiously.

"No," she said. She rubbed her wrist.

"We'll go to a doctor. In Luray. We'll have him look at your hand and then we'll—"

"It's no use, Jeff," Annie said. "I can't leave him. I have to see the dreams through to the end."

I pulled the car over to the edge of the road and stopped. "The end? What end? What if Lee goes on dreaming for a hundred years? What if he decides to dream the whole damn Civil War?" I said bitterly. "Are you going to dream it for him?"

"If I have to."

"Why? They're not your dreams. They're Lee's. He's the one who ordered all those boys back into battle. Let him dream them himself. Let his daughter Annie dream them for him, if she wants to, it's her father. But not you."

"I have to."

"Why?"

"Because I can't bear it," she said, and started to cry. "Poor man, poor man, I have to help him. I can't stand to see him suffer so."

I took her hand in mine and rubbed the wrist gently. "And I can't stand to see what they're doing to you," I said. I brought her hand up to my chest and held it there. " 'I would that I were wounded in your stead,' " I said. "Lee said that when they told him Stonewall Jackson had been wounded at Chancellorsville."

She looked up at me, the tears running down her face. Her tears, not Lee's, not Lee's daughter's. And it was me she was looking at this time.

"I would, you know," I said. "If there was any way I could, I'd have the dreams for you."

I listened to what I'd said and looked at her dear, tear-streaked face. "Which is what you're trying to do, isn't it? Have the dreams for Lee, so he won't suffer."

"Yes," she said.

"All right," I said. I let go of her hand and turned the car around. "We'll find a place in Fredericksburg that has fried chicken. And we'll hope to God you don't dream about Brandy Station."

She didn't. She dreamed about a chicken. And Annie Lee's grave.

CHAPTER TWELVE

At the battle of the Wilderness, Lee yelled to the Texas brigade to form a line of battle and then spurred Traveller through an opening between the guns and up to the front of the line to lead the attack. "Go back, General Lee!" the soldiers shouted. "Go back!" A sergeant grabbed hold of Traveller's bridle, and General Gregg rode up to head him off. The soldiers stopped in their attack and shouted, "We won't go on unless you go back," but Lee seemed not to hear them.

We read galleys after we got back, me in the green chair with my feet on the bed, Annie propped up against the pillows with the copyedited manuscript on her knees. Broun had written himself off the battlefield finally, and into a makeshift hospital near Winchester, where Ben had been taken with his wounded foot and was being nursed by a sixteen-year-old girl named Nelly.

In these chapters Broun introduced a lot of new characters: an overworked, alcoholic surgeon who had been a horse doctor before the war, a battle-ax nurse named Mrs. Macklin, a fast-talking private named Caleb who was all of fifteen.

Theoretically, it was a bad idea to bring in so many new characters so late in the book, but Broun didn't have any choice. Like Lee, he'd killed off everybody else, and now it was time to bring in the old men and the boys. And the women.

"Where'd you get shot?" (Annie read) *the boy in the bed next to Ben said. "I got it in the foot."*

"Me, too," Ben said, and turned his head carefully to look at him. He was afraid if he moved too quickly he would pass out. He had passed out in the wagon. The ambulance detail had propped him up in the back of it with his arms over the sides, and he had watched blood drip from under the wagon onto the dirt road. He had had the idea it was all his blood, and after he had bled more than any one person could possibly bleed, he had fainted.

He had come to when they tried to get him up the stairs, but one of them, a big, mean-looking woman, had hit his foot against the bannister, and he had passed out again.

"I ain't shot bad," the boy said proudly. He had a friendly, sunburned face. "I'm goin' back soon's they let me. My name's Caleb. What's yours?"

Ben had tried to answer him, but then it was dark and there was the sound of a horse whinnying. Ben's heart pounded. "Malachi?" he said.

"Promise me you'll hold my hand," somebody said pitifully, and Ben was afraid he was the one who had said it, but the voice went on, "Nothing bad can happen so long's you are holdin' it," and Ben knew that wasn't true so he decided he must not be the one talking. The horse whinnied again, and Ben recognized it as a scream this time.

"I promise," a girl's voice said, gravely, kindly, and then it was morning and the girl was standing over him saying, "I've brought you your medicine. Can you sit up and take it?"

She was beautiful. She had light, fine hair pulled back into a bun. When she bent over, to set the brown bottle on a chair, Ben could see the part in her hair. She was wearing an apron and a gray dress that looked like it had faded from blue.

"Course I kin sit up for you," the boy named Caleb said. He was sitting up on top of the covers. "For you I could git up out of this bed and go dancing, but would you dance with me? No. You're breaking my heart, Miss Nelly, you know that, don't you?"

"I do not think you are quite ready for dancing yet," Nelly said, pouring the laudanum into a tin spoon. Caleb's leg was bandaged with

157

heavy white strips of linen, but Ben could see that there wasn't a foot there at all. He wondered if he himself had a foot.

Ben gulped the laudanum down.

"I am willing to dance with you this very day," Caleb said, grabbing for Nelly's hand. "We shall push the beds back against the wall, Miss Nelly, and you," he waved his hand at Ben, "shall play us a jig tune."

"Nelly! Come away from there!" a woman's voice said. She came and stood at the foot of the bed where Ben could see her. It was the woman who had hit his foot bringing him up the stairs.

"Have one of the others do that!" she barked. "We got another wagonload coming in, and here you are flirting with the menfolks." She glared at Caleb. "You woke every soul in the house with your screaming last night."

He grinned at her. "I dreamed Miss Nelly wouldn't marry me," he said.

"You can't marry Nelly," Ben tried to say. "I love her."

Nelly set the bottle of laudanum down on the chair and went out of Ben's range of vision. Caleb swung his legs over the side of the bed and leaned across to pick up the bottle. "I dreamed Miss Nelly said she wouldn't marry me and old Mrs. Macklin said she would." He winked at Ben. "It was a nightmare, that's what it was."

I watched Annie read, her head bent over the manuscript so I could see the part in her hair. "It's the war," Broun had said when I had refused to believe that Ben could fall in love with Nelly after only one day in the hospital. "A spoonful of laudanum, and Ben will do anything for her," I had said, and Broun had answered, "People did things like that in a war, fell in love, sacrificed themselves."

Maybe it was the war. We had been through a lot together— Fredericksburg and Chancellorsville and Brandy Station. I had explained her dreams to her, held her hand while she slept, dried her tears. All that was bound to produce feelings of camaraderie, affection. But I knew it wasn't true. I had loved her since the moment I saw her standing there in the solarium in her gray coat.

I insisted on finding a restaurant that served fried chicken, as if that had been why we intended to go to Shenandoah.

Annie brought home a drumstick wrapped in a napkin for the cat.

"You'll kill it with kindness," I told her. "You're not supposed to feed them chicken bones," but the cat was nowhere to be found. It had come out to the car when we got back in the afternoon, meowing reproaches, but now it wasn't on the outside steps or over in front of the coffee shop.

"He'll be back," I said. "Cats always come back."

"Tom Tita didn't. He was locked in. He couldn't get out."

"The cat isn't locked in. He's probably found some other pushover to feed him, that's all. You notice Tom Tita didn't try very hard to get out. He was perfectly happy in the attic with all those mice, and when Markie Williams let him out he didn't go racing back to Lee. He didn't even miss Lee as long as the Union soldiers would feed him."

"Lee missed him," she said. "Cats don't have any sense of loyalty, do they?"

"Their first loyalty is to themselves. What good would it have done Tom Tita to follow Lee through the Civil War? He would just have gotten himself killed. And the Union soldiers took good care of him, the way somebody's taking good care of this cat right now."

"You're right," she said. "Somebody's taking care of him, and he's fine," but she stripped the meat off the drumstick and left it in a little pile at the bottom of the steps before we went in.

She went to bed at eight, and I tried to call Broun at the Westgate in San Diego again. There was no answer. I called the answering machine.

"I'm still in San Diego, Jeff," Broun said. "I didn't get in to see the endocrinologist. He was called out of town. I'm going to a place called Dreamtime while I wait for him to get back. Probably a bunch of quacks, but you never know." I waited, thinking there'd be a message from Richard, but there wasn't.

Annie tapped lightly on my door. "I had a dream about a chicken," she said.

"Are you sure this is one of Lee's dreams and not just something you ate?" I asked her, giddy with relief that I hadn't inflicted Brandy Station on her.

"I'm sure," she said. She leaned against the door. She was wearing the blue robe over her nightgown, and her eyes were bluer than I had ever seen them. Her short hair was tangled from sleeping on it. She looked beautiful. "The chicken was on the porch of my house. She acted like she belonged there. Did Lee have a chicken?"

"He had a horse," I said. "He had a cat. I refuse to believe he had a chicken. It sounds to me like this dream is one of your own, brought on by that southern fried chicken we had for dinner. I told you I was giving you bad dreams."

She went back to bed. I put the chain on the door and moved the chair over next to it, balanced the book on the arm. I corrected galleys for a while, read Freeman for a while, napped for a while, but I couldn't sleep in spite of the fact that I had had maybe three hours' sleep in the last two nights. It was a good thing.

Annie got out of bed, put on her robe, and tied the belt, all so calmly I thought she was awake. She pushed the chair out of the way. The book thumped onto the carpeted floor, making less noise than I thought it should. She reached for the chain.

"Where are you going, Annie?" I said quietly.

"My fault," she said. She unfastened the chain.

"It's not your fault. Let's go back to bed." I hooked the chain and led her carefully back to bed, my hand barely touching her arm. She didn't resist at all. She stopped next to the bed and took off her robe.

"What happened to them?" she asked.

The chicken? Tom Tita? Or all those yellow-haired boys?

"We'll find them," I said. She got into bed and lay down. I covered her up. Fifteen minutes later we went through the whole thing again. After I had her back in bed, I wedged the chair under the doorknob and waited.

It took half an hour that time, and then she stood up again, put her robe on, tied the belt, and tried to move the chair. It wouldn't budge. She turned and looked at me. "What happened to them?" she said angrily, as if I had hidden them from her.

"We'll find them," I said, and started back to the bed, my

hand lightly on her arm, but halfway there she stopped and took two steps toward the windows.

"My fault," she said softly. "My fault."

We were at Gettysburg again, in the woods that were like an oven, watching the soldiers struggle back from Pickett's Charge.

"My fault," she whispered, took a few faltering steps forward, and sank down on her knees, her face in her hands.

"What is it, Annie?" I said, squatting beside her. "Is it Gettysburg? Is it Pickett's Charge?"

She took her hands away from her face and sat back on her heels, staring blindly at whatever it was.

"Can you wake up, Annie? Can you tell me what you're dreaming?"

She stretched her hand out toward something on the floor in front of her and then drew it back. "She's dead, isn't she?"

She knelt there for over an hour, me squatting beside her until my legs cramped and I had to switch positions, talking to her, trying to wake her up, trying to get her back to bed. In the end I picked her up and carried her, placing her arms around my neck so she wouldn't fall back, unfastening them when I had her in bed.

"What happened to them?" she asked when I covered her up.

"I don't know," I said, "but I'll find out. I promise."

Five minutes later she stood up again, put on her robe, and went over to the door.

"Annie, you've got to wake up," I said tiredly.

She stopped pushing on the chair, straightened up, looked at the door, at me. "Did I do it again? Did I go outside?"

"You were trying your darnedest to," I said. "Where were you? Gettysburg?"

"No," she said, sitting down in the chair. "I was at Arlington again. It had snowed, like in the first dream, and I was looking for the cat. He was out under the apple tree, and I went out to get him, and I stepped on something. It was a Union soldier. He was lying face-down, with his rifle underneath him, and his name pinned to his sleeve."

She was clutching the tie belt of her robe the way she had

161

clutched the African violet in Broun's solarium that first night. "I bent down to unpin the paper, but when I did, it wasn't a blue uniform sleeve, it was white. And then I saw it wasn't a dead soldier, it was a girl in a white nightgown, asleep under the apple tree."

She didn't ask me where it was or what the dream meant. She sat for a while in the chair, looking toward the middle of the room as if she could still see the apple tree and the girl asleep under it.

"I'm sorry I was sleepwalking again, Jeff," she said. "Maybe you should tie me to the bed." She took off her robe and lay down, her arms stiffly at her sides, as if she were willing herself not to walk in her sleep.

She lay that way the rest of the night. I didn't know if she was asleep. She didn't move when I picked up Freeman from where it had fallen on the floor and went into my room to get the other three volumes, when I locked the connecting door to my room and pulled the desk across it, or when I moved the lamp over by the green chair so I could read by its light.

There weren't very many index references to Annie Lee, in spite of her having been Lee's favorite daughter. I looked up the last one first. "I have always promised myself to go, and I think if I am to accomplish it, I have no time to lose," he had written his son Rooney in 1870. "I wish to witness Annie's quiet sleep." She had died during the war at White Sulphur Springs, North Carolina. She was twenty-three years old.

"He was a good man," Annie had said. His soldiers loved him, his children loved him, and he had had to sacrifice them all to the war, even his favorite daughter. Annie Lee had died of a fever, but she was as much a casualty of the Civil War as any soldier, dying young and far away from home. At least Lee had had the comfort of knowing where she was buried. He had gone to visit her grave in 1870. "I wish to witness Annie's quiet sleep."

Poor man. When he had gotten the letter of her death, he had not shown any outward emotion. He had read the letter and then gone on answering his official correspondence with his aide. But when the aide had come back into the tent a few minutes later, he found Lee weeping.

It was four o'clock, one in California. I called Broun at the Westgate in San Diego, at the L.A. number. I called directory assistance and got the number for Dreamtime. There was no answer anywhere.

Just before dawn, Annie got out of bed and put on her blue robe. I put out a restraining hand, afraid she was sleepwalking again. She went over to the window. "Did you find out what the dream meant?" she asked.

I told her about Annie Lee. "She died in 1862," I said. "Right before Fredericksburg."

"Willie Lincoln died in 1862. He was Lincoln's favorite son," she said, hugging her arms to herself. "What did she die of?"

"I don't know. A fever of some kind."

"Poor man," she said, and I wondered which man she meant, or if she would know if I asked her.

We spent the morning trying to sleep, gave up, and went to see the last tourist attraction in town, Hugh Mercer's apothecary shop. We looked at silver-plated pills and brown glass laudanum bottles and handwritten prescriptions for curing fevers.

We spent the rest of the day in the library. Annie took notes on Lincoln. I read Lee's letters and tried to find out what Annie had died from. Nobody seemed to know. I found the chicken, though. Its name was Little Hen. She had walked uninvited into Lee's tent one day, and Lee had kept her for over a year. She laid an egg under Lee's camp cot every day and sat on Traveller's back, which delighted the soldiers.

We looked for the cat after dinner, but it was nowhere to be found. The neat pile of chicken scraps Annie had left for it was still on the step. "It's probably holed up someplace warm," I said. "It's supposed to turn cold tomorrow." We went back to the room, and I barricaded the doors, as if I thought I could somehow keep the dreams out.

I needn't have bothered. Annie didn't sleepwalk. She lay quietly, and watching her I thought the dreams must not be as bad, though when she told me about them, they were worse than ever.

Her house was on fire and a rider handed her a message

which she tried to open with one hand. The message was wrapped around three cigars, and she couldn't open it because her hands were bandaged. She handed it to the redheaded waitress and she couldn't open it either, there was something wrong with her arm, and it wasn't the waitress, it was a girl in a white nightgown and the message wasn't wrapped around cigars, it was a letter, and Annie was afraid to read it.

She dreamed she stood on the porch of Arlington and argued with Richard, who was wearing slippers. The vet was in the dream, too. He handed Richard a message, and Richard tore it into little pieces and threw them on the ground.

"Who is the vet?" she asked me.

"I don't know," I said. "Pickett maybe? Longstreet?"

"No," she said bitterly. "Richard is always Longstreet."

She dreamed about Gettysburg, the retreating soldiers sometimes coming back into the orchard from a burning house, sometimes carrying a chicken in their arms. She tried to re-form them under the apple tree, but she couldn't because Annie Lee was asleep under the tree.

There were no tears or sleepwalking during the dreams, and afterwards she recited her horrors to me gravely and I explained them as best I could, but she scarcely heard me. She seemed to be conserving all her strength for the dreams, lying perfectly still under the green-and-white coverlet. Her cheeks no longer burned, and when I touched her hands or her forehead, they were cold.

In the early hours of the morning I called the answering machine. Richard said, "Annie's records show low levels of serotonin, which is indicative of a suicidal depression. The symbolism of her dream corroborates that. The rifle represents the desire to inflict harm, the dead soldier is obviously herself."

"I was right about the Dreamtime thing," Broun said. "They were a bunch of quacks. Imaginative quacks, though. They said the dreams were warnings sent by Willie Lincoln to his dad, and when I asked them how Willie Lincoln happened to be sending messages, and why, if they knew what was going to happen, the rest of the dead didn't warn us of impending disaster, they came back with this theory that the dead nor-

mally sleep peacefully, but that Willie's rest had been disturbed
when Lincoln dug him up.

"I'm flying up to Sacramento Wednesday to a sleep clinic
there. I'll be home sometime Tuesday. I've got an autograph
party Saturday in L.A. and an appointment on Monday. I
hope you're doing okay on the galleys, son. I'm going to be
impossible to get in touch with for the next few days."

"I know," I said.

I didn't get any sleep to speak of. "Did you manage to get
some sleep, Jeff?" Annie asked at breakfast. She looked as if she
hadn't. Her face was pale and there were dark, bruised-looking
shadows around her eyes. She sat stiffly in the booth, as if her
back hurt, and occasionally rubbed her hand along her arm.

"Some. How about you?"

"I'll be all right," she said, and handed me the stack of
manuscript. She let the waitress pour her some coffee while
she tried to find the place we'd left off.

"You know that big front they were talking about?" the
waitress said. "It got stalled over the Midwest for a few days,
but now it's moving again. We're supposed to get six inches of
snow tonight. Can you believe that? In April."

"Where are we?" Annie said after she left.

"Page six-fifty-six," I said. "Where it starts, ' "No," Nelly
said.' Page six-fifty-six." I separated the manuscript into two
piles, one only fifty or so pages thick. We were almost done,
and what would we do then while we waited for the dreams?

"No," Nelly said, (Annie read) *"and Ben tried to come awake to
help her, but it was like trying to roll out from under the horse that had
fallen on Malachi.*

*"He's dead," Mrs. Macklin said. She sounded impatient, as if
Nelly had done something stupid.*

*"I know he's dead," Nelly said, and the need in her voice brought
Ben completely awake. He pushed himself up in the bed. Pain roared
out from his ankle, and he opened and closed his mouth in little gasps,
trying to keep from screaming, pinned down by the pain.*

*He turned his head and looked at Nelly. She was sitting on a
wooden chair next to Caleb's bed. She was holding Caleb's hand,
gently, as she had every night since he had been brought in. His fingers*

clung to hers, and his eyes were closed, but he didn't look like he was asleep. He must have been dead the whole night.

"You can't do anything for him," Mrs. Macklin said, and took hold of Nelly's wrist.

"Let go of her," Ben said, and then had to breathe in and out rapidly again so the pain wouldn't overtake him. "Leave her be."

Mrs. Macklin ignored him. "Twenty men downstairs half-dead and you sit here," she said accusingly. "Let go of his hand." Still holding Nelly by the wrist, she yanked her to standing, and Caleb's arm came up smartly, as if he were saluting.

"No," Nelly said desperately, "please," and Ben lunged for Mrs. Macklin, but he didn't make it. His foot got shot off again, worse than the first time, and he thought they must have had to cut it off at the knee.

When he opened his eyes to see, Nelly was still sitting beside the bed, but the boy's body was gone, and somebody had laid a gray blanket over the ticking.

"I'm sorry," Ben said.

Nelly rubbed her wrist. It looked red and puffy. "Do you know what he said to me yesterday?" she said. "He said that as long as I was holding on to him he had beautiful dreams." She rubbed at her wrist, making it redder.

"You done the best you could," Ben said. "He ain't dreaming no more now anyways," and he wanted to take her hand and hold tight, but he knew he'd be shot again before he reached the edge of the bed.

"I broke my promise," she said.

"My friend Toby Banks that I told you about promised his mama he'd come home athout a scratch on him. Some promises they just . . . you done the best you could. After he was," he stopped and cast around for some way to say 'dead,' "after he was passed on to glory, he couldn't feel whether you was holding on nohow."

"Promise me you won't reenlist when your foot gets better," she said.

"I promise," he said, but she went on sitting by the bed, rubbing her wrist.

After a while Mrs. Macklin came in and asked to look at Nelly's wrist. "No," Nelly said.

"It's all swollen," Mrs. Macklin said angrily. "I'm a nurse. It's my duty to tend to . . ."

Nelly stood up, knocking the wooden chair over. "Don't you talk to me about duty," she said, cradling her arm like a baby against her, "not when you wouldn't let me do mine."

Annie stopped reading. "I want to go to Arlington," she said.

We had been through all this before. "There's no reason to go to Arlington. We know what the dreams mean. Lee blamed himself for Annie's death. Maybe he thought it wouldn't have happened if Annie had been at home, if they hadn't had to leave Arlington. We even know what the message is. It's the letter telling him Annie's dead. There isn't any reason to go back to Arlington."

"I have to . . ." She didn't finish what she was going to say. "The dreams are going in circles. It's like when I kept dreaming about the cat, and then when we went out to Arlington, it helped."

Helped who? I wondered. You or Lee? She was helping him have the dreams, helping him sleep in that marble tomb of his at Lexington, and what was he doing to her?

"I think he is trying to atone," Annie had said. Lee had loved his daughter. Surely he wouldn't do anything to hurt Annie. I wished I could believe that. I wished I could believe this atonement of his didn't mean dragging Annie through the Civil War till both their hearts were broken.

"Look," I said, "you heard what the waitress said. The weather's supposed to get bad, and anyway the vet's not back from his conference. I think we should wait till we hear from him. That way we can finish the galleys, too. We can take them up to New York and stop at Arlington on the way."

The waitress brought our eggs. "It's snowing in Charleston," she said. "I just heard it on the radio."

"See?" I said, as if that settled it.

Annie cut her ham up but didn't eat it. She just kept cutting it into smaller and smaller pieces. "It isn't supposed to snow till tonight," she said. "You could call the vet from Broun's, Jeff. We could take the galleys with us and finish them in D.C." She put the knife down and rubbed her wrist.

"Annie, you're not in any shape to go to Arlington or

167

anywhere else. You haven't had any sleep for two days, and your wrist is obviously hurting."

She stopped rubbing it. "I'll be all right."

"You could have sprained it when you hit it on the dashboard. Maybe we should go have a doctor look at it."

"No," she said and put it in her lap as if to hide it from me. "It isn't sprained."

"But it hurts. And you're exhausted. We're both too tired to think straight. I think the best thing for both of us to do is take some aspirin and try to get some sleep, and then we'll talk about Arlington."

"All right," she said and looked, I thought, relieved.

We went back to the inn, and Annie did what I'd told her to, even though she protested that her wrist really didn't hurt, took some aspirin and went straight to bed. I called Broun's West Coast agent. He would know where Broun was if anybody did, and I had meant what I said about our being too tired to think straight. Broun wouldn't be dead on his feet. He would know what to do, how to help.

His agent's call referral service told me he was in New York. When I said I was trying to get in touch with Broun, she gave me a number to call. It was the number of Broun's answering machine.

Broun hadn't left any new messages. Richard had. I fast-forwarded over it to see if Broun had left a hotel name or a number and found a call from Broun's agent. "You've got to get the galleys in now," she said. "McLaws and Herndon is screaming bloody murder. They're not the only ones who've called. Everybody's looking for you. I got a call from a Dr. Stone, head of the . . ." there was a pause and a rustle while she looked at the message, "head of the Sleep Institute. He called to say that he had checked out the Gordon thing for you, and—"

"The Gordon thing?" I said. Gordon? I didn't remember any Gordon.

"—that there was no clinical verification for Dr. Gordon's theory that dreams can prefigure illness. You're supposed to call him for the results."

I called Broun's agent and told her the galleys were almost

done. "You don't know how I can get in touch with Broun, do you?" I said. "There are a few errors I want to check out with him before I turn in the galleys."

"All I've got is his West Coast agent's number," she said. "If you do get in touch with him, have him call me. I've got a lot of messages for him. What's he doing out there?"

"He's working on a new book about Lincoln's dreams."

"Oh, good," she said. "I was afraid he was still messing with *The Duty Bound.* Oh, and Jeff, there was a call for you. A Dr. Richard Madison. He said it was urgent that he get in touch with you. I thought you were in California with Broun, so that's what I told him. I'm sorry."

"That's okay. I've been hiding out trying to get the galleys done. When did he call?"

"Oh, gee, it was two or three days ago. He didn't leave a number. Shall I try to find him in the phone book?"

"No!" I said and then laughed, hoping it sounded apologetic and not unstrung. "I've got to get these damn galleys in before I talk to anybody. If he calls back, I'm still in California, okay?"

"Okay." There was a pause. I was so used to talking to the answering machine I almost punched in the erase code. "Jeff, all these psychiatrists are just helping Broun with his research, right?"

"Yeah. He's trying to find out what caused Lincoln's dreams."

"Oh, good," she said. "He had so much trouble with *The Duty Bound* I thought maybe . . . I've been worried about him."

"He's fine. I'll have the galleys in to McLaws and Herndon by Monday."

I went in to check on Annie. She was already asleep, one hand cradling the other. I wondered if I had done the right thing, trying to get her to sleep, or if I was only letting her in for more nightmares. I knew how Lee felt sending his son Rob back in at Antietam. I had told her I would try to get some sleep, too, but I doubted if I'd be able to. I was too worried about her. I took my shoes off and settled down in the green chair with the acknowledgments sheets for *The Duty Bound.*

*   *   *

"I'm going to the battlefield, Jeff," Annie said, bending over me. She had on her gray coat. "Go ahead and sleep."

"Are they open at night?" I said. I sat up, spilling the acknowledgments everywhere. I had fallen asleep and she had dreamed about Fredericksburg again. "I don't think they're open at night."

"It's three o'clock," she said, and picked up her purse and the room key. "Go back to sleep."

It was almost dark in the room. She had turned on the lamp by her bed. Three o'clock. I couldn't let her go out to the battlefield in the middle of the night. I had to get up and get dressed and go with her.

"I'll go with you," I said, and bent over to put on my shoes. "Wait for me."

"Go back to sleep," she said, and shut the door behind her.

I stood up, still convinced that it was three o'clock in the morning and surprised to find myself dressed. I must have slept through the afternoon and on into the night while Annie dreamed about Fredericksburg or worse. Asleep on duty. They shot soldiers for that.

I grabbed my coat and racketed down the outside stairs to the little parking lot, but the car was still there. She wasn't in it. I stood looking around the parking lot for a long, stupid minute, trying to think where she had gone and waking up to the fact that it was not the middle of the night.

It was getting dark out, and some cars had their lights on. The weather the waitress had predicted had come in. It was windy, and the sky was a gray blanket of cloud. The waitress was right, I thought, and would have given anything if she'd been hovering by my shoulder waiting to pour me a cup of coffee to wake me up.

And where was Annie? What if she hadn't gone out to the battlefield at all? What if she'd caught a bus to Arlington? What if she'd taken off altogether, afraid I was going to try to stop the dreams, afraid I was going to put Thorazine in her food like Richard?

Richard. He had called Broun's agent. Who else had he called? Nobody knows where we are, I thought desperately. But what if Annie had told Richard her second dream after all, and he had recognized it as Antietam? And when we weren't in Antietam, he had gone on to the next battle? Which was Fredericksburg.

I raced back up the stairs, across the hall, and down to the desk. "Did you see a man in here, about my height, dressed like a doctor?"

The clerk grinned. "You looking for Mrs. Davis?" he said, emphasizing the *Mrs.* "She asked us to call her a taxi."

A taxi? She wasn't in a car with Richard, drugged and helpless, on her way back to Washington. She had taken a taxi to Arlington because I wouldn't take her. "Did she say where she was going?"

"She didn't say anything to me," he said, still grinning. "When she called for the taxi, though, I heard her say she wanted to go out to Fredericksburg battlefield."

I took the stairs two at a time, grabbed my car keys, and raced back out to the car and across town. But before I'd gone two blocks I knew I was too late.

Lincoln pardoned the sentries who fell asleep on duty, saying it was hard for farm boys to break their country habits. He wouldn't pardon me. I had let Annie go out to the battlefield by herself, and it was starting to snow.

171

CHAPTER THIRTEEN

Lee never forgot his love for horses, even at the end. One of his chief concerns that last week, while Five Forks fell and Sheridan cut off all hope of escape to the north, was with the starving mules and horses. He had had to give their rations of parched corn to the men.

The morning of the surrender Colonel John Haskell rode up "like the wind" with news that Fitz Lee had learned of a road over which the army might still be able to escape. He had only one arm, and he couldn't get his horse stopped until he was nearly a hundred yards past Lee. "What is it?" Lee cried, running up to the winded horse. "Oh, why did you do it? You have killed your beautiful horse!"

The blue taxi was sitting just outside the National Park gates. I tore up the terraced slopes to the cemetery. I didn't even look for her in the Visitors' Center or on the brick paths. There was only one place she was going to be.

She was standing on Marye's Heights where Lee must have stood, the skirt of her gray coat whipping around her in the wind. It was snowing, stray angled flakes like rifle fire. Annie was holding a brochure but not looking at it. And what was she looking at? The flash and shine of sun on metal, the whipping of flags, the breathless hush before the men on the naked plain were cut to ribbons, the flags toppling one by one and the horses going down? Or the graves, terraced row on row below her?

I came up the last step, panting. "Are you all right?" I said, and had to take a breath every other word.

"Yes," she said, and smiled at me, her face grave and kind.

"You should have woken me up," I said. "I would have brought you out here."

"You needed to get some sleep. I've been worried about you. You stay up with me all night and don't get any sleep."

She turned and looked down the long terraced slope at the graves.

"They didn't build this cemetery until after the war," I said, still having trouble getting my breath. "It isn't like they buried the soldiers here after the battle. This wasn't made into a national cemetery until 1865. A lot of the soldiers buried here probably didn't even die in the war."

She looked down at the brick path we were standing on. There were grave markers set into the path. She bent and swept snow off the granite square. "This is where the unknowns are buried, isn't it?"

"None of these graves are Confederate dead," I said. "They're not even from the battle of Fredericksburg. The Confederate soldiers are all buried in the city cemetery."

She stood up and looked at the brochure. "This says there are over twelve thousand unknown soldiers buried here," she said, "but there aren't really, you know. There aren't any."

I took the brochure away from her and pretended to read it. The snow was melting on it in big spots that blurred the ink.

"You said nobody knows what happened to the chicken, but it isn't true," she said. "I know what happened to it. It got killed. One of the soldiers wrung its neck for dinner."

"You don't know that. Maybe it ran away into the woods and became a wild chicken. Maybe some little girl found it and kept it for a pet."

"The brochure says nobody knows what happened to the soldier that's buried under this marker, but that isn't true either. After the war, when he didn't come back, the people who were waiting for him knew. His mother or his sweetheart or his daughter. They knew he was dead because he didn't come back."

"Some of the soldiers just never went home after the war. Some of them lit out for California and the gold mines, and they wrote letters home that got lost in the mails, and they weren't dead after all."

The wind had stopped and the snow was falling slowly, covering the numbers on the marker at our feet, burying the boys with their yellow hair and their outflung arms, blurring the charred pieces of paper they had pinned to their sleeves.

"What happens to Ben in *The Duty Bound*?" Annie asked.

I had no idea how Broun had ended the book. He had killed off Malachi and Toby and Caleb. Maybe he had an epidemic of typhoid in the last chapter and killed everybody else. "I don't know," I said.

"Does he die?"

"Die? Ben? He's the hero. Of course he doesn't die. He marries Nelly and they go back to Hillsboro and have ten kids and live happily ever after. Broun loves happy endings."

The marker was completely covered with snow. You couldn't even tell it was there in the path.

"I'm sorry I got you into all this Jeff," she said, still looking at the marker. "I needed your help. I didn't even think how it would be for you." She looked up at me. "I had another dream."

"When? This afternoon? Is that why you came out here by yourself?"

"Last night," she said. "I didn't tell you."

"Because you didn't want to wake me up?"

"Because I didn't want to have the dream. Because I already knew what it meant."

"You don't have to tell me your dream," I said. "Let me take you back to the inn. It's starting to snow. You'll catch pneumonia."

"Did you know that when Willie Lincoln had pneumonia, Bud Taft held his hand the whole time?"

"Annie . . ."

"Bud fell asleep once, and Lincoln picked him up and

carried him off to another room. He shouldn't have done that. Willie might have called for him."

"Bud was only a little boy," I said.

"Right before he died, Willie clutched Bud's hand and said his name." She was still watching the snow sift down onto the graves. "What happened to Lee after the war?"

"He lived for years. He became president of Washington College. Miley came out and took his picture, and tourists came and pulled hairs out of Traveller's tail. Lee said he looked like a plucked chicken. He took little girls for rides on Traveller and let them hang daisy chains on him. They lived for years."

"I think the war is almost over," she said. "I think that's what my dream means."

"Did you know Traveller saved Lee's life up here?" I said, sounding like a frantic tour guide. "A shell burst and Traveller reared up on his hind legs or they'd both have been killed. The shell went right under them."

She didn't even hear me.

"I was asleep," she said, looking at the snow falling on the graves. "In the dream. I was sleeping out under the apple tree in the bed I had when I was a little girl, only in the dream it had a green-and-white coverlet. I was asleep and the pharmacist came and woke me up and told me it was time to go and I got up and got dressed. I put on a dress with a red sash I had for Easter the year I was ten, and a blue cape. I knew I had to look as nice as possible, and at the last minute, when I was all dressed and they were all waiting for me, I stopped and made my bed. I asked the pharmacist to help me. He was getting dressed, too. He was putting his cuff links in, but he stopped to help me, and all the time we worked on the bed he was crying. 'It's time to go,' he said. The whole time I was dreaming I had the feeling it was Easter Sunday."

She stopped and turned to look at me, expectantly, waiting for me to help her. And I could no more help her than Ben could keep them from taking away Caleb's body.

And what had I expected? I had brought her here to this town that was all graveyard and told her about other graveyards— Arlington and Chancellorsville and Gettysburg—and, as if that

175

weren't enough, I had read her a whole book on the subject of Duty, hundreds and hundreds of pages of people who had just signed up they didn't know why, of people who had had to see it through even though they hadn't counted on getting kilt.

Where had I thought it would lead, this road "past the second Manassas, to Chancellorsville," except here? I should have known from the beginning that to get her away from Arlington, to help her past Fredericksburg and Jackson's death, past even Gettysburg, was bound to lead to this, that all the roads Traveller carried Lee over had to converge here in an apple orchard near Appomattox Court House. She had dreamed about an apple orchard in the very first dream, an apple orchard and a house with a porch. I should have known then.

Lee had lost a third of his men at Sayler's Creek. The day after, April seventh, Grant wrote offering surrender terms. Sheridan was moving west and north to block Lee's retreat at Appomattox Station, and Meade had the rear guard under attack. The infantry wasn't strong enough to fight its way through. Its only chance was to try to escape to the west, into the mountains, slipping around the Union flank, and for the next two days they tried that.

At dawn on April ninth, Palm Sunday, they attempted to break out near Appomattox Station, but the attack failed. Lee met with his officers in an apple orchard outside Appomattox Court House and told them he had arranged to meet with General Grant. The surrender terms were signed in the house of Wilmer McLean, a man who had originally lived near Manassas Junction. After the second battle of Bull Run, he had moved to the little village of Appomattox Court House, "where the sound of battle would never reach them." The house was a two-story brick farmhouse. It had a covered wooden porch that ran the length of the building.

"We can't stay out here in this snow," I said. "It's getting dark. Why don't we go have some supper? Our waitress won't know what to do with herself if we're not there to have our coffee cups refilled."

Annie's uncovered hair was getting wet. It curled up around her face.

"Please," she said, and held her hand out to me, and she

was as far away from me as Ben had been from Nelly, distanced not so much by the dead man between them as by his own pain.

Maybe Annie was right, and the dream meant the war was almost over. Maybe the dreams were almost over, too, and we could both go home together, paroled. At Appomattox Lee had gotten Grant to let the men keep their horses.

"It's not Easter," I said, looking down across the graves, past the souvenir shops and the roofs and trees to the line of river, wondering if Lee had been thinking of Traveller when he asked Grant not to confiscate the horses. "It's Palm Sunday."

Lee had gotten up and dressed in his best, his dress uniform and a red sash and his blue military cape because, as he said, he was likely to be taken prisoner. "There is nothing left for me to do but go and see General Grant," he told his officers, "and I would rather die a thousand deaths." Lee asked advice of Longstreet and the other officers, and then mounted Traveller and rode to the McLean house. Along the way he saw Sam McGowan, his staff officer, struggling out of his muddy clothes and into a dress uniform, weeping like a child.

Annie and I went back down the hill, she holding my hand, the terraced steps already slippery, the graves hardly visible in the coming dark. The taxi was still there, its motor running and its windshield wipers going, the driver waiting patient as a horse.

I sent him home and took Annie to the coffee shop and told her about the last days before the surrender. Our waitress poured us cups of coffee that steamed the windows up so we couldn't see out into the snowy darkness.

"They say it's supposed to warm up tomorrow and turn into rain, but I don't believe it," she told us. "I hope you aren't going anywhere."

"No," I said, and wished it were true. "We aren't going anywhere."

I took Annie up to the room and put her to bed. "I'll be right here," I said, as if she were going away, and held her hand till she fell asleep. Then I finished the acknowledgments and went and stood by the window and waited.

She lay perfectly still under the coverlet, one hand resting on her chest, the other at her side, her cheeks pale as marble. After a long time, she sat up in the bed, the green-and-white sprigged muslin over her hunched knees like a crinoline, and put her hands over her face.

"What is it?" I asked. "What did you dream?"

She looked up at me and tried to speak, her eyes full of tears.

"Did you dream about Appomattox?" I asked.

She nodded, looking straight ahead, the tears welling up, and she didn't have to tell me what she had dreamed. I knew.

They met in the parlor of the McLean house in the early afternoon. Grant told Lee that they'd met before in Mexico and that he would have known him anywhere. He apologized to Lee for being in a field uniform and muddy boots. He and Lee discussed the terms of surrender, Grant doing his best to "let 'em up easy," as Lincoln had ordered him to.

Lee told Grant that in the Confederate army the cavalry and artillery units owned their own horses, and asked that they be allowed to keep them since most of the men were small farmers and would need them for the spring planting. Arrangements were made to feed Lee's army from Union supplies. The terms of surrender were drawn up and signed.

When it was all over, Lee came out of the house and stood by Traveller while the orderly buckled the bridle. Lee slipped Traveller's forelock over the brow-band and smoothed it, absently patting the gray's forehead. Then he mounted the horse that had carried him from "Fredericksburg, the last day at Chancellorsville, to Pennsylvania, at Gettysburg, and back to the Rappahannock" and rode back to the apple orchard to tell his men. "Men, we have fought through the war together," he told them, "and I have done the best I could for you."

The men, boys most of them, barefoot and hungry and dead on their feet, his men crowded around him, yelling out, "We'll go on fightin' for you, General!" and "I love you just as well as ever!" and "Goodbye!," but most of them couldn't speak at all and they reached out to touch Traveller's mane and side and flanks. Lee looked straight ahead, his face set, tears in his eyes, but Traveller tossed his head all down the line, as if the cheers were for him.

"It's all right," I said. "You won't dream anymore. The war's over."

She held out her arms to me, and I took her and held her and never let her go.

CHAPTER FOURTEEN

Lee seemed to understand the need for surrender before any of his generals did. By the time they made it to the apple orchard, half of his army had been destroyed. Nothing was left of the infantry but a few brigades and Longstreet's and Gordon's corps, and none of them had had anything to eat in days. Yet, when he showed Grant's first letter of surrender terms to General Longstreet, Longstreet snapped, "Not yet," and when he asked Venable what kind of answer he should send, Venable said stiffly, "I would not answer such a letter." "Ah, but it must be answered," Lee said.

The last night before the surrender he slept, all alone, under an apple tree, holding on to Traveller's bridle.

We went on reading galleys in the coffee shop the next day as if nothing had happened and we would do this every morning for the rest of our lives. During the night the snow had turned to a cold rain.

"We should be able to finish them off this afternoon," I said, "and then tomorrow we can run them up to New York and hand them to the publishers. What's the weather like?" I asked our waitress.

"It's raining hard north of here. Some truckers in here were talking about flooding."

Annie yawned. She looked beautiful, rested, her cheeks as pink as that first night when she had come to me for help. I took hold of her hand.

"Why don't you go back to bed?" I said. "You've got a lot of catching up on sleep to do. I'll call McLaws and Herndon." The waitress frowned. "And the highway patrol."

We went back up to the room. I called the answering machine to make sure Broun hadn't decided to come home. Broun had left a message. "Pay dirt," he said, sounding excited. "I knew I was on the right track. The sleep clinic has some TB patients they've been studying because the fever makes them have more REM sleep. All of them dream about being buried alive. They say they can feel the cold wet dirt being shoveled in on them. The doctors say it's the night sweats, but I talked to them and some of them started having these dreams before they had any other symptoms.

"Not only that, but as the disease progresses the dreams get clearer and less symbolic and they dream their own symptoms, fevers and coughing and blood, and sometimes they dream about dying, being at their own funeral, being in the coffin. That's why Lincoln dreamed the coffin dream that last week. His acromegaly was getting worse.

"But here's the best part. One of the patients is this kid who was reading *Treasure Island.* I asked him about it and he said Robert Louis Stevenson was his hero because he had TB as a kid, too. He said Stevenson had dreamed about being buried alive, too. Robert Louis Stevenson dreamed the same dream over a hundred years ago!"

He didn't say where he was. He had an autograph party in L.A. on Saturday and an appointment with a neurologist on Monday. He would be home sometime Tuesday if he finished with the prodromic-dreams thing.

Broun's agent had left another message. "I told McLaws and Herndon the galleys would be in Monday at the latest. If you can't reach Broun, they'll have to go in as is."

Before she had even stopped talking, Richard said, "You have to call me immediately."

"The hell I do," I said, and hung up. I took the galleys

and went back into Annie's room. Annie was asleep, on top of
the covers, her legs pulled up against her body. She was cradling her left arm in her right, as if it hurt. I took the folded-up
blanket at the foot of the bed and put it over her.

There were only a few pages of *The Duty Bound* left to go.
Mrs. Macklin had broken Nelly's wrist trying to get her away
from her dead private. The alcoholic surgeon had had to take
time off from sawing at arms to set hers and put it in a sling.
Mrs. Macklin wanted her to go home. *"You can't do any good
here," she said.*

*"You told me that once before," Nelly said. "You have your duty. I
have mine," and kept working as long as they had a hospital, which
wasn't long. The armies swarmed around and past Winchester, and
the hospital had to be moved and then dismantled and the soldiers too
hurt to walk taken off in wagons. When Ben's unit marched past on its
way to Fredericksburg, Ben went with them.*

"No," Nelly said when he told her he was going.

Annie sat up in the bed and screamed. I jerked as if I'd
been shot. I dropped the galleys and stood up. My foot was
asleep and I half-fell onto the bed. She screamed again and
put up her hands to ward me off. I grabbed her wrists. "Wake
up, Annie. You're having a bad dream. Wake up!"

I could feel her heartbeat through her wrists, fast and
light. "No!" she said, and her voice was full of desperation. She
tried to pull away from my grip.

"Annie, wake up! It's just a dream."

"I'm so cold," she said, and I thought for a minute she was
awake. "It got so cold. In the church." She was shivering and
her breath was coming in gasps, as if she had been running.
"The meeting took so long."

What meeting? Not the meeting with Longstreet at Gettysburg. That was in a school, not a church. Dunker Church?
Surely she wasn't going to dream Antietam, not now, when the
dreams were supposed to be over.

"They couldn't decide . . . I finally said . . . so cold!" Her
teeth were chattering. I let go of her wrists and wrapped the
blanket around her shoulders. I pulled the sides of the coverlet
up and over her legs.

"What were they meeting about?"

She tried to say something through her chattering teeth, closed her eyes, and turned on her side. She gasped and shifted, as if her arm hurt. She put her hand up to cradle her elbow and murmured something I could not make out. Then she turned again, still holding her arm, and said clearly, "Tell Hill to come up."

And now I knew what church she'd dreamed about. I shut my eyes.

She slept for another hour. I sat with her awhile and then went into the other room, hobbling on my still half-asleep foot, stripped the bed, and piled the blankets over her.

The phone rang. It was the vet's wife with a message. Dr. Barton had called home from the horse-disease conference. He had two things he wanted to tell me. One was that he had gotten to talking about me with some of the other veterinarians at the convention, and one of them mentioned that he had just read an article about acromegaly in one of the science magazines. He thought I might be interested. She didn't know which magazine, she was just relaying the message.

The second thing was that he had finally gotten in touch with his sister. She didn't remember Dr. Barton—she meant Dr. Barton's father—ever saying anything about dreaming about coffins or boats, and she thought he would have mentioned it. He was very interested in dreams because of his study of the Egyptians. He had had a recurring dream for months before he died that he was convinced was warning him of his death. He had dreamed he was lying dead out under the apple tree in his backyard.

"What did he die of?" I asked. "The acromegaly?"

"No," the vet's wife said. "He died of a heart attack."

"What symptoms did he have? Before the heart attack?"

"Gosh, I don't know. He was living with Hank's sister, and we didn't see much of him. He complained of his arm hurting a lot, I know, because Hank's sister thought it was arthritis, but afterwards the doctor told her it was probably angina, and I remember he rubbed his wrist all the time."

I thanked her for giving me the message and hung up the phone. Then I went and stood by the window, looking out at the Rappahannock. My precious Annie.

When Annie woke up, I said, as casually as I could, "The weather's supposed to get worse tonight. Maybe we should go on up this afternoon."

"I thought you said tomorrow," she said.

"I did, but I don't want to get caught in a blizzard the way I did on my way back from West Virginia."

She stood up, still cradling the arm. "What about the galleys?"

"We can stop somewhere for lunch along the way and finish them off. There are only a few pages left."

She was looking at the tangled heap of blankets. "What happened?" she said. "Did I have another dream?" She turned to me, her face innocent and trusting, as if this dream were like all the others and I would say it was Antietam or The Further Adventures of Little Hen. There was nothing in her face to show she had realized there was something terribly wrong, that with the surrender the dreams were supposed to be over. Over.

"I don't know," I said. I pushed the blankets aside and laid her open suitcase on the bed. "You muttered something about being cold a couple of times. It was cold in here. I put some more blankets on you and I wrapped you up in the bedspread."

"I'm still a little cold," she said, and shivered. She began taking things out of the closet and putting them in the suitcase, and I noticed that now that she was awake she was using both hands, but she moved a little stiffly, as if her back hurt.

"I'll go check us out downstairs," I said.

"Wait a minute. What about Dr. Barton? Weren't you going to wait till he got back?"

"He called," I said. "His sister said their father never mentioned any dreams." I shut the door and went down the stairs, thinking how easy that had been, as easy as emptying a capsule into her food. For her own good.

I went across the street to the phone booth in the coffee shop and called the hospital. "I have a friend who's sick," I said, and then stopped. I would never get her to a hospital. They would want to know the name of her doctor, they would have a thousand forms and while I was filling them out she would call a taxi and disappear.

I called the Sleep Institute and asked for Dr. Stone. "I'm
sorry," the receptionist said. "Dr. Stone's in California. Can I
take a message?" I called Broun's hotel in L.A. He had checked
out. I asked the clerk whether Broun had mentioned where he
was going, and he repeated, "Mr. Broun has checked out."

He had checked out, and I didn't know where his autograph party was being held today or who the neurologist was
he was going to see on Monday, and he wouldn't be home till
Tuesday, which was three days from now.

Annie insisted on having lunch at the coffee shop so she
could say goodbye to the redheaded waitress, but she was not
there. Her little girl was sick, the manager told us. "Tell her
goodbye for me," Annie said and went on reading galleys as if
we were not now cut off from everyone, the rear guard destroyed at Sayler's Creek, Sheridan already at Appomattox
Station, and Meade in the rear and coming up fast, Grant
already writing the terms of surrender.

*"No," Nelly said when he told her, and he could hear the despera-
tion in her voice, but this time he was the cause of it and there was
nothing he could do. "The army won't take you. You can't even
march."*

*"I'm walking pretty good," Ben said. "Mebbe they won't take me
now, but there's a time when they will and glad of me."*

"Why are you doing this?"

*"I gotta. I don't know why. It's the same as when I signed up. I
just gotta."*

"I will never know what happened to you," she said.

*"I been thinkin' on that," he said. He pulled a piece of folded
paper out of his shirt pocket. "Friend of mine told me to put my name
and my kin in my shoe, but that didn't do no good. The boot was shot
clean off and the paper with it. I want you should keep this."*

"What good will that do?"

*Ben thought of her sitting by Caleb's bed, holding his dead hand.
"After the war's over, you show them this paper and you point at one of
them bodies and say, 'That's him,' and they'll put my name on a grave
and write my kin, so's they'll know what happened to me."*

"All right," she said.

*After he was gone she opened up the paper and read it. "Toby
Banks," it said. "Big Sewell Mountain, Virginia."*

Annie stopped.

"I did have a dream," she said. "I remember it now. I think I was in our church, the Presbyterian church on Main Street back home, and they were taking up the collection, only it wasn't a church service. It was a meeting of some kind."

A vestry meeting. At Grace Church.

"I don't remember very much of it. It wasn't like the other dreams." Some of the panic came back in her face as she tried to remember. "It was cold. I remember thinking I should have worn my other coat and wishing they'd stop arguing so I could go home."

They had been arguing over a raise of fifty-five dollars for the minister. The meeting had gone on for three hours, and finally Lee had said, "I will give that sum," just so it could be over. Lee had only worn his military cape, and he walked home through the chilly rain.

The family was waiting for him at the tea table. He sat down heavily on the sofa, cradling his left arm, and his wife said, half-joking, "Where have you been? You've kept us waiting a long time," and asked him to say grace. He stood up and looked as though he were trying to say something, and then collapsed onto the sofa.

"What is it?" Annie said.

"It's probably Dunker Church at Antietam. Let's go."

"I didn't say goodbye to the cat." She insisted on going around to the outside steps. It wasn't there, and the scraps of chicken were half-buried in the snow. "What if something happened to it, Jeff?" Annie said, rubbing her wrist.

"Nothing happened to it. It's holed up someplace nice and warm, in an attic full of mice maybe. There's no sense waiting around for it to come back. Come on. Let's go."

She slept the whole way up as if she had been drugged. She didn't even wake up when I stopped at a filling station just outside Woodbridge. It was raining there, a chilly, autumn-feeling rain that might turn to snow any minute.

I went inside and called the answering machine again. "Pay dirt," Broun said. "I knew I was on the right track." I hadn't erased the messages. I listened to the whole message repeat itself, trying to pick up some clue to where Broun was.

Broun's agent said, "I told McLaws and Herndon the galleys would be in by Monday at the latest. If you can't reach Broun, they'll have to go in as is."

"You have to call me immediately," Richard said. I had hung up on him before, but now I listened to the message hoping that Broun had called again to tell me where he was, afraid to fast-forward for fear I'd go right over it and miss it. "I just got the test results back from the lab. There's a problem with the EKG. I don't know for sure what it is. Have you noticed any chest pains? Any pains in the wrist or the back or down the arm? If it's unstable we could be looking at a myocardial infarction anytime. You've got to come back immediately." There were no more messages. The machine ran on to the end and then switched off by itself.

Broun's West Coast agent's number was busy. I bought a cup of coffee to go and went back out to the car. Annie was still asleep, curled up in the passenger seat with her left arm cradled against her body. Her short hair was brushed back off her flushed cheeks. I took the lid off the Styrofoam cup, put the cup between my knees, and started the car. Annie shifted slightly and brought her other arm up to support her left arm. "Strike the tent," she said.

I turned off the car. After a while I opened the door and poured the coffee out onto the ground and went back inside and called Richard.

CHAPTER FIFTEEN

After the surrender, Lee was offered the job of president of a little college in Lexington. He rode up on Traveller to arrange for a home for his family. "He starts tomorrow," his wife wrote, "on horseback because he prefers it that way and besides, does not like to part even for a time from his beloved steed, the companion of many a hard-fought battle."

In Lexington he rode Traveller every day, stopping to give rides to little girls and to talk to the students. Lucy Long, the mare that had been stolen, was found and bought back, and one of Lee's daughters would accompany him on the mare when he exercised Traveller. As time went on Traveller's hard trot fatigued him more and more, and when he went on a speaking tour, he took the train. "Tell him I miss him dreadfully and have repented of our separation but once," Lee wrote his wife, "and that is the whole time since we parted."

I took Annie to Broun's. "We can take the galleys over to Federal Express later," I said. "This stuff's going to turn into snow if we go any farther north. I'm not driving up to New York tonight. I need to check for messages and look at the mail."

I had told Richard to park several streets over so Annie

wouldn't see the car, but the front door wasn't locked and Broun's Siamese was crouched on the bottom step. My first thought was that it had somehow gotten locked in when we left for Fredericksburg, but then I saw that the mail was neatly stacked on the hall table and that there was a jacket hanging over the bannister. Annie was standing in the door of the solarium with her gray coat and her gloves still on, and her left arm still cradled in her right, looking at the African violets. They had been watered—there was muddy water standing in puddles on the table.

"Is that you, Jeff?" Broun said, and came clattering down the stairs. He was wearing a black overcoat that looked like he'd slept in it. "Thank God!" he said, and hugged me. His beard hadn't grown at all in the week we'd been gone, and the rough stubble scratched my ear. "Are you all right? I called every motel in Fredericksburg, but nobody had you registered." He pushed me out to arm's length and peered at me with his sharp little eyes. "You got Richard's message then?"

"What message?" I said. I pulled away from him, and shrugged out of my coat. "I'm fine, now that the damn galleys are finished. What a mess! Transposed chapters, missing chapters, the works. I finally called Annie here and talked her into coming down to help me finish them. You remember my boss, don't you, Annie?" I said. I draped my coat over the newel post. "The man who is responsible for all our misery these last few days? Broun, you remember Annie?"

"Yes, of course," Broun said, and shook hands with her.

"Hello," she said gravely. I couldn't read her face at all.

"It's freezing out here in the hall," I said. "Didn't you turn the heat up? Let's go in the solarium." I took Annie's arm and led her into the room. "Good, it's warmer in here. Annie, let me take that wet coat."

Broun came and stood in the doorway. "Why didn't you tell me you were sick, Jeff?" he said. "I thought there was something wrong that night you got in from Springfield. Why didn't you tell me you were having chest pains? I would have canceled my trip. Have you been to see a doctor?"

"The records from the family doctor show a problem with the EKG," Richard had said. "Have you noticed any chest pains?" Broun had thought the message was about me, had flown home to help me, but it was too late. I looked at Annie. She had taken her gloves off and had backed up until she was against the table that held the African violets. She stood there twisting her gloves and watching me, waiting to hear what I would say.

"I'm not the one who's sick," I said. "Annie is. I brought her home to put her in the hospital." I took hold of her hands. "I called Richard," I said. "He'll be here any time."

She stood very still for a moment, as though she were going to speak, and then lurched forward, the way Lee had when Traveller bolted, the gloves still in her hands.

"You're suffering from angina," I said. "That's what's making your wrist hurt. Lee had angina all through the war, pains in his shoulder, along his arm, in his back. He died of a heart attack. The dreams are a warning. You've got to see a doctor."

"And so you called Richard."

"Yes."

She sat down on the couch. "You promised," she said.

"That was before I knew the dreams were killing you. I'm doing this for your own good."

"Like Richard," she said, twisting the gloves in her lap.

I knelt beside her. "Annie, listen to me, the dream you had this morning, it wasn't about Antietam. I lied to you. The meeting you dreamed was at Grace Church in Lexington. Lee went to that meeting and sat there all afternoon in the cold and then walked home in the rain and had a heart attack! I'm not going to let that happen to you!"

"I have to do this." She twisted the gloves. "I have to see it through. Please try to understand," she said, gravely, kindly. "I can't leave him. I promised to have his dreams. Poor man . . . I have to try and help him. I can't leave him. He's dying."

"He's not dying, Annie!" I shouted. "He's dead. He's been dead over a hundred years. You're holding on to the hand of a corpse. You can't do anything for him! Don't you see that?"

"I promised."

"And I made some promises, too, but I'm damned if I'm going to let you die for the sake of a goddamned answering machine! That's what it is, some kind of biological prerecorded message that switches on when you're going to have a heart attack and leaves a message for you to call the doctor."

"No, they're not," Annie said. "They're Lee's dreams."

"Lee's dreams," Broun said. He took hold of the door jamb and leaned against it as if he couldn't stand.

"They're prodromic dreams, Annie! They're caused by the angina!"

Broun took a step toward Annie. "Are you having Robert E. Lee's dreams?" he said in a labored, uncertain voice, as if he could not get his breath.

"No," I said.

"Yes," Annie said.

Broun groped blindly behind him for a chair and sat down heavily. "Lee's dreams," he said.

"Annie, don't you understand?" I said. "You're in danger. I have to get you to a hospital."

"I can't. I promised."

"What did you promise? To march up to the Bloody Angle and get yourself killed? You're not one of Lee's soldiers! His soldiers *had* to stay with him. They'd have been shot for deserting."

"That isn't why they stayed," Annie said.

It was true, barefoot and bleeding, they still hadn't deserted him, not even at the end. We'll go on fightin' for you, Marse Robert.

"Lee's soldiers knew when they signed up they could get killed. You didn't. You didn't sign up at all."

"I did sign up," Annie said. "That day we went to Shenandoah. I realized then that I couldn't leave him, that I had to stay and help him have the dreams."

"That day we went to Shenandoah you didn't know you had angina!"

"Yes, I did." She put the gloves down on her lap. "I figured it out that morning in the library. My wrist hurt, and I thought maybe it was a side effect of the drugs I'd been taking, so I looked it up. It said Elavil was contraindicated for patients with heart conditions."

"Elavil?" I said stupidly.

"A year ago when I went to my doctor for the insomnia, he told me I had a minor heart condition."

"Why didn't you tell me? I could have taken you to a doctor."

"I couldn't go to a doctor." She looked at me. "The dreams are a symptom. If you cure the disease, the symptoms go away. And I can't leave him."

"Why didn't you tell me?" I said again.

She didn't say anything. She sat with her hands in her lap.

"Because I would have tried to stop the dreams," I said for her. Like I was doing now.

The doorbell rang. Broun put his hands on the arms of the chair and made a motion to get up, then sat down again watching Annie. She stood up. Her gloves fell to the floor, unnoticed. "You promised," she said.

"I'm doing this for your own good," I said, and opened the door to Richard.

He didn't have a coat on. His sweater and jeans were wet clear through. His hair was wet, too, and he looked tired and worried, the way he had the night of the reception when he was still my old roommate, still my friend.

"Where is she?" he said, and swept past me into the solarium.

Annie had backed into the table holding the African violets and was standing there, her hands at her sides. She had knocked one of the violets over, and muddy water dripped off the edge of the table onto the floor.

"Thank God you're all right!" he said, and took hold of her wrist. "I've called the hospital, and they'll have a room ready when we get there. Are you feeling any pain?"

"Yes," she said, and looked across the room at me. Broun stood up.

"Where? In your arm?"

"No," she said, still looking at me. "Not in my arm."

"Well, where then? Back, jaw, where? This is important!" he said angrily, but he didn't wait for her answer. He turned to look at Broun, and as he did he pulled Annie with him, her arm coming up smartly, like a corpse's.

"Call an ambulance," he said.

"No," Annie said, to Broun, not to me. "Please."

I had thought I could do it. She had already lived through that other surrender. I had not thought this one would be so bad. But that surrender had been different. Lincoln had told Grant to "let 'em up easy," and Grant had. He hadn't taken Lee prisoner at Appomattox. He hadn't even demanded Lee's sword. He had arranged for rations to be distributed to the men and for the officers to keep their horses, and then he had let Lee go.

I looked at Broun standing there in his black overcoat, his arms hanging at his sides as if he were overcome with fatigue or sorrow, and then back at Richard. I could have surrendered to Lincoln, I thought. I could have surrendered to Grant. But not to Longstreet. Not to Longstreet.

"Let go of her," I said. Richard turned and looked at me. "There's no need for an ambulance. We've already been to see a doctor. In Fredericksburg. Dr. Barton."

"What did he say? Why didn't he have her admitted to a hospital?"

"He did. He took her in and did an EKG on her and ran blood tests. He asked her if she'd been taking any drugs, and she told him Elavil." I waited to see what effect that had on him.

"You didn't say anything about this on the phone."

"Doctor Barton wanted to know why somebody had pre-scribed Elavil for a heart condition."

Annie and Broun stood perfectly still, watching him. The room was so quiet I could hear the water from the African violet dripping onto the floor.

"A mild sedative was indicated for the patient's insomnia," he said in his Good Shrink voice. "The record from Annie's family doctor indicated nothing more than a functional heart murmur, and her EKG confirmed that. There were no symp-toms of heart disease, and Elavil is only contraindicated in cases of maximum and long-term dosage. I prescribed a mild dose, monitored the patient carefully, and removed her from the drug immediately when it failed to have any effect on her symptoms."

"Her symptoms," I said. "You mean the dreams?"

193

"Yes," he said. He still didn't let go of Annie's wrist.

"I asked Dr. Barton about the dreams," I said. "He said he didn't know what was causing them until he saw her blood tests this morning. They showed traces of Thorazine. He said the Thorazine was probably causing the dreams. He asked Annie who'd prescribed Thorazine for her, and she said nobody. She said she didn't know what he was talking about, that she'd never taken any Thorazine."

"Thorazine was indicated," he said. "It's routinely prescribed in cases of sleep disorders."

"Dr. Barton said that Thorazine is prescribed for institutionalized mental patients, not for people with bad dreams."

"That's what this is all about, isn't it? You still believe she's having Robert E. Lee's dreams."

"Dr. Barton said it was a crime for a doctor to give a patient a drug without this knowledge. He said a doctor could lose his license for that. Is that true, Richard? Could you lose your license?"

"You bastard," my old roommate said, and let go of Annie's wrist. "I was only trying to help you, Annie. I had a duty as a doctor."

"Don't you talk to me about duty," Annie said, cradling her arm like a baby against her, "not when you wouldn't let me do mine."

Broun made a sound. His face under the beard was deathly pale. He looked sick, like a writer who had just heard the words he wrote spoken in earnest.

"Call the ambulance," Richard said to Broun.

"No," Broun said. "She's having Robert E. Lee's dreams."

"You've convinced him, too, haven't you?" he said to me. "You're all crazy, you know that?"

"Like Lincoln?" Broun said.

"Call an ambulance," Richard said, and Broun turned and stumbled up the stairs.

"I told Annie I was going to prescribe Thorazine for her and informed her of its side effects," the Good Shrink said. "She took the first dose herself. Thorazine will sometimes temporarily impair the patient's short-term memory."

"After the Civil War, Longstreet wrote long, involved ex-

planations of how he hadn't let Lee down at Pickett's Charge,"
I said, "how it was all Lee's fault. But it didn't work. There
were too many eyewitnesses."

"Is this supposed to be something Robert E. Lee dreamed?"

"No," I said. "It's supposed to be a warning. I have two
Thorazine capsules and all those messages you left on the
answering machine on tape. You leave her alone or I'll send
them to your boss, Dr. Stone, at the Sleep Institute. I'll tell him
you gave a patient Thorazine without her knowledge. I'll tell
him you gave Elavil to a patient with a heart condition."

Broun came down the stairs, carrying the answering machine. He had wrenched it out of the wall. The shredded ends
of the wire dragged on the floor beside him.

"If you still want to call an ambulance, you'll have to use
the phone next door, Richard," I said, "only I doubt if our
neighbor will let you in. Not after she had you arrested once."

"You bastard," he said again. "I'm not going to let you get
away with this. I called you, did you know that? To tell you I
had a patient who was having terrible dreams and I didn't
know what to do. I called you and you weren't home."

"Did you call me for help or were you trying to establish
an alibi?" I said, but he had already slammed the door shut
behind him.

I pulled my coat on. "He may try to follow us," I said.
"He's parked at least a block away. If we go right now, we can
lose him." I grabbed up Annie's gloves and thrust them at her.

"Do you have any money?" I said to Broun. He fumbled in
his pockets and came up with a twenty and some change. "Is
that all?" I said, shouting at him as if I were trying to wake him
up.

He reached into the inside pocket of the jacket that was
still hanging over the bannister with his right hand, still holding the answering machine in the other, and pulled out a wad
of bills. He handed it to me and then sat down heavily on the
loveseat.

"Thank you," I said. I snatched up Annie's suitcase and
hustled her out the door. Broun didn't answer me. I could see
him through the solarium window when I started the car, still

sitting there cradling the answering machine against him, like a man asleep.

The rain was trying to turn into snow. I took side streets as far as Ohio Drive and then turned onto the Memorial Parkway. After we'd crossed the bridge, I looked behind me and then went on past the Washington Memorial Parkway exit.

"I'm not going to take you to the airport," I said. "Richard may not be that far behind us," I went on hastily so she wouldn't think this was another trap and that I was taking her to a hospital. "I'm going to take you to the Arlington Metro stop. You can take the Metro to the airport, if you want, or to the train station or the bus, and Richard won't have any idea where you've gone." And neither will I, I thought.

Annie nodded without looking at me, her gloved hands clasped tightly in her lap. I pulled the car over next to the white stones that marked the entrance to the Metro station and stopped.

"I had a dream about you. On the way up today," she said, still looking straight ahead. "I was in my room at home, in bed, propped up against the pillows, and you came in and said, 'I'll drive you to Fredericksburg,' and I wanted to go with you, but I couldn't. I couldn't even answer you. I just shook my head." She turned to me, her eyes filled with tears. "It was the first time I ever dreamed about you. I've dreamed about Richard and Broun, but never you, Jeff. Who do you suppose you were? I was so glad to see you."

"I don't know," I said, though I had guessed almost from the beginning what part I played. "Lee's doctor maybe? I would drive you to Fredericksburg, you know. Or anywhere at all."

Would I? Knowing where the dreams were leading her, would I be able to take her there? Or would I call Richard again? I got out of the car and took her suitcase out of the trunk and put it on the top of the steps. I opened the door for her. She folded a piece of paper, put it in her pocket, and then got out.

I gave her Broun's money and all the cash I had. "There's about five hundred here. That should get you home or wherever you want to go."

"Thank you," she said.

"This is the Blue Line. You can take it straight to the airport. If you want Amtrak, change to the Red Line at Metro Center and that'll take you to Union Station."

She bent her head to fumble in her purse and put the money away. "I won't know what happened to you," I said. "Promise me you'll go see a doctor."

"After the war," she said. She took the folded piece of paper out of her pocket and handed it to me.

I nodded. "After the war."

She reached up and brushed the hair off my forehead. "I was so glad to see you," she said. She picked her suitcase up in her left hand, put it down on the wet sidewalk and picked it up in her right, and went down the stairs.

I went out to the edge of the platform and stood there long enough for her to get away, holding the folded paper and looking up the hill toward Arlington House. It started to snow. I put the piece of paper in my coat pocket and went back home.

I didn't look at it until the next day for fear she had written the address of that house with the wide porch and the apple orchard, and that I, like Richard, would try to follow her.

It was still wet. I unfolded it carefully, so it wouldn't tear, and read it. She had written in blue proofreader's pencil, "Tom Tita, Arlington House."

CHAPTER SIXTEEN

Lee only lasted two weeks after the rainy afternoon in Grace Church. For most of that time he lay in silence or dozed. Outside it rained, and the rivers around Lexington rose till it was impossible for Rob to make it to his bedside. For several nights the aurora borealis lit up the sky, as it had at Fredericksburg. Lee talked very little, though he sometimes muttered in his dreams, but when the doctor told him, "You must make haste to get well; Traveller has been standing so long in the stable that he needs exercise," he only shook his head, unable to speak.

He died on the twelfth of October, saying, "Strike the tent," and then moving off to some old battle, leaving Traveller behind. Traveller walked in the funeral procession, his head bent, his saddle and bridle covered with black crepe. Then he was taken home to his stable to wait out the end. Did he dream of Lee? I wonder. Do horses dream?

When I got home, Broun was still sitting on the loveseat in the solarium. The Siamese had jumped up on his lap, and he had set the answering machine down on the loveseat beside him so he could pet the cat.

He stood up as soon as I came in, dumping the cat on the floor to come and put his arm around my shoulders. He didn't ask me what had happened, and because he didn't, because he didn't say, "How could you let her go like that? She's sick. She needs a doctor," I told him I had taken her to the Metro station, and then I told him everything else.

He didn't say, "They're only dreams," or tell me any of the theories he had picked up in California. He only said quietly, "It was a terrible war, the Civil War. So many young people . . . I had no business going to California. Out on a wild goose chase after Lincoln's dreams when I should have been here."

"It's not your fault," I said, and went up to bed even though it was still early afternoon, and slept for two days. When I woke up, an electrician was there, fixing the wires on the answering machine, putting it back in the wall.

"In case she calls," Broun said.

I took the galleys up to New York. When I got back, we started the Lincoln's dreams novel. I did Broun's legwork for him, drove him places, looked up obscure facts that didn't matter to anyone, and dreamed of Annie.

While we were in Fredericksburg, I had not had any dreams at all, as if Annie were dreaming enough for both of us, but now I dreamed nearly every night, and in the dreams Annie was fine. I dreamed that she had left a message on the answering machine. "I'm fine," she said. "I didn't want you to worry."

"Where are you?" I asked, even though I knew it was only a message, that she wasn't really there. I had never been able to break myself of the habit of replying to people who were not there, and if I could not, how did I think Annie could, Lee whispering to her night after night, telling her his dreams?

"I'm fine, Jeff," she told me in the dream. "They're taking good care of me." It was not a message. It was really her on the phone, and she was fine, fine. She had gone home to that house with the wide porch and the apple tree and when she got there she had gone to see the doctor. "I thought you were afraid they'd stop the dreams," I said into the phone.

"I was, but then I thought about what you said about Tom Tita. What good would it have done for me to follow Lee through the Civil War? I would just have gotten myself killed. My first loyalty was to myself."

"That was what you meant in the message," I said, clutching the receiver. "That was what you meant when you wrote Tom Tita's name."

"Of course," she said. "What did you think the message meant?"

"That you were locked in. That you couldn't get out."

"I'm fine," she said. "They're taking good care of me."

We worked on the book all summer. In the fall, *The Duty Bound* came out, and we went to New York to promote the book. "I'm glad to see Broun looking so well," his agent told me at the McLaws and Herndon reception. "I was afraid all that running around in California would be too much for him, but he looks wonderful. I also can't tell you how relieved I am to see that book in print," she said, jabbing her finger at a stand-up display card of *The Duty Bound*. "Did you know he called me after the galleys were in and wanted to change the ending? He wanted to have Ben and Nelly get married. Can you believe that?"

"When did he do that?" I asked.

"Oh, I don't know. After you brought the galleys up. Luckily, he called me first and not McLaws and Herndon. I managed to convince him it wouldn't work at all."

"No, I suppose not."

"Well, I mean, it was obvious from the very beginning she was in love with that boy who died, what was his name?"

We were in New York till after Christmas, doing autograph signings and talk shows. On the day we got home, while I was next door getting the Siamese cat back from Broun's neighbor, Broun had a heart attack. It was very small. There was hardly any damage. He was only in the hospital a week, and he seemed more upset about the fact that a battle-ax of a nurse had shaved his beard off than he did about the heart attack.

"Didn't you have any symptoms?" I demanded of him. He was lying in the hospital bed, propped up against the pillows.

"A little indigestion," he said. "Or what I thought was indigestion."

"Didn't your arm hurt? Or your wrist?"

"No," he said. "I thought I'd eaten too much."

"Didn't you dream anything?"

"I was awake when I had it, son," he said gently.

"Before the attack," I yelled. "What did you dream about?"

Broun's doctor pulled me out into the hall. "I know you're under a lot of stress, but so is he." He looked at Broun's chart. "And so am I. I don't want him having a third heart attack on me."

"A third?" I said.

"Of course," he said, still frowning at the chart. He looked up and saw the expression on my face. "Why, the old son of a gun! He never told you, did he? It was three years ago," he pulled back several pages on the chart, "in September. September twenty-eighth. You were out of town, I think. He said he called you."

Three years ago in September I had been in Springfield, looking at Lincoln's tomb and being driven crazy by Broun, and halfway through the trip the calls had stopped, the messages had stopped, and when I got home, he was willing to let me do his legwork for him.

"How bad was the first one?" I asked.

"Bad enough to scare him. He was convinced he was going to die. That's why I believed he'd told you." He let the pages fall back and tucked the chart under his arm. "Now, I'll agree he needs yelling at for not telling you, but as his doctor I'm not going to let you back in to see him unless you promise not to mention this heart attack thing to him until he's in better shape than he is right now. He must have had his reasons for not telling you about the heart attack."

"Yeah," I said.

I went back into the room and apologized for yelling at him. "I didn't have any dreams before my heart attack," Broun said. "I didn't have any warning at all."

"Annie did," I said. "The dreams were trying to warn her. Only she wouldn't listen."

He leaned back against the pillows. "If I'd dreamed I was in a boat before my heart attack, traveling toward a shadowy, indefinite shore, I wouldn't have listened either. If Lincoln was letting me dream his dreams for him, there is nothing on this earth I would let stop me. Not even somebody I loved."

"Even if you ended up having a heart attack? Even if it killed you?"

"Even then," he said softly. "Maybe she's all right. Maybe she went to see a doctor when she got home, like she promised."

Broun started back to work on the Lincoln book as soon as he was out of the hospital, in direct defiance of doctor's orders. "I'm going to finish this damn book if it kills me," he said, scratching at his unshaven chin. He was trying to grow another beard.

"Which it will at this rate," I said. "At least let me do the legwork for you."

"Fine," he said, and sent me to the White House to take notes on the purple-hung Guest Room where Willie Lincoln died and the stairs Lincoln had descended in his dream and the East Room, where Willie's coffin and then his father's had lain.

I was having a new dream now. In it, I dreamed I woke and heard the sound of crying, but when I went downstairs I couldn't see anyone. There was a guard standing at the door of the solarium, and I asked him, "Who is dead in the White House?" but when he turned around to answer me, it wasn't the guard at all, it was Annie. She was wearing her gray coat, and she looked beautiful, fresh and rested.

"Are you all right?" I asked her. "Did you go see a doctor?"

"A doctor?"

"A doctor," I said urgently. "The dreams were a warning."

"I know. They were trying to warn us about Broun's heart attack, but we didn't understand them. We were looking at all the wrong clues."

"Broun isn't going to have another heart attack, is he?"

She shook her head. "The dreams have stopped."

"And you're all right?"

She smiled at me, a sweet smile with no sadness in it. "I'm fine."

In April, Broun was hospitalized again with chest pains. "I've been thinking about what caused Annie's dreams," he said, lying against the pillows. He was refusing to let the nurses near him for fear they might shave his beard, and he looked terrible, grubby and disreputable. "Do you remember Dreamtime?"

"The quacks in San Diego?"

"Yes," he said. "Remember they had that theory that the dead sleep peacefully until something disturbs them, like Willie Lincoln being dug up, and then they start dreaming. Well, what if something like that happened with Lee? What if they moved his body and that's what started him dreaming?"

"Lee's body hasn't been moved," I said. "It's still buried in the chapel at Lexington."

"Maybe the dreams weren't because of the angina. Maybe they started because his body was disturbed some way. Was his daughter Annie's body moved?"

"No. She's still buried in North Carolina where she died."

He lay silently for a while, glaring at the door whenever a nurse passed, and then said, "They moved Lincoln's body. First they moved it to Springfield on the funeral train, stopping at every damned one-horse town and whistle stop along the way." He pushed himself up against the pillows, and the line on the EKG screen behind his head spiked suddenly. "And then there was that kidnap plot and the guard moved him out of the tomb and buried him in a passage of the Memorial Hall."

"Annie didn't have Lincoln's dreams," I said calmly, reasonably, watching the screen. "They were Lee's dreams."

"In 1901, they moved Lincoln back into the tomb again. He was moved four times altogether, not counting the funeral train." The screen jerked in sharp, dangerous lines. "What if those Dreamtime quacks were right, and all that jostling woke him up?"

"They weren't Lincoln's dreams," I said. "They were Lee's."

"Maybe," he said, sitting up with a motion that sent the EKG lines to the top of the screen. "I want you to bring me some books."

He asked for books the next three days, and by the end of the week he had half his library in his hospital room. "I've got it all worked out," he said. He was able to sit up by then without setting off the EKG. "They were Lincoln's dreams."

He had it all worked out. Lincoln had been the one who had dreams, not Lee, and their dreams wouldn't have been all that different. They would both have dreamed about Gettysburg and Appomattox. Lincoln had known about Special Order 191 before Lee did, and the cat didn't have to be Tom Tita, did it? It could have been one of Lincoln's kittens. Lincoln loved kittens. He had it all worked out.

"What if they were Lincoln's dreams?" I said when I couldn't take it anymore. "What would that prove?"

"Lincoln tried to save Willie's pony from the burning stable. That's what the house on fire really is, not Chancellorsville."

"They weren't Lincoln's dreams, damn it," I shouted. "They were Lee's."

"I know," he said quietly, and the EKG line above his head went right off the screen. "I know they're not Lincoln's dreams."

"Then why did you do all this?"

"Because then she'd be all right. If they were warnings from Lincoln, they wouldn't have been about apple orchards, they'd have been about boats. I thought if I could make them Lincoln's dreams, then that would mean she was all right."

"He's in no shape to be upset," Broun's doctor said. He had yanked me out into the hall again and down to an empty room. The EKG had set off an alarm at the nurses' station that brought everybody running.

"I know," I said.

"You look as bad as he does," he said. "How are you sleeping?"

"I'm not," I said. If I slept I dreamed about Annie. She was standing on the porch of Arlington with her arms around my neck, crying, and I kept saying over and over, "I don't want you to leave."

"Would you like me to prescribe something for you? To help you sleep?"

"What did you have in mind? Thorazine?"

He didn't get the joke. He pulled out a prescription pad. "Who's your regular doctor?"

"I don't have one. Do you want my family doctor? He's in Connecticut."

"I don't like to prescribe without seeing a patient's records." He wrote busily on the prescription pad. "I'll give you something mild for now and then wait till I have your records to put you on anything stronger. You don't have any health problems I should know about, do you? Diabetes, heart condition?"

"No." I told him my doctor's name. "How long will it take to get the records?"

"Depends. If they're computerized, we'll have them in a few days. If not, it could take several weeks. Why? Are you having that much trouble sleeping?"

"No," I said and pocketed the prescription without looking at it. But Annie had been having trouble sleeping. She had been having so much trouble sleeping that Richard had put her on Elavil right away. He hadn't done an EKG. He had told me in that phone message that the EKG was just back from the lab, but EKGs didn't have to go to the lab. Broun's doctors read his as they came off the machine. He had said Annie's records showed a functional heart murmur, but how could they when it took two weeks to a month to get the records? Annie had told me he put her on Elavil right away. Richard hadn't done an EKG, and he hadn't waited for the records from her family doctor. The Elavil had made the dreams worse, but Richard hadn't taken her off the Elavil then. He had taken her off of it when her records came, when he saw she had a minor heart condition and he had had no business putting her on Elavil in the first place.

He had panicked and called me, only I wasn't there. I was in West Virginia. What if I had been there? Would he have told me the truth, that he had been so frantic with worry that he had made a terrible mistake, that when he had seen the dreams and what they did to Annie, all he could think about was stopping them and how the hell could he wait for the family doctor's records when they might take a month to get there? Or would he have used his Good Shrink voice on me even then?

Why had he put her on the Thorazine? To try to stop the dreams? Thorazine could have stopped a train, and it wasn't contraindicated. (*Note*: Sudden death apparently due to cardiac arrest, has been reported, but there is not sufficient evidence to establish a relationship between such deaths and the administration of the drug.) Or did he give it to her to keep her from going back to the Institute, from telling Dr. Stone he'd given her a medicine that was explicitly contraindicated for heart patients? Why didn't Longstreet send his troops up at Pickett's Charge?

Lee never gave any indication after the war that he considered Longstreet's actions at Gettysburg as anything more than "the error of a good soldier." But after the battle, when Colonel Venable said bitterly, "I heard you direct General Longstreet to send Hood's division up," Lee had blamed him. And I blamed Richard. I'm trying to do my duty as a doctor. I have your best interests at heart.

I took the prescription out of my pocket and looked at it. Broun's doctor had written a prescription for Elavil.

In July Broun finally let his doctor perform the bypass he had been resisting. He came through it fine, jubilant because nobody had shaved his beard off while he was under the anesthetic, but he didn't show any interest in working on the Lincoln book.

He sent me to Springfield, complaining that he couldn't go any farther with the book till he knew where Willie Lincoln had been buried. I spent nearly a month there trying to find out, and then came back and started through the grave registries of the D.C. cemeteries. I had had the prescription for the Elavil filled while I was in Springfield. It stopped the dreams completely, repressing REM sleep the way it was supposed to.

Broun still wasn't doing any work on the book, even though Willie Lincoln's burial site was a fact he could add after he got it. He had me do a lot of research he never even bothered to look at, and in the fall he started having chest pains again.

In October he insisted I take him out to the Lincoln Memorial. "I don't think this is a good idea," I said. "It has steps. You know you're supposed to take it easy on steps."

He climbed the steps, shaking off my assistance, and went into the memorial to look at the statue of Lincoln. "You know what theory nobody came up with in all that traipsing around California?" he said, looking at Lincoln sitting in the big marble chair with his too-big ears and wide nose and his too-long legs, his too-large hands resting on the marble armrests. "That he was lying about the dreams."

"Lying?" I said.

"He loved the Union," he said. "He would have done

anything he could to save it, even if it meant trumping up some dream about a boat and a shadowy shore to keep the Cabinet off his back." His words echoed in the cold room. "He would have sacrificed his own son to save his precious Union."

"He didn't sacrifice Willie," I said. "He loved Willie. He would never have done anything to hurt him. Willie died of typhoid."

"He should have been home taking care of him instead of off gallivanting around some battlefield," he said.

"What are you talking about?" I said. "He wasn't off gallivanting. He was right there by Willie's side the whole time."

"I never should have gone to California," Broun said, still looking at Lincoln. "I should have stayed home."

"It isn't your fault," I said.

Broun let me help him back down the stairs. At the bottom he turned and looked back up at the memorial. "It's been over a year, hasn't it?"

"A year and a half," I said.

I was almost out of the Elavil. I called Broun's doctor and asked him if I could refill the prescription. "Is it helping you sleep?" he asked me. "You're not having any side effects, are you?"

"No," I said.

"Your records are here. I want to check them, and then if everything's okay I'll call it in for you. By the way, is Broun still interested in Lincoln's dreams?"

"I don't know."

"Well, if he is, there's a paper by a psychiatrist he might be interested in, a Dr. Madison. He has a theory that you can dream yourself into ulcers or asthma—"

"Or a heart attack?"

"Yeah. Interesting theory." He read me the title of the paper and the journal he'd read it in. "It says here Dr. Madison's degree is from Duke University. You went to Duke, didn't you? Maybe you know him. Richard Madison?"

Longstreet became quite successful after the war, in spite of Southern criticism that the failure of Pickett's Charge had been his fault, becoming president of a cotton factory and then an ambassador to Turkey. He wrote articles and a book, and in them he defended his actions at Gettysburg until I think finally he convinced even himself that he had done the right thing and was not to blame for anything that had happened.

"No," I said. "I don't know him." I started taking the Elavil two at a time.

After that trip to the Lincoln Memorial, Broun had put the Lincoln book aside, boxing up all the research and the rough draft and having me carry it up to the attic for him. I spent most of my time at the library. I was still trying to find out where Willie Lincoln was buried, even though Broun wasn't interested anymore. I checked all the grave registries in the towns around Washington and even called Arlington, thinking maybe Commander Meigs had buried Willie in the front lawn of Lee's house.

I ran out of Elavil again, but I didn't call the doctor back. I didn't dream very much, and when I did, Annie wasn't in the dreams. I dreamed of a place I'd never seen before, a place with green hills and white fences. For some reason, I thought it was in West Virginia.

In February I found out what had happened to Willie Lincoln. He had been buried at Oak Hill Cemetery in George-town, in a vault belonging to William Thomas Carroll, a clerk of the Supreme Court and a friend of the Lincolns.

The information was in a biography of Mary Todd Lincoln at the branch library, and when I read it, I slammed the book shut, grabbed it up, and went running out. Alarms clanged, and Kate ran out on the steps and shouted after me, "Jeff, are you all right?" I didn't answer her. I leaped in the car and went tearing out to the cemetery.

The narrow roads between the graves were blocked with snow so deep most of the gravestones were buried, but I got out of the car and walked through the snow to the tomb and looked at it, as if I thought Willie was still there, as if I thought, disturbed out of his sleep, he would tell me where Annie was and what had happened to her.

But he wasn't there. He was in Springfield, lying beside his father. I had thought that finding his grave would tell me what had happened to Willie, but I already knew that, didn't I?

It was the same thing that had happened to all of them—Ben and Tom Tita and Little Hen. They had died in the war. Willie's pony had been burned alive and Annie Lee had died of a fever, but they were Civil War dead, and they were all buried together at Fredericksburg, along with Stonewall Jackson's arm, under a numbered granite square no larger than a scrap of paper. I knew what had happened to all of them except Annie. And Traveller. So I walked back through the snow and went home and got out Freeman.

I knew that Traveller had outlived Lee because I remembered reading that he was part of Lee's funeral procession, but there was no mention of him after that in the last chapter of Freeman and nothing at all about him in Davis or even Robert E. Lee, Jr.'s recollections of his father.

I went downstairs to the solarium and found Sanborn's *Robert E. Lee.* I went back up to the study and sorted through the stacks of books Broun had piled on his desk and the leather chair, looking for any mention of Traveller. Pierson mentioned almost in passing that Traveller had been boarded out at a friend's farm because Mrs. Lee was too ill to care for him. Lovesey's *Man and Horse* said he had "lived on for two years, waiting faithfully for the master who would never come again." Hinsdale said he was kept on at the stable Lee had built for him until he picked up a nail, contracted lockjaw, and had to be shot.

I looked at that for a while and then went back to the last chapter of Freeman, though I already knew everything there was to know: Traveller had had the misfortune to outlive the person he loved, he had waited for nearly two years, and where he had been those two years didn't matter any more than where Willie Lincoln had spent those last three years of the war, and then he had died. Freeman couldn't tell me any more than that, but I went back anyway, writing down the page numbers after "Traveller" in the index as if they were the Roll of Honor numbers on some soldier's grave, because I couldn't face the idea that Freeman, who had loved Lee enough to write four volumes about him, would have forgotten Traveller, and he hadn't.

It was in one of the appendices in volume one. He wrote

that Traveller had died of lockjaw and been buried on the grounds of Washington and Lee University. His bones had been disinterred by the Daughters of the Confederacy and put in the basement of the Lee Memorial Chapel. Near Lee's tomb.

In March I took Broun to see his doctor, and he got a clean bill of health.

"He told me I could do anything I wanted, climb stairs, write a book," he said on the way home. "I want to write a book about Robert E. Lee." He waited to see what I would say.

"And Traveller," I said.

"Of course Traveller."

We started work on the new book. Broun sent me out to Arlington to take notes on the porch and the parlor and the attic where Tom Tita had been imprisoned. There was going to be a military funeral in the afternoon, and they had blocked off the drives. I had to park the car in the visitors' parking lot and walk up the hill. It was a warm day, the first one in over two months, and the snow that had fallen in February was just now starting to melt. The water ran in rivers along the curving drives.

Custis Walk was blocked off, too. I had to cut across the grass to get to Arlington House. I made it as far as the grave. The workmen had trampled the snow down till you could see the grass in places. They had used a backhoe to dig the grave, heaping dirty snow at the sides, and it was melting, too, and running across the grass and the snow in muddy rivulets.

The workmen had gone off to eat lunch or smoke a cigarette. They had left a metal clipboard lying under a tree on the far side of the grave, with a piece of paper clipped to it. It would have the name of who the grave was for written on it, and I wanted to walk over to the tree and read it, but I was afraid that I would not be able to get back, that the ground would give way, and I would step on all their mangled bodies.

"It has something to do with Arlington and the unknown soldier and a message," Annie had said, trying to understand the dreams. "I think he was trying to atone," and I should have asked her, "How is he trying to atone?" instead of shouting at her. Because of course the dreams were an atonement.

He was trying to warn her. His daughter Annie had died,

and he hadn't been able to do anything to save her. He hadn't been able to save any of them, Stonewall Jackson or the ragged soldiers he had to keep sending back into battle or the Confederacy. But he could save Annie. She reminded him of his daughter, and she was twenty-three years old. He was trying to warn her.

The dreams were terrifying, full of images of death and dying. They were meant to frighten her, to make her go see a doctor before it was too late, a warning as clear, as easy to interpret as Lincoln's seeing himself in a coffin, only nobody saw it. Except Annie, and she wouldn't listen.

"It's the war," Broun had said. "People do things like that in a war, sacrifice themselves, fall in love." They had been together night after night, through battle after heartbreaking battle. She was bound to fall in love with him, wasn't she? And then, even though she knew the dreams were a warning, even though the warnings got plainer and more terrifying, Lee willing even to dream Appomattox again, to dream his own death for her, to warn her, she couldn't leave him.

She had stayed with him to the end, as she had promised, and when the snow melted a little more I would be able to see her body, face-down, her arm flung out, still holding on to her Springfield rifle. I leaned against the backhoe, unable to stand.

I could see the square white subway entrances looking like gravestones and beyond them, across the river, the square white tomb of the Lincoln Memorial. I thought about the statue inside, Lincoln sitting with his long legs planted in front of him and his hands on the arms of the chair, looking like a man who has lost a child.

Lincoln had gone out to the cemetery in Georgetown and had the vault opened twice, trying, I think, to convince himself that Willie was really dead, but it hadn't helped. It hadn't helped, and he couldn't sleep, and his grief nearly drove him insane. Until finally, in Broun's words, Willie's face had come in dreams to comfort him. As Annie's face had come to comfort me, though she was dead.

Though she was dead.

It took me a long time to get back to the road, high-stepping like a cat among the snowy graves, and an even

211

longer time to drive home. When I got there, Broun was in the solarium, watering his African violets.

I stood against the door, still in my coat, watching him spill water out of the already-full pots onto the table. He will never look like Lincoln. The heart attacks have aged and somehow saddened his face, and his beard, which has finally, after almost two years, grown in the way he wanted it, is nearly white. He looks like Lee.

I wondered why I had never noticed it before, why I had kept instead the image I had had of him the night of the reception, of someone sharp and disreputable and not to be trusted. He has been nothing but kind to me. And one snowy night he sold me to Annie, who was having someone else's dreams.

"Jeff'll take good care of her," Broun had said, like a man trying to make a deal, "won't you, Jeff?"

And I had said, "I'll take good care of her. I promise."

I think some part of me has blamed him for that all this time, in spite of the fact that he has been nothing but kind, loves me as much, I think, as Lincoln loved Willie, is down here now not because the violets need watering, but because he wondered where I was, because he didn't know what had happened to me.

I have blamed him for something that wasn't even his fault. It was love at first sight for both of them, wasn't it? Didn't Lee call him "my colt" even before he bought him?

I belonged to her from the minute I saw her standing there in her gray coat, and she took me, her faithful, following companion, from Fredericksburg to Chancellorsville and Gettysburg and finally to Appomattox, and then left me behind.

"I had no business sending you out there," Broun says.

I cannot answer. I stand there by the door with my head down, winded, blown. Poor Traveller. Did he know that Lee was dead, or, poor dumb animal that he was, had he waited every day for two years for him to come back?

"What happened?" Broun says, alarmed. "What's wrong?"

"I have picked up a nail."